WHEN I WAS JOE

"Thoughtful and well-crafted."
The Financial Times

"An intelligent and gripping debut."
Julia Eccleshare at *LoveReading4Kids*

"Ms David has really managed to get inside the
head of a teenage boy."
The BookZone for Boys

"Simply a stunningly good book."
The Bookwitch

Praise for

ALMOST TRUE

"A book about big questions . . . Perhaps
Keren David's biggest achievement, however,
is that these issues play second fiddle to the
psychological authenticity of her troubled hero,
and the longing she rouses in the reader
for Ty's ultimate redemption."
Books for Keeps

"A thrilling adventure . . . an emotional roller coaster."
Julia Eccleshare *Lovereading.co.uk*

WHEN I WAS JOE

KEREN DAVID

F

FRANCES LINCOLN
CHILDREN'S BOOKS

Quarto is the authority on a wide range of topics.

Quarto educates, entertains and enriches the lives of
our readers—enthusiasts and lovers of hands-on living.

www.quartoknows.com

First published in Great Britain and the USA in 2010 by
Frances Lincoln Children's Books,
74-77 White Lion Street,
London N1 9PF
www.franceslincoln.com

First published in paperback in Great Britain and the USA in 2012

A CIP cataloguing in publication record for this book is
available from the British Library.

978-1-84780-379-5

Set in Palatino

Printed in the UK

MIX
Paper from
responsible sources
FSC
www.fsc.org   FSC® C013604

For Laurence, Phoebe and Judah
Remembering Daniel with love and sorrow

CHAPTER 1
Statement

It's one thing watching someone get killed. It's quite another talking about it. When it happened I didn't even realise exactly what I was seeing, and my heart was thumping so loud I couldn't hear anything else. My mind was whizzing around at hyperdrive speed – trying to work out what to do, trying to sort out what was going on. And I ran away as fast as I could.

But now I'm sitting in the police station telling three officers what happened and they're asking so many questions about every detail that it's as if they've put the whole thing into slow-mo. It's like being trapped watching a really sick horror film and not being able to close your eyes. And I can't run away this time.

Twice – when I tell them how the blood splashed into the mud, and then about the tangle of bodies on the ground – I think I'm going to vomit, and Nicki – that's my mum – has to ask them to stop their tape while I lean forward and try and gulp it back.

She puts her hand on my back and uses her best lawyer-in-training voice: 'Is this really necessary? He's here to help you. He's just a kid of fourteen.' And the main guy asking questions says, 'So was the boy who died, Miss Lewis.' They get me a glass of water and then they start again. I'm wondering if they'll ever let me leave.

They make me look at loads of photographs. Some are just faces and it's easy to pick out the ones I've told them about. Some are close-ups of the cuts and wounds that I've already seen. But they look different in pictures than they did at the park yesterday – was it only yesterday?

At the park it was nearly dark, and I got a quick glimpse, and looked away. Now they make me look and look at the way the flesh is split and curved and meat-like, and it's been photographed in bright white light and I know I'm never going to forget it. I think they're trying to shock me into confessing something. They warn me that I might get charged, tell me that I can stay silent. Nicki says again, 'Is this really necessary? He's here to help you.'

The police officers change around, but one guy always stays. He's called Detective Inspector Morris and he's the only one that's black and he's older than the rest.

He's quiet, hardly says anything and leaves it to the others to ask me again and again, louder and louder: was I involved? Was I fighting? Did I know what was going to happen? How near was I when the knife went in? Was I the lookout?

No, I say, keeping my voice steady. No, not very close, no. I was just watching, not involved, just a witness. All the time, every question they ask, I'm trying to focus. I'm trying to think only about those boys fighting – who pushed, who hit, which knife went where.

After hours of questions, after taking my fingerprints and scraping my mouth – 'for DNA' – they leave Nicki and me alone. She's looking completely knackered, her eyes are puffy and I feel incredibly guilty that she has to sit through all this. 'I'm really sorry Nic,' I say, and she says, 'Don't worry about me, you're doing the right thing.' But she doesn't look very sure.

Then one of the policemen shows us the canteen. 'I'll bet you're hungry,' he says, but when we get there the hatches are closed and we have to make do with what's in the vending machines. So my supper is hot chocolate and crisps and stale custard creams. It's about midnight. Eventually I fall asleep, head cushioned on my crossed arms, slumped forward over the table.

When I wake up, DI Morris is sitting at the table, talking to Nicki. I keep my head down while I work out if they are saying anything interesting.

'We're satisfied with his story,' says DI Morris.

Nicki asks, 'Can I take him home now? He's got school in the morning.'

'We're going to have to think very carefully about whether you can go home,' he says. 'It may be safer for you not to.'

She frowns. 'What do you mean? We can't stay here.'

'We'll take care of you,' he says. 'Ty's named some dangerous people in his statement and we don't want them trying to silence him.'

I sit up, shivering and blinking in the fluorescent light of the canteen. 'Where would we go?' I ask. I'm hoping that wherever it is it won't involve crossing London to get to school for 8.30 am, although it would be typical of my mum to make me go. She's bonkers about my education.

'We'll take you to a hotel, and assess the situation,' he says. 'It may be necessary to take you into our witness protection programme.'

'What do you mean. . . What's that?' asks Nicki. I don't like that word *protection*. It brings back bad memories.

'We rehouse vulnerable witnesses; give them a new identity, a new home, a lump sum to start a new life.

We'll do our utmost to keep you safe.'

'No way,' she says. 'Absolutely not. I'm sure that won't be necessary.'

'Well, maybe we should just take you to a hotel for a few days and see how things go,' he says, finishing his tea and getting up. He reaches out and shakes our hands. 'Good to meet you, Ty,' he says to me. 'We very much appreciate your co-operation.'

Next they bring me my statement all written out. I don't want to read it. I don't want to think about what did and didn't happen in that park. But they make me read every word and initial all the pages and sign it at the bottom.

A uniformed policeman drives us back to our flat through dark and empty streets in an unmarked police car. 'You've got half an hour to pack some bags,' he says. 'You'd better pack carefully because you may not be able to come back again.' Nicki starts protesting that we're only going to a hotel for a few days but I look at his face and I can see that he thinks she's kidding herself.

How do you choose what to take when you've just been told you may never see your home again? I think about people who lose their homes in floods and tsunamis and earthquakes, people you see on the news living in refugee camps because their country is at war. You think their troubles are so huge they probably don't have much time to worry about losing the odd photograph or old toy. You imagine that in a crisis the little things don't matter any more.

I pretend we're surrounded by rising flood waters, grabbing a few things before helicopter evacuation. It makes it slightly less real. But it doesn't help much when it comes to leaving stuff like the desk that my grandad made for my mum before I was even born.

I zip my laptop into its case, but the policeman says, 'You'll have to leave that. We're going to want to have a look at it.'

'But it's mine. . .' It's the most precious thing I own. Gran had to save up for ages to get it as a present when I went to secondary school. He shakes his head: 'We'll be getting a warrant and we'll have to check the hard drive. What about the clothes you were wearing yesterday? I'd better take them.' I search through the dirty washing pile and pull out some jeans and a grey hoodie. Luckily I have lots of pairs of jeans and Gran bought the hoodie in a three-pack at Asda.

I pack my iPod. I pack my Manchester United scarf, which is the only thing I have from my dad. I pack my school uniform and books because I reckon Nicki will probably wangle it somehow so I'll be going back to school. And I take some clothes and stuff as well. I root around under my bed and pull out the Tesco bag which

I need to sort out somehow. But the main things I want to take – they can't be packed.

Nicki and I live in a little flat above a newsagent's on a main road. It's not so special, and when the windows are open the noise of traffic means we have to shout to be heard. But I like having my own room, even if it's tiny, and we've painted it a cool purple-blue colour and plastered it with football posters. And I like the way the sunlight comes into my room in the evening so I can sit on the windowsill and watch whatever's going on.

I never feel lonely because there are shops and people all around, and I love hearing all their different languages. It makes me feel like all the world's represented on our street, and East London must be a great place if everyone came so far to live here.

Nicki shoves some stuff into a bag, pretty much at random, and then starts arguing with the policeman again. 'We're not leaving here forever,' she says. 'I have a job and Ty's at a very good school.'

'It's not up to me,' he says. And then, 'What's that?'

We can all hear it . . . a crashing noise. The tinkle of glass breaking. It's a pretty rough area that we live in, but this is really close. It's downstairs. Then I sniff something sweet and metallic . . . not perfume . . . I know that smell but I can't think what it is.

'Come on,' he yells. 'Quickly, down the stairs.'

We tumble down the steep steps that lead up to our flat, dragging our bags with us. Halfway down there's a huge bang – I miss a step, the building seems to shake – a crackling noise, and a choking smell . . . and there's smoke . . . smoke in the air of the stairwell . . . but we're out of our door and into the night.

Mr Patel's shop is on fire. The newsagent's that he's so proud of, and spends so long cleaning. Flames are eating up all the sweets and magazines. There's a huge hole in the front window and glass all over the pavement. Nicki's screaming and bashing on doors, ringing bells, yelling, 'You've got to get out!' to all the people who live in the flats above the shops.

I'm just standing still among the glass on the pavement, staring at the flames. Did whoever did this know that we had our own front door? If we hadn't . . . could we have escaped?

Our policeman is on his radio, calling for help. 'Petrol bomb, newsagent's shop . . . we need to evacuate, urgently. . .' And then he grabs Nicki as she's about to run further up the road and says, 'No, stop, we need to move you now.' And he bundles our bags into his car, and we jump in the back and he's driving us away, just as our neighbours start to come out on to the pavement.

'Oh my God,' says Nicki. 'What the hell was that?' She's crying. 'Will they get everyone out? Poor Mr Patel.

That shop is everything to him. What about Mrs Papadopoulos? She's deaf, she won't have heard. . . Some of those flats have a lot of people stuffed into a few rooms. . .'

She puts her arms around me and we sit huddled together. I can hardly believe what I've just seen. I love that shop. I hang out there a lot, especially when Nicki has friends round to drink wine and watch soppy DVDs.

Mr Patel's a really nice man. He teaches me Urdu and he lets me borrow any magazine I want, apart from the ones on the top shelf. He gave me my pick of the paper round routes, and when I need man-to-man advice on stuff, he's the person I ask.

'What happened?' I ask, and my wobbly voice sounds like I'm ten, a scared little boy. 'Was it a bomb?' Fire engines rush past us, and the quiet night is full of screaming sirens.

'That's why we're getting you away from here,' says the policeman. 'Some people will stop at nothing.'

I sit and think about all the stuff that's going to get destroyed by the fire. Everything we didn't pack. My laptop. All the things Nicki'd bought from the market to jazz up the flat – a fluffy sheepskin rug and pink silky cushions, and a stupid beaded curtain which divided the kitchen area from the living room. I used to moan about it looking too girly but right now I'm missing that curtain and those pink cushions.

Nicki fumbles for her mobile, but the policeman says, 'No calls.'

'But I have to let my mum know we're OK. She'll go frantic when she hears about this. . .' and he says, 'Let's make sure you are OK first, shall we?' And he drives on until we leave London behind and we're heading into nothingness.

CHAPTER 2
Makeover

Eventually he pulls in at a service station. I think we're going to have a pee and something to eat, but instead he walks over to a blue Ford Mondeo, and talks briefly to the driver.

'This is Doug,' he says, 'He'll take you from here.'

Doug's a big guy, looks a bit like Simon Cowell – bad hair, weird trousers, smug smile – and he's got a look on his face like he's decided that we haven't got much talent. Nicki's looking hopeful. 'Can't we just get a coffee?' she asks, but Doug says, 'No, love. Too risky,' and we have to get into his car.

We drive on for about an hour, and then he pulls in at a hotel. It's a Travel Lodgey sort of place but not quite as exciting – I'm surprised I can still make jokes, but it's as if the shocked and terrified part of my brain has got so much work to do that it's taken itself off somewhere very remote. I'm left pretty much normal but completely numb, not feeling anything at all. I don't want to imagine what it'll be like when that bit comes back. Maybe it won't, and I'll spend the rest of my life feeling as though I'm standing behind some very thick glass.

He books us in as Jane and David Smith. It's not the sort of hotel you'd want to spend a holiday in. They show us to our room, which is tiny, just enough room for twin beds and a big TV. There's a chest of drawers with two drawers, so we can't even unpack properly. Not that we care right now. Nicki and I both fall asleep right away, with all our clothes on. I don't even brush my teeth.

It's about midday when I wake up and I can't quite think where I am. Or why I'm sharing a room with my mum. Everything that's happened feels like a film or a nightmare. She's already had a shower and she's getting dressed.

'I'm going to sort all this out today,' she says, slapping on blusher and frowning at the mirror. 'It's ridiculous. We're helping them. They can't keep us here. That fire, it must have been a coincidence. Just vandals, stupid kids messing around. Racists, something like that.'

We go downstairs and discover that there's no

breakfast on offer after 10 am, and after that, the hotel doesn't do any food at all until 7 am the next morning. I suggest finding a cafe for a fry up, and Nicki wrinkles her nose, and then two men walk in through the front door. Doug from last night and DI Morris from the police station.

'We need to talk to you,' says DI Morris and I open my mouth to explain about no breakfast, but Nicki says, 'OK,' and we end up going back to the tiny bedroom.They sit on Nicki's bed and we sit on mine. My stomach is making strange gurgling noises, but everyone pretends not to hear.

DI Morris goes into a long boring explanation of how he's in charge of the murder investigation and Doug is a Witness Protection Liaison Officer, someone who looks after people like me. Vulnerable witnesses. He drones on for a bit and then he gets to the point.

'We're sure that the petrol bomb in the shop last night was designed to intimidate you.' he says. There's a silence. I'm thinking that someone wants me dead. He never actually said 'dead', but that's what he means. I'm not stupid. It's lucky that I'm not doing feelings at the moment, because if I was I might be pretty scared.

'Your only sensible decision now is to be taken into the witness protection programme,' he says. 'Doug will look after you. You really have no choice.'

Nicki opens her mouth to argue, then closes it again. Doug says, 'I'll have to take your phones because there's no easier way to trace someone than the mobile network,' and she puts up a bit of a fight, but you can see her heart isn't in it. My phone is pretty naff, so I don't care that much. Maybe they'll give me a cool new one.

'Is there anything you need right away?' asks DI Morris. 'Because it'll be about three weeks before we can rehouse you and provide you with your new identities. Until then you'll be staying here with your heads down.'

'Breakfast,' I say very quickly before Nicki can say anything else first, and they all laugh and then Doug takes us in his car to a Little Chef where I eat a massive plate of sausage and egg and Nicki drinks black coffee and pretends she's not crying.

We have three long weeks in the sodding hotel, spending most of the time at the launderette as neither of us packed enough clothes. That's quite useful though, because one day I manage to send Nicki off to the chemist and I tell her I'll start doing the washing by myself. I've smuggled the secret Tesco bag with me and I take the contents and dump them in the machine with three packets of stain remover. And, when they come out, everything's gone and now I have an extra grey hoodie and another pair of jeans.

We buy sandwiches every day but it's never enough for me and I'm permanently starving and cross with her for not noticing. The lack of food doesn't bother her because she's always preferred coffee and cigarettes to actually eating. And she's forever nagging me about keeping up with my schoolwork, which is impossible when there's no school to go to. She snaps at me all the time when she falls over my feet or my bag, so after about two days we're hardly speaking.

There's Sky Sports on the hotel television and I watch it most of the time. Football, basketball, handball, whatever. When Nicki tries to talk to me I turn the volume up. And I get friendly with Marek who works as a cleaner at the hotel and try to get him to teach me Polish, but when Doug finds out – Nicki tells him, thanks a lot Nic – he tells me not to talk to anyone, not even someone who only knows ten words of English.

It's so boring that we're even quite pleased to see Doug when he arrives at the hotel one day. He announces that he's taking us to McDonald's which he seems to think is a treat, although if he'd bothered to ask he'd have found out that we both hate the food there.

'What do you want?' he asks. Nicki goes for a salad and a coffee, and I order two portions of fries, two quarter-pounders and two milkshakes on the basis that at least it's not sandwiches. I don't care if I feel sick for hours afterwards. Doug raises his eyebrows and I can see he thinks I'm a greedy pig.

He takes us to sit upstairs where we're all on our own and he hands Nicki a cheque-book and some bank statements. The name on the account is Ms M Andrews.

'Michelle,' says Doug. 'And Joe. Recently moved from Redbridge. Michelle, you're looking for a job. Joe's changing schools.'

'Why Joe?' I ask through a mouthful of fries. It's as good a name as any I suppose, but I'm curious.

'If you forget when you're writing, then it's easy to turn a T into a J,' he says.

'Oh, right,' I say, slurping the chocolate milkshake, although I think it's much more likely that I'd forget when I was talking. Or listening. . . How am I ever going to remember that my name's meant to be Joe?

He lectures us about staying as anonymous as possible, not making too many friends, never phoning anyone in London, never giving out our address. 'Best not to invite anyone home,' he adds. We'll be allowed the occasional phone call or letter to Gran and my aunties every six weeks or so. 'We'd have more rights if we were in prison,' says Nicki.

'What about our mobiles?' I ask – I've moved on to the strawberry milkshake now and I'm not feeling all that great – and he says he'll be giving us new ones, 'but I'll be checking your statements. No phoning London, no phoning family or friends. You're just getting them to be able to communicate with each other really.' He's obviously not planning for us to actually have a life. It's going to be hard to know what I can tell people and what I have to hide. How do you lie about everything?

He lets us write letters to Gran. I chew my pen and can't think what to write. 'I'm missing you a lot. Love, Ty,' is what I put in the end. 'Can I write to Mr Patel to say sorry about the shop?' I ask, and Doug says, 'No, I think that might complicate matters.' I would argue about it but I'm trying to stop myself throwing up mixed milkshake all over the table.

'So,' says Nicki, 'when does this end? I mean presumably after the trial we'll be going home again.'

Doug just looks at her like she's the most stupid person he's ever met. The bit of my brain that does emotions, the bit that's gone missing for the last few weeks, suddenly reappears, and I feel such hate boiling up inside me – *how dare he disrespect my mum?* – that I choke on my burger. By the time I've stopped coughing and she's stopped slapping me on my back and a little bit of quarter-pounder has flown across the table and been brushed off Doug's sleeve, we've all realised that she's asked the wrong question. 'It's not going to end, is it?' she says, and her voice is flat and empty and there's no argument left in it.

And he's still wiping his sleeve and looking completely revolted and says, 'We'll have to see.'

One day it's pouring with rain and I'm lying on my bed watching some football match from prehistoric times. Nicki's reading a set book from her Open University law course and telling me to turn the sound off.

'I don't know why you're bothering with that,' I say. 'You've missed so many assignments now that you'll fail anyway.'

She makes a face at me.

'And I bet you'll lose all your credits for the last three years too, because you'll be called Michelle Andrews and have a new address and everything.'

I don't know why I'm being so mean. That course means the world to her. She lifts her head up and says in a dangerous voice, 'Why don't you just shut up now, Ty?'

'I'm just trying to save you from wasting your time,'

And the next thing the book is flying through the air towards me, and I dodge it, totally lose my balance, fall off the bed and crash into the bedside table, breaking a glass and cutting my hand.

'Ow!' I screech. 'What was that for?'

'It wasn't going to hit you anyway,' she hisses.

There's a knock at the door and Doug walks in.

'What's going on?' he asks, and we both mumble, 'Nothing. . .' and I get up off the floor, push the table back into place, shove the broken glass under the bed and grab a tissue to mop up the blood. It really stings. Doug looks suspicious, but stands aside to let someone else into the room.

'This is Maureen,' he says, and she's smiling at us, an older woman with a big black suitcase.

'It's Extreme Makeover day,' she says. 'We've got to change the way you look,' she explains, adding, 'I hope you've been growing your hair, young man.' I have – one of the things I hated most about St Saviour's was the army-type haircut – and my fringe is already falling over my eyes.

Maureen nods her approval and then looks me up and down. 'There's not much I can do really. You've already got very anonymous clothes. Wear your hood up as much as possible – there, you don't expect the police to tell you that. I've got some more clothes for you in my bag and I think Doug's already sorted your school uniform.'

School uniform? I didn't even know I had a school.

'He's a nice-looking lad,' she adds, as if I'm not there. 'His eyes are very striking, aren't they? An unusual colour, that light green; we'll have to do something about that. And I think we'll have to darken the hair . . . although you'll have to keep it going, because we don't want his roots showing.' She and Nicki start giggling at what must be a look of complete horror on my face. I'm praying none of the boys from school will ever hear about this.

She turns the tiny hotel bathroom into a salon, and tackles Nicki first. Nicki's raging from the moment she sees Maureen's scissors. 'These extensions cost me a fortune,' she says, as they hit the tiles. 'I can't believe you have to do this. Isn't it enough to drag us away from our home?'

But I remember the flames eating up everything from *TV Quick* to *Playboy* and I doubt our home even exists any more, so I don't complain when Maureen slaps some foul-smelling muck on to my hair and then smears something which prickles and burns on to my eyebrows too.

She washes my hair and wraps it up in a towel, which looks completely stupid, and then makes me sit down on the bed. 'Eyes wide open,' she says, then jabs her finger at them. I slam backwards, yelling out loud with pain. Who said the police could torture me? 'It's only a contact lens,' says Maureen, but I won't let her near me again. Eventually, after a huge amount of agony,

I master putting them in myself.

Maureen dries my hair, and scrubs my eyebrows with a flannel, Nicki clucking strangely in the background. Then I'm allowed to look in the big mirror. Somehow I'm still expecting to see green eyes and light brown hair looking back at me. But instead I see a white face, black shaggy hair, amazing black eyebrows and dark brown eyes – very bloodshot eyes. Only the pointed chin is recognisably mine, and it's a lot more pointy than it used to be because I seem to have lost any sign of chubbiness around the face. In fact my whole body is leaner than it ever was before.

'What do you think?' asks Maureen.

'I look like a bloody Goth,' I mutter, giving the eyebrows an experimental wiggle. Actually I rather like it. I look a lot older – I seem to have grown taller, cooped up in captivity – and the messy black hair is excellent.

She turns to Nicki. 'I think I've done a pretty good job there.' But Nic's gloomily examining her brunette helmet-hair frump-of-the-year look, and doesn't even look at me. With one crappy haircut and some unisex sweatshirts, Maureen's managed to turn her from someone who looked a bit like Nadine Coyle into a complete minger. She's gone from looking twenty-five, max, to around forty. Poor old Nic. She's actually only thirty-one. If they ever made a TV show called

Ten Years Older then Maureen could get a job as presenter.

Doug comes in the room and says, 'Well done Maureen, good job. I've settled up so we can leave now – by the back stairs please. I don't want anyone here seeing what you look like now. It won't take long to pack up, will it?'

He's right, it'll take about five minutes – there was never any space to unpack in the first place. 'We're going now?' says Nicki. 'But where?' And Doug says he'll explain everything in the car.

She sits in the front with him and I sit in the back with Maureen and we drive and drive. He tells us the name of the town where we're going to be living, but neither of us have ever heard of it. It's about fifty miles out of London – far enough away to be really boring but not far enough for people to have strange accents.

He says I'm going to be starting school on Monday and he points it out, Parkview Academy, as we pass it halfway up a hill.

'You'll be in year eight,' he says.

'No, I'm in year nine.'

'You'll be in year eight because it's safer. We want to make you as different from your old self as possible. And luckily' – he smirks – 'you don't look too old for your age.'

Stupid tosser. 'So what is my age?'

'We've made you thirteen; your new birthday is September the fifth.'

Brilliant. A whole year lost. A new birthday. Outstanding. 'You're an idiot,' I mutter, but I say it in Urdu so he won't understand.

He glances in the mirror and sees the look on my face. 'What's that? It's very important that you take this seriously, *Joe.*' He's started using our new names, speaking slightly too loud like we're deaf or foreign or stupid. 'If you screw up then we'll have to move you elsewhere, give you another identity. Some people have to do this three or four times. Let's try and avoid that, eh lad?'

'Yeah, yeah. . .' Three or four times? He can't be serious.

'You'd better change your attitude fast, lad,' he says, 'because it's a matter of life or death.'

There's nothing I can say. Doug's the only person who knows Joe Andrews and Doug already thinks he's stupid, greedy and revolting. Maybe everyone else will think the same. I look out of the window and wonder why Joe and Michelle have chosen to live in such a dump.

And then we're driving down a high street with the same shops that you see everywhere, and we're into an estate where all the houses look identically dull and shabby, and we're pulling up outside a semi with a red front door. This is it. Our new home. A safe house. But can we ever be safe again?

CHAPTER 3
Ellie

School is the only place where I feel calm. Everywhere else I'm looking out for exploding shops and heavies bursting from the shadows. It's completely exhausting because nothing actually ever happens, so I'm wasting tons of energy watching and worrying.

But once I go through the school gates I feel better. No one can find me here. I'm camouflaged among hundreds of other kids all dressed the same. It's not like London where everyone looks different. In the playground, pretty much everyone is the same colour, has the same sort of look. I never even knew you could be this invisible.

My invisibility doesn't hold up in the classroom though. My class is full of babies. The boy who sits on my left – Max – is about seven inches smaller than me, and his voice is as high as James Blunt's. The girl in front of me – Claire – is even smaller. She looks like an eight-year-old who's borrowed a uniform five sizes too big for her.

I'd been quite interested in the idea of sharing a classroom with girls. But even the ones who look thirteen seem incredibly young. There're only one or two who make a real effort with make up and stuff.

Among this lot I really stick out. I'm the tallest. I sometimes look like I might need to shave. I know everything – it's so helpful that St Saviour's was unbelievably strict and made us work so hard. Redoing year eight is a breeze. A boring one.

Today I'm dozing in English class, thinking about a picture I once saw in a magazine of a woman member of a tribe somewhere in Indonesia. Her left hand had only two fingers; the rest had been hacked off, one finger for every family member she'd lost. It was her tribe's way of remembering the dead. I can't see it catching on in England, but right now I think it's got possibilities. People would know something about you right from the start, without asking questions. So you never forget, and you carry the truth on your body.

Some losses don't really deserve a whole finger though. When my dad left, I was only about two and he just kind of faded out of my life. Now he's gone forever, I suppose. He'd never find us even if he looked. Maybe he's worth a little toe. What about losing a friend?

What about seeing someone die?

Brian, who sits on my right, pokes his elbow in my ribs and I'm suddenly aware that the classroom has gone strangely quiet and everyone is looking at me. A few of the girls are giggling. 'Joe Andrews?' says the teacher. 'Are you still with us, Joe?' Damn. I wonder how long he's been calling on me. 'Yes, sir,' I say, which is what they expected at St Saviour's, but it gets a big laugh here. Bugger.

'Wake up, young man,' says Mr Brown. 'Late night last night?' I shrug, then half nod, so he can take it as agreement if he wants.

'Perhaps you'd like to tell us, Joe, something about Prospero's magic in *The Tempest*?'

He's trying to catch me out. Big mistake. I deal with his question really easily – I even quote from the play, that's how good I am – and then I sit there trying not to look smug.

All the girls are giggling now. Even little Claire sneaks a look at me from under her long droopy fringe. I'm getting quite a bit of female attention. Pity I can't take advantage without feeling like a child-molester.

The bell goes, and Mr Brown scowls and stomps out of the room. Brian slaps me on the back and he and his mates walk with me to the dining room to get lunch.

Ty Lewis at St Saviour's never made people laugh

or had an instant gang. He – I – he was just Arron's sidekick. I never made any friends of my own, I was too worried he'd go off with some new mates.

I've never been in a school without Arron. We made friends when we walked to school together on our first day in reception at St Luke's, because our mums knew each other from some evening class. He was really happy to be going to big school – he knew everything about it because his brother Nathan had been there for three years already.

I was pretending I was happy too, for my mum and gran, but I was actually a little bit nervous and I didn't like our teacher because she kept on calling me Tyrone. Arron showed me where to put my coat, and how the lock on the loo door worked. He taught me to climb the climbing frame, and he explained to Miss Eagles that I was really called Tyler. And he'd always been there every school day since. Until now.

Now I'm always looking around for him. Sometimes I see a tall dark boy at the end of a corridor and I try to catch up – then realise that it's not him after all. It can't be him. Every time I feel sick, every time the same – I'm not sure – disappointment? Relief?

As we're queuing for our lunches – stodgy lasagne, excellent because I'm lucky to get a boiled egg at home – some girls wander up to us. They're the most confident girls in year eight, the ones who've discovered make-up and short skirts and – if I'm not mistaken – push-up bras.

Their leader is called Ashley Jenkins and I have a vague impression that she's loud and annoying. Her eyelashes curl like fat spider-legs, her lips are glossed like snail's slime. I try and ignore her. It doesn't work.

'That was cool, the way you tricked Mr Brown,' says Ashley, patting her hair.

'I suppose so. I wasn't really tricking him.'

Ashley shrugs: 'Whatever. I was wondering, do you want to come for a walk with me after school? Maybe we could go up the shopping centre?'

My practical experience with girls is pretty minimal after two and a half years at an all-boys' school, although Arron and I had talked a lot about the theory. Arron gave me basic instructions based on eight weeks of tussling in the park with Shannon Travis – eight weeks when I felt left out and left behind. We'd never imagined that I would be asked out in front of a huge crowd of people. In fact, we'd never really imagined I'd be asked out at all.

From the way the year eight boys around me glance at each other, it looks like I am being offered their ultimate fantasy. Ashley doesn't look like someone to offend. Ty would have been speechless, but luckily

Joe is a supercool dude. There's a poster on the wall, and I improvise. 'Great offer, Ashley, but I can't do tonight. I'm training with the athletics squad. Really sorry.'

Ashley looks impressed but not exactly like she believes me, and likewise Brian and his friends. And there's a look of surprise on the face of the teacher right in front of us in the queue who – I realise too late – is Mr Henderson. He has taken me for all of two PE lessons and certainly never mentioned anything about athletic talent. But, fair play to him, he turns around and says, 'We're looking forward to having you in the squad, er, Joe. Make sure you're there prompt at 3.30 and bring your kit. I'll have cabbage and carrots, and go easy on the custard,' he adds, turning back to the dinner lady.

Ashley pouts and says, 'When are you free then?' and I say, 'I'll let you know,' impressing Brian's gang almost as much as my fantasy place in the athletics squad. The girls find another table, and I'm left with the impossible questions of the boys. When was I chosen? What did he say to me? Had I ever competed before? Did I realise that everyone else in the squad was at least sixteen?

The same criteria apply to Ashley: 'She's never looked at anyone in our year before,' says Brian. 'She's only just split up with Dan Kingston in year ten. She won't like it that you didn't say yes right away, Ashley gets whatever she wants. Aren't you the lucky one?' Everyone laughs and jeers and the lasagne sticks in my throat. It tastes like lumpy cement.

I'm sure Mr Henderson won't make me train. They take PE really seriously at this school, much more so than at St Saviour's where we were lucky to get a game of football in our concrete playground. Here they have fields and a running track, a gym and even a swimming pool. The school is a designated sports academy, whatever that is, and the athletics squad is made up of people who compete for the county. I am an idiot.

But when your whole life is a lie then one more doesn't seem like a big deal. It's ironic really, I'm only at this school because I'm trying to tell the truth.

The final bell arrives soon enough and I text home to say I'll be a bit late, and walk slowly over to the sports staff office, which is right by the running track. I'll tell Mr Henderson that I made a stupid mistake. But when I get there there's a girl sitting at his desk. She's older than me and she's not wearing school uniform, but she's too young to be a teacher.

I stand there feeling awkward while she looks me up and down. She takes her time.

'Are you Joe?' she asks. 'Umm . . . yes,' I reply uncomfortably. 'I'm Ellie,' she says. 'Mr Henderson asked me to watch you run and try you out. I'll report back to him.'

I shift from one foot to another. 'Umm, you see, the thing is I'm not really meant to be here.'

She looks up at me. Grey eyes, blonde fringe, a smile that could be friendly or might be laughing at me. 'But you are here.'

'Yes but I'm not meant to be. I wasn't spotted, or asked to join the squad or anything like that. I just . . . umm . . . made a mistake.'

'It may not be a mistake. That's what Mr Henderson wants me to find out.' She takes her hands off the desk and reaches down and kind of glides towards me, and I suddenly realise that she's sitting in a wheelchair. I go all hot and cold with embarrassment.

'If you'll just open the door for me then I'll go out to the track and meet you there when you're ready,' she says.

I just stand there, probably with my mouth open. She assumes I'm shy. 'Don't worry, Joe, the others are training in the gym today. There's no one to watch.'

'I . . . you . . . you're in a wheelchair?' It comes out as a question. Duh! How dim can you get? I am never going to speak to this girl again. Luckily she laughs and says, 'Wow, you're really observant. Don't let it scare you off. Now go and get out of your clothes and

I'll see you in a minute.'

And she wheels away, leaving me completely crushed and absolutely determined to impress her. I rush to open the door. 'Hurry up,' she says, and I do.

Twenty minutes later I've warmed up and stretched, following her instructions, and I'm pounding round the track. It's amazing how good it feels, how concentrating on breathing and moving make all the worry of the last few weeks fade away.

When I run it doesn't matter if I'm Joe or Ty. Running isn't just about escaping, it's about power and strength, chasing away the fear of the unknown, these people who want me silenced. When I was eight I thought I could grow up to be a superhero; here I am flying around the track as fast as Spiderman, as strong as the Incredible Hulk.

I've always loved running. Mr Patel thought it was great that I would volunteer to do the longest paper rounds. It wasn't just because of the money that I wanted them, it was because once I'd delivered the last *Daily Mail* I could run all the way home through the park. In those days I wasn't scared of the park. In those days I loved the park.

I come to a halt beside Ellie, blinking, sweating and feeling a bit dazed. She hands me a bottle of water and I gulp it down, wishing I'd brought a towel.

'That was not bad at all,' she says, sounding pleased. 'Really promising, actually. If you're prepared to work I think you could achieve something.'

Neither of us has noticed, but Mr Henderson has joined us. 'I'm pleased to hear that, Joe,' he says, drily. 'It's not every day someone announces that they've appointed themselves to the squad.'

'I'm really sorry—' I begin, but he waves his hand dismissively. 'I don't know any of the details but I gather you've had problems at your last school.'

I open my mouth to protest, then close it again. I wonder what story the school has been told. 'I'm a great believer in new starts,' continues Mr Henderson, which is very nice of him considering he probably thinks I'm disruptive, violent and thick. 'I'm interested that you chose the athletics squad to get out of a tight spot, and if Ellie agrees I'm going to make a suggestion.'

Ellie nods, and he continues. 'Ellie here is a bit of a local celebrity. She's a very successful athlete and she's working for a place in the Paralympics. She's been given sponsorship by various local businesses and the council to back her training and she's also working towards a qualification in sports science. We're very proud of her.

'Ellie needs a case study as part of her course-work, and she's happy to work with you. You may even be able to join the athletics squad for real one day. It's a challenge for both of you, but if you work hard and do what you're told, then who knows what you can achieve. What do you think?'

What I'm mostly thinking is that PC Plod, aka Doug, isn't going to like this at all. 'Keep your head down' is the advice he's given me, and special training from some local celebrity blonde paraplegic isn't exactly what he meant. On the other hand, how can I say no? Isn't that just going to get more attention? And Mr Henderson and Ellie obviously think I'm being given something very special, although I'm not altogether sure that competing in running races is actually my thing.

'Well?' asks Mr Henderson and I nod and mutter my thanks. Ellie tells me to go and get a shower or I'll freeze, standing around all sweaty, and she'll see me here same time tomorrow. She's certainly bossy, but she says it all in a nice way and there's something quite soothing about obeying her orders. I don't think she's put off by sweat. She gives me a really nice smile.

I'll do the training, I decide, and then find a way out of competing if the problem arises. Sprain an ankle or something. It's certainly a good idea to be as fit as possible, just in case. Even Doug should see that. If I tell him.

After all, you never know when you might need to run away, and, right now, there's quite a lot I might need to run away from.

CHAPTER 4
Home

Walking home is the worst part of the day. I try to vary my route, partly in case I am being followed, mainly to make it last longer. My mum's no fun to be around right now, and I'm not used to her being home when I get there anyway.

She used to finish work hours later than me, and when she did come home she was either studying, chatting to her mates on the mobile, or getting ready to go to the pub for karaoke. She was singing and happy and laughing and I loved the way she buzzed around, doing five things at once.

But now she spends all her time sitting at the kitchen table, smoking. She never bothers to straighten her hair and her eyebrows look weirdly heavier. I haven't heard her have an argument for days, even with Doug, and she never switches the radio on. It's not so nice to see her like this and sooner or later she's going to start calling her sisters and her friends and we'll be found by the wrong people. The petrol bomb guys.

I reach the High Street, dodge into WH Smith, just in case there is anyone following me, then out and on to a bus. No one gets on with me, so I feel reasonably safe. I get home, dump my bag and blazer and call out, 'Mum . . . I'm home. . .'

It may not seem like a big deal to call your mother Mum but it is for us. She was only sixteen when I was born and she never seemed old enough to be called Mum somehow, and anyway Gran was more like my real mother. But since she became Michelle I can't call her that and I can't call her Nicki. So I'm calling her Mum, thinking of her as Mum and hoping like hell she'll be up to taking on the role. She hates it, says it makes her feel old and makes a little protesting face every time I say it.

She's smoking in the kitchen as usual, ash speckled over the white Formica. In WH Smith I'd bought the local paper to encourage her to look for a job. I spread it open in front of her, hoping she'll get interested. 'Look, several office administrator jobs and two for PAs. Can't you apply?'

She has a look, but shakes her head: 'I don't think so. What would I say on my CV? What about references?'

Where is Doug when I need him? Surely this is something he ought to be helping with. I'm worried that the money the police have given us is going to run out sooner or later, and with no job for her or paper round for me, then what are we going to live on?

'Mum, the police will give you fake references and stuff. I'm sure Doug said something about that. Look, save it to show him when he comes here.'

I slide out the jobs page and at least she takes it and puts it into a drawer. As I fold up the paper I spot the back page and can't believe my eyes. There's a big picture of Ellie, grinning away, and a headline – 'Gold again for brave Ellie'.

Reading on, I discover that Ellie has just won a crucial qualifying race for the Paralympics – that's like the Olympic games but for disabled people, which sounds to me like a really complicated thing to organise – and that she lost the use of her legs when she broke her back in a gymnastics accident aged twelve.

She's now seventeen – only just three years older than me, but when the three years are between a fourteen-year-old boy and a seventeen-year-old girl, frankly, she might as well have been thirty. Particularly when the fourteen-year-old boy is pretending to be only thirteen. It's not fair, I think, considering girls like Ashley Jenkins can have their pick of anyone of any age.

Not, of course, that I fancy Ellie, it's just the principle which is sexist.

There's also the wheelchair, which is kind of intriguing because it's possible that it makes it hard for her to get a boyfriend, which might cancel out the age difference. . . I mean, she might be really interested in someone a tiny bit younger who's not prejudiced about disabilities, and who'd be happy to push the chair and carry stuff. I don't think I'm prejudiced about disabilities at all . . . it would depend on what other people would say . . . but in theory I'm not. Not when it's someone as pretty as Ellie.

OK, I admit it. I do sort of fancy Ellie. We could be a really unconventional couple, like . . . like . . . umm . . . Paul McCartney and Heather Mills McCartney if it was her who was massively older than him instead of the other way round and if they hadn't decided to hate each other and get divorced, obviously.

'I suppose you want supper,' says my mum, who is really talented at interrupting my most interesting thoughts, and she starts poking about vaguely in the fridge as if she hopes some food might suddenly magically appear. Of course nothing does, so I take charge and find some ancient cheese and onions which are trying to turn into plants. I chop the onions and fry them and grate the cheese and make spaghetti.

We haven't got any kind of food shopping routine, which isn't surprising because we never did have, but we always used to have Gran to cook things for us and the kebab shop three doors away was really good, and sometimes we'd go on the bus to Tesco. Now I suspect that Mum hasn't left the house for days, but I don't want her to burst into tears so I haven't bullied her into going to the supermarket.

It's not even a very nice house to be stuck in. It's bigger than anywhere we've ever lived in before – three bedrooms, a proper bathroom, not just a shower, and a separate kitchen which is big enough for its own table. But compared to our cosy pink and blue flat, this house will never be home. Everything is beige or brown – carpets, furniture, curtains – the magnolia walls have no pictures and the kitchen is painfully white like a dentist's surgery.

At home our fridge was covered with photos and Capital Radio blared out and I could look out of the window and see people getting tattoos and manicures. Queuing for buses. Arguing, kissing, shouting at their kids. Buying plantain, coriander, kebabs, ice-cream, okra – you could buy anything on our street. I could smell meat and buses, curry and hairspray. Everything was interesting. Every day was different.

Here it's always quiet and all you see from the

window are grey houses and the biggest excitement is when the bloke across the road washes his car, which he does every Sunday. No wonder she's a bit down.

As we eat – or rather as I eat and she twirls spaghetti on her fork and then drops it again – I ask, 'Mum, do you know who the police are hiding us from? Has Doug told you anything?'

I'm wondering whether Nathan is involved. Arron's brother is big and tough, he knows how to fight and he has some dodgy-looking friends. Arron really looked up to Nathan, so we spent a lot of time trying to hang out with him and his mates, down the bowling alley mostly. Sometimes they let us join in and sometimes they told us to buzz off. Not in precisely those words, obviously.

I can see that Nathan would be pretty scary if you didn't know him and you were stupid enough to get into a fight with him. And he definitely wants me to keep quiet, because he told me so, but I don't think he would actually want to kill me. Nathan always seemed to quite like me – at least, I thought he did. He sometimes told Arron to look out for me. And he used to do a paper round for Mr Patel. Surely he wouldn't attack his shop?

Mum's looking worried. I don't know whether that's because she has information she's not telling me or whether she's as clueless as I am. 'I don't know much, Ty, and I don't think they're going to tell us. But it seems

41

to me that it's something very big and very organised. Don't you think?'

I do think. But I don't like to think any further.

CHAPTER 5
Intimidation

F riday afternoon, walking home from school, the weekend stretches ahead. I suppose I could go down to the shopping centre tomorrow, meet up with some of the kids from school, but it seems a bit unfair to abandon my mum, even though we don't do anything together except occasionally bicker.

I suppose it's good to get a chance to stop pretending all the time, but sometimes I think it's only the pretending that keeps me going.

I come through our front door and hear male voices in the living room. I freeze, trying to overhear what's going on. I catch the phrase 'only temporary,' then Doug emerges, saying cheerily, 'Hello young man. How's life at your new school?'

I ignore him and walk into the room. Mum is sitting there drinking tea with DI Morris and one of his sidekicks, youngish with red hair and freckles. I vaguely remember him as one of the less shouty ones at the police station. He introduces himself as Detective Constable Bettany.

Mum says, 'He's just come in from school. Can I at least get him a snack?' like they're here to ship me off to prison, and rushes away. She brings me tea and some biscuits, then goes back to the kitchen with Doug. I hope she's going to discuss her job prospects.

'So, Ty, how are you settling into your new life here?' says DI Morris. Unlike Doug he seems genuinely interested. 'It can't be easy.'

I shrug. 'It's OK.'

'Good. Making friends?'

'Suppose so.'

'How about your schoolwork? What's your favourite subject?'

'I suppose French.'

I find languages really easy. At home, as well as learning Urdu from Mr Patel, I'd picked up a lot of Turkish from the kebab shop guys and I'd just got a Saturday job cleaning up the tattoo parlour across the road and had persuaded Maria, the receptionist, to teach me Portuguese. I'm pretty upset to have lost these opportunities.

My ultimate ambition is to be fluent in about twenty

languages and be one of those interpreters who work for Premiership football teams. Scoring Portuguese lessons was a really big thing for me because obviously it's a key footballing language. I never talk much about it though. My mum has her heart set on me earning megabucks in the City and, according to Arron, languages are gay.

'School's boring because I've done it all before. The sport is good though. Amazing facilities.'

DI Morris doesn't know it but he's discovered more about my life as Joe than Mum and Doug have. He asks a bit about sport, but he's more interested in football than athletics, so I don't feel the need to tell him about extra training with Ellie. Come to that, I'm more interested in football than athletics. We establish that he supports West Ham and I support Man Utd – I know it's wrong for a Londoner, but Manchester's where my dad went to university – and he moves on to the point of his visit.

'Ty, we'd like to chat to you about the events leading up to the attack in the park. Just general background. Also I'm sure you've got some questions you'd like to ask us. It's nothing to worry about.'

Too right I've got some questions, I think, but I just nod. DC Bettany is taking notes, just like he did at the police station. They're making out it's all very friendly, but I'm not feeling too relaxed.

DC Bettany produces a book of photographs.

45

'Anyone here you recognise? Not just that afternoon at the park, but from any time?' I do see a few faces I know and point them out. They ask about St Saviour's, which guys Arron and I hung around with. They ask about the paper round. They ask about what we did after school – mostly homework, I reply. I'm not sure they believe me.

They ask about gangs. Had anyone ever asked me to join one? Would I have liked to join one? It depends. It depends a lot on what you think a gang is. According to the newspapers they're mostly for black boys and they've got names and rules and tattoos and things. So I answer no without any worries.

I'm tired, and I stifle a big yawn. The policemen glance at each other. DI Morris asks, 'You'd been friendly with Arron since you were what, five years old?'

I nod. 'You were the only boys from your primary school to go to St Saviour's, yes? Most of the rest went to St Jude's or Tollington?' The names of the schools seem like something from a film or a book – far away and fictional. I nod again.

'So you and Arron were quite close in your first year at secondary school. Did things remain that way?' I nod again. The room is hot, and my throat feels incredibly sore, like someone inside me has been slashing with a razor. My arm is aching so that I can hardly lift the mug of tea. It must be all the training.

'But you made new friends? Your circle increased?' asks DI Morris. I find my voice.

'Arron, he was good at making friends. People wanted to be around him.'

'I see.'

He asks a bit more. Boring stuff. Nothing to worry about. But I don't like the way he seems to think it's OK to ask about any part of my life. It makes me feel a bit exposed. Like I'm in the Big Brother house, except that would be way cooler than this dump.

And then he says, 'OK, Ty, thank you for answering our questions. I realise this is not at all easy for you. Now you can ask what you like, although I'm sorry to say that there may well be things that we cannot tell you.'

'Why are there things you can't tell me, when I have to tell you everything?' I ask.

'As a witness, you can't be told about our investigation, because that could affect your account. It's a high-profile case and it is good that you are removed from the local area.'

'What do you mean, high profile?'

'There's a suggestion that there may be racism involved. Feelings are running high locally.'

'But there wasn't. . . No one said anything racist. . .' I say.

'You'll understand why people think that, though,' he says, but I don't really, when I think about Arron's black mum and various white dads and the way he and his brother and sisters were all different shades of brown.

'Who are these people that want to kill me?' I ask. 'Who bombed the shop? Can they find me here? Is it . . . are they . . . people we know, or someone else?'

I think of Nathan, his face close to mine, sweat pouring from his forehead to his eyes, so it looks like he's crying, spitting out the words. 'Keep your mouth shut, or I'll make sure it stays shut.' How would he make sure?

DI Morris looks hard at me, as if weighing up something, then makes up his mind.

'As you know, Ty, we are dealing with three suspects here. Three people have been charged with a very serious offence. Because there are three of them, their lawyers will all be trying to shift the blame, one to the other, and also they are casting doubt on your integrity as a witness. We need to be absolutely sure that you are telling the truth. You will almost certainly be asked difficult questions in court.

'After the petrol bomb incident we are concerned that you may be subject to witness intimidation. That's why we are taking extra care of you and your mother in the run up to the trial, and, if we deem it necessary, beyond.'

'Who are they? What else do they do? Why can't you catch them? Why do they want to shut me up?'

DI Morris hesitates. 'We are confident that we can protect you,' he says, which doesn't even begin to answer my questions.

'What about my gran, and my aunties? Are you looking after them?'

'We will keep an eye on them, yes. Luckily only your gran lives very locally, doesn't she?'

'Yes, but there's my aunties too.'

'We're doing our best, Ty, but I'd be lying to you if I said we could protect every single member of your family.'

Why not? It's just three more people, not a huge clan.

'When will the trial be?'

'Courts take their time. I'd be hoping for something by late autumn. The earlier the better.'

'So I'll be Joe until then?'

'Yes, unless there is a reason to move you. But the most likely reason for that would be if you or your mother does something unwise, like contacting family or old friends, going back to London to visit, or telling people here about your former identities.'

'What does everyone think? Why do they think we have left?'

'It's entirely possible that many people think you were involved in the fight in the park that night, Ty. The defendants are all juveniles, and their names will not be made public, so no one really knows who they are. Others think you have moved away. Your mother's job, for example – they think that she was offered another post in a different part of the country and moved away.'

Oh yeah? I can't see anyone actually believing that. First, my mum loved her job. Second, if she was leaving, she'd have thrown the biggest party ever, ending up with her karaoke version of 'Love Machine' with my aunties doubling up as the rest of Girls Aloud. They're famous for it. People think they ought to go on X Factor.

'The defendants – are they in prison?'

'They are in a Young Offender Institution and so far bail has been denied.' I must look blank, because he adds, 'That means they will probably stay there until the trial.'

'What happens after the trial? Will I go on being Joe?'

'It's possible. When you give evidence we will certainly apply for your identity to be protected – but after the trial it may be safer to move you. I'd think of this time as a temporary phase.'

I want to ask about Arron, and his family, but the

slasher feeling in my throat is back. I say, 'Can my mum get a job? Can you help her? I don't think we will have enough money.'

'Doug is here to help with that, and he should make sure that there is enough money either way, job or no job.' DI Morris leans forward. 'Would it be better for her if she had a job? Is she a bit depressed and lonely, do you think?'

Of course she is, I want to shout, but instead I just nod. DI Morris says, 'OK then, I'll speak to Doug. Try not to worry too much. Thanks Ty,' and he hands me his card. 'If you want to speak to me then call this number.'

Why would I want to do that? Talking to him is like watching a film with the sound turned down. You know there are important bits that you're missing but you can only guess at them. You're left filling the gaps with stuff that might be worse than reality.

There's a lot that he's not telling me. But does he realise how much I'm not telling him?

CHAPTER 6
Red Bus

I'm jittery and sleepless, jumpy with nerves. I have a constant buzz of nausea, which buggers my appetite completely. I'm pretty much existing on a diet of raw caffeine, Coke Lite to be specific. I've helped myself to a few of Mum's cigarettes.

This is not the greatest state in which to start a heavy new training programme. Ellie sat down with me on the first day and went through a set of health questions, and I told her exactly what she wanted to hear. So, I sleep for nine hours a night, eat a healthy balanced diet and have never smoked. More or less true six months ago, give or take the odd kebab. Mostly true just a few weeks ago. But now I'm forcing myself to nibble a handful of crisps, which is all I've eaten today before facing her for the third training session this week.

It's a bright sunny day, but instead of going to the

running track we head for the school gym. It's not like any school gym I've ever been in. They call it the Fitness Suite and it's full of expensive equipment.

It's very quiet because most people are outside. She sorts out a programme for me, shows me how things work and writes it all down. 'I'm not going to be able to give you as much time as this in the next few weeks,' she says. 'I've got a big competition coming up. So you need a programme you can work at on your own.' It all sounds like hard work.

'What you need is an access card,' she adds.

'A what?'

'An access card, so you can use all the sports facilities of the school out of hours. The only thing is they don't hand them out to anyone as young as you, but I can go and have a word with Mr Henderson if you like.'

She smiles, then ruins it. 'Anyway, you seem much older than your age. I can't believe you're still only twelve.'

'I'm not *twelve*,' I say, devastated, adding lamely, 'I'm nearly fourteen, actually.' What an insult. I'm going to be fifteen in November.

She grins. 'Sorry! Let me ask anyway.' She tells me which buttons to press to set up the treadmill to let me run for forty minutes, and says, 'I'll be back soon.'

It's strange running on a treadmill, and I don't like it so much. I feel like I'm about to fall backwards or wobble off. It takes a few stops and starts to get going, and eventually I find the easiest thing is to shut my eyes and imagine that I'm outdoors. At first it's hard going, then the rhythm of the breathing takes over, and the physical motion gets easier and easier.

I run and run and in my head there's a long road leading to London. And then I'm back in the park, running and running, heart thumping in my chest. Thoughts scuttling round my head like rats on a rubbish tip: ambulance, Arron, ambulance, Arron.

I'm running and running and there's no one to help me; and then I see the red bus on the road and I know I can get help and I know I can help Arron and the red bus is red blood and it's flooding the white shirt. . .

I slam my hand down flat on the treadmill's emergency stop button and stagger off the machine. I'm going to faint or throw up or something. I drop to my knees on the mat and curl into a ball; I'm trying to stop the shaking which has taken me over. I'm still like this when Ellie comes back.

'Oh my God,' she says. 'Are you all right?'

I can't speak. I concentrate on stopping shaking. She stretches her hand out, leans down to me, pats my shoulder and asks urgently, 'Joe, what's happened? Are you OK?'

With a huge effort I sit up. But I can't speak. I breathe deep and hug my arms around my knees. I have to stop shaking, I have to stop seeing the blood, the mud, the meaty flesh – stop thinking about the ambulance, stop the panic. Christ, Ty, get a grip.

Ellie hands me a bottle of some sugary sports drink. 'Try this. Maybe you're dehydrated.' I sip a little. It helps. 'Shall I call for help? Are you in pain?'

I shake my head, no, filled with shame. I want to speak, but every time I open my mouth I shut it again because I'm very scared that what's going to come out is going to sound something like a scream.

Ellie moves her hand on my shoulder and I reach up and grab it. It feels like she's the only thing keeping me anchored to safety. I glance around. Thank goodness we're all alone. Ellie keeps hold of my hand, and I gradually calm down. It's strange looking up at her when I've only ever looked down.

We seem to sit there in silence for hours, but eventually she says, 'You're looking better now. Can you tell me what happened?'

I'm still holding her hand, like a pathetic baby. I let it go right away. She straightens up and I think how uncomfortable it must have been for her, leaning over the chair to reach me. I'd like to run away but I owe her a little bit of truth. 'I closed my eyes when I was running and I lost touch of where I was. It was like a flashback.'

'A flashback to something pretty scary?' she says, obviously dying to know more.

'And I haven't had much to eat today, and I suppose that didn't help.'

She looks at her watch. 'It's six o clock now. Are you OK to go and get changed? Then we could go down to the High Street and get a coffee and a snack and have a chat. I don't want this happening every time you're training, especially if I'm not always going to be around. And look. . .' she reaches into her pocket, 'I got you an access card. But there was a big fuss about it. That's why I was so long. There's a boy in your year – Carl someone – who's the captain of the under-fourteen football team. He was furious that he and his team weren't getting cards too. Argued for ages. But Mr Henderson said he could make an exception for one but if he let them in he'd have to let in hundreds. I hope you don't get any hassle about it.'

I shrug. 'Thanks, anyway.'

She looks thoughtful. 'Unless, maybe, this has put you off training completely. Do you think it could happen again?'

I consider. 'No. I like training. Mostly it makes me feel a lot better. It's just today I wasn't in great shape.'

'Good. Can you get up? You ought to stretch a bit too.'

I get up. I stretch. And thirty minutes later we are sitting in an organic health food cafe on the High Street – 'I don't think we'll find any of your fan club in here. They'll be having frappuccinos at Starbucks,' says Ellie – and she orders some brown rice stir-fry for both of us.

'What do you mean, my fan club?'

Ellie laughs. 'Joe, you must realise that you've taken the school by storm. Most of the girls in year eight – and years seven and nine for that matter – are crazy about you. You're the talk of the town.'

She's got to be joking. 'How would you know?' I ask cautiously.

'Oh, I have impeccable sources,' she says. 'I have a sister in year eight, plus I run a group mentoring young sportswomen. Believe me, I know everything.'

'You have a sister in year eight?' I'm wondering how I've missed an Ellie lookalike, particularly one who has her eye on me.

'In your class. Claire. Of course,' she adds hastily, 'she's just reporting to me on what the other girls think. She's not one to follow the crowd.'

Claire? The tiny little mouse who sits in front of me?

How can she be Ellie's sister? 'Oh yes. She doesn't talk much.' I'm trying to think how to find out more without sounding big-headed.

'They all think you're older than you are. That's why I was teasing you about only being twelve. Apparently you're very mysterious. And there are the cheekbones as well.'

Oh. I think she's probably still teasing, but it sounds like my disguise isn't holding up too well. I'm chewing my lip, which is what I do when I'm worried.

Ellie asks, 'You don't like that? It's good, isn't it?'

'I don't know. It's all a bit complicated.'

'I can see that.'

'Ellie, please, you won't tell anyone what happened?'

'Of course not. I wish you hadn't been on your own though. If you had passed out on the treadmill you could have injured yourself.'

'Yeah, yeah. But I didn't. I mean, I didn't even pass out.'

'How much are you eating Joe? That was all crap wasn't it, when we did the health survey?'

'Err, well it wasn't really, because mostly I do eat healthy and sleep and everything. It's just that the last few weeks have been a bit . . . umm . . . difficult. I mean I was just answering on a general basis.'

I was answering from the time when Gran was around to keep an eye on me, to tell the truth.

'So, right now, how's your eating? And sleeping, smoking and drinking?'

'Well, we've just moved, so eating's a bit chaotic. I mean, we haven't got a routine or local shops or stuff. And I've been finding it difficult to sleep. And my mum says smoking is good for her nerves so I thought I'd just try and see if it helps.' I poke at the brown rice. It's weird, but nice, to have a proper meal that I haven't had to make.

'For God's sake, Joe, are you mad? You get the chance to join one of the best school athletics squads in the country and you take up smoking?'

'Er, well. . .'

'Why did you move in the first place?'

Why? Hmm. . . 'My mum broke up with her boyfriend and she wanted a new start.' I think that's a pretty good cover story to invent, off the cuff.

'And what about your dad?'

'I never see him.'

I suddenly remember something my gran once said about my dad. 'That Danny Tyler,' she grumbled, 'so bloody good-looking that he had his own fan club. Of course your mum had to outdo all the rest.' Gran didn't seem to like my dad much but Ellie's comment about my fan club makes me feel quite close to him. I'm called Tyler after my dad, and changing my name meant losing that little link.

'So you and your mum must be a bit lonely, in a new town, making a new start, then?'

'We're OK.'

She says, 'I used to get a bit shaky like that when I was in hospital, when I'd just had my accident.' I'm amazed by how easily she can talk about it even though her whole life must have been shattered. I know a bit how that feels. 'I was in a terrible state. I blamed myself, everyone else. . . I couldn't see a future. All I wanted was to go back in time.

'One day a physiotherapist came to see me. I refused to do any work with her. I just shouted and screamed. And she said, "Scream all you like, nothing's going to change unless you do."'

'What happened? Why did you change?'

She smiles. 'She gave me something to think about and it really helped. I started working for myself, to take control. But the best thing was discovering that being in a wheelchair wasn't necessarily all bad.'

'Why not?' I ask.

'When you race a wheelchair it feels like you're flying. Honestly Joe, it's better than cycling or skiing.'

I wonder if one day in the future I'll be Ty again, and

able to say, 'Once I had to go into hiding because I witnessed a crime. It wasn't all bad, when I was Joe.' It's unimaginable. This is never going to be something that I can own, that I can talk about.

'Right Joe,' she says, 'you've got to leave the past behind. Forget it. Be really positive and focus on what you can achieve now. Because you could do incredibly well. You could go right to the top.'

I shrug. 'I'll try.' I wish I could, but the past won't leave me alone. Some other people have come into the cafe, and I can feel myself getting jumpy again as I check them out.

Ellie thumps the table. 'That is not good enough. Don't sit there shrugging and acting cool. Am I just wasting my time? I want you to show a bit of commitment. God, it's frustrating to see someone with such potential giving less than 100 per cent.'

I don't know what to say. People are looking. 'I'll do my best.'

'You'd better.' She's a bit scary when she's like this. I don't mind being nagged by her though, because she's so incredibly pretty.

She writes out a suggested training diet for me and asks if I can try and keep to it for a week and see how I feel. She asks if I can play music on my iPod to keep my mind busy when I train – yes, very good idea.

She says I must never just run on the treadmill, I must do interval training so I have to keep concentrating and changing the settings. She says, 'You've got to promise me to keep off those cigarettes or I'm going to come and talk to your mum.'

'Oh, bloody hell, Ellie.'

'I would, you know.'

She would too. I'd better keep them apart.

We leave the cafe, and arrange a time for training the next day. Coming out of the cafe she has to manoeuvre carefully around a pothole, and I wonder whether I should have offered to push her home or whether she'd think I was being crass. I have no idea how to act around the wheelchair. Mostly I just pretend it's not there.

It must be such a pain for her, never just being normal. And if you're stuck in a wheelchair it must be more than irritating to see people with no disabilities failing to make the most of life. People like me. I'm going to try my best for Ellie.

Then I run all the way home because I want to get back before it gets dark.

Opening the front door I know immediately that something is wrong. The smell is not the usual mixture of dust and cigarettes. It's stronger . . . smokier – Jesus, there's something on fire.

I yank the kitchen door open – nothing – then the living room. The television is on, sound turned off. And there's Mum, sprawled on the sofa, head down, not moving, with thick black smoke all around.

CHAPTER 7
Balamory

I run to her, grip her under the armpits and drag her to the front door. She's alive. She starts waking up and coughing, choking and retching in the fresh air. I leave her to it, grab a towel from a pile of dirty washing that's been sitting in the kitchen for about a week and run back into the room.

Petrol bomb . . . arson . . . I'm panicking, but I realise this is completely different. There's no actual fire anywhere, no flames. It's the sofa that's smouldering – the smoke is pouring from a black-edged hole in the beige fabric. I smother it with the towel, then look around. I can still hear Nicki coughing away on the front step.

Has someone attacked her? Beaten her up, left her unconscious, then set the place on fire? I look around but there's no sign of fighting, nothing broken or anything like that.

There are bottles scattered on the brown carpet. She's been shopping at last, down to the off licence to get a six-pack of alcopops. By the look of it, she's drunk them all. There's a cigarette stub lying on the sofa. If I hadn't got back when I did then, she'd have been dead.

I open all the windows, throw away the bottles, make sure the fire is completely out. Then I go and find her, right when she spews up all the Breezers and Coolers and whatever on to the front path. A neighbour walking by looks revolted and rushes away. I wish I could. Instead, I get a glass of water for her, then find the mop and bleach and slosh some water around on the path.

She's crying. 'I'm sorry, so sorry, Ty.'

'Bloody hell, *Mum*, shut it, will you? Wait until we're inside the house.'

She sobs and I mop in the dark, and after a bit we go inside and shut the front door. Everything still stinks of smoke. We sit in the kitchen and I make her a cup of tea. When I look for milk in the fridge, I realise that she'd actually bought some chicken and vegetables for supper. If only I'd come straight home.

Of course I've seen my mum drunk before. If she goes out with her mates they all have a few drinks, possibly quite a lot of drinks. I've seen her giggly and I've seen her merry and sometimes she gets a bit loud.

But she's happy and singing and fun. When she's planning a really big night out I get packed off to my gran's and all I see is the headache and pale face the next day. But she's never done this before. Drinking all alone? Passing out?

She can't stop crying. I can't find any tissues, so I get a loo roll and put it on the kitchen table in front of her. Then we just sit there, her weeping, me with arms crossed, silent. It's like I'm the stern father and she's the naughty teenager.

'Ty, I was just feeling so lonely. I thought a drink might cheer me up.'

'A drink or six.'

'I didn't know where you were. I was worrying about you. I thought, I'll just have another one. And then I lost track of time.'

This is not my fault. 'You mean you passed out smoking and started a fire.'

'I'm sorry, I'm so sorry. I'm such a bad mother.'

I know she wants me to wrap my arms around her and tell her how much I love her and what a great mum she is. Ty would have done that, but Joe is hard and cold and unforgiving. I despise the old Ty almost as much as I hate her. 'Pretty boy,' Arron used to call me sometimes, and I burned with shame. Now Joe's going to be tough and mean.

I say the words that will hurt her most. 'I wish Gran had come here with me and not you.' Then I go and turn off the television. There's still a foul smell in there, but I have to lock the windows so we can go to sleep and know that no one can break in. It's only when I move the towel from the sofa that I see it. Mum's mobile. What was she doing with that while she was drunk?

I pick it up and hit the call history button. My gran's number flashes up. I knew it. I knew she'd done something incredibly stupid. I remember Doug telling us that mobile networks are incredibly insecure. What if someone's spying on Gran's calls? What do I do now? Do I have to tell Doug? Does this mean I can't be Joe any more?

I go back into the kitchen. I give her the mobile, and she looks at me. She's wondering if I know what she's done. I'm not telling. 'It's really late and we should go to bed,' I say, but as I lie awake in my empty room I hear her crying downstairs for a long, long time. I can't sleep. I've opened all the windows in our bedrooms so we won't die of smoke inhalation, and it's freezing.

I'm remembering a time when I was about six, and staying at Gran's. I was under the table, parking my cars, and Auntie Louise was talking to Gran. Lou said, 'Nicki needs to get her act together a bit better, otherwise this'll keep on happening and you'll get lumbered.'

And Gran said, 'Louise, you know I'll always be there for my darling.' And I drove my cars – *brrrrrm* – out from their garage, and they stopped talking. I'd not understood what they meant but I'd always remembered it. And even though I'm Joe, the hard man, the cool dude, I wish I could go and stay with Gran and be her darling again.

In the morning Mum is still asleep when I need to leave the house to go to school. I sit at the table in my uniform wondering what to do. In the end I pick up the phone and call the school office. 'I'm Joe Andrews in 8R and I'm not coming to school today,' I say. I can't do any more lies. 'My mum is ill and I have to look after her.'

The secretary at the other end is surprised. 'Are you her sole carer?' she asks.

'She doesn't usually need a carer. But today she does, and it's me.'

'I'm not sure. I may have to enter this as an unauthorised absence.'

'Whatever.' I put the phone down. Next, I have a look in Mum's purse and lift fifty pounds. I take the bus to the supermarket and buy eggs and wholemeal bread, brown rice and pasta, milk, vegetables and fruit. All the things from Ellie's list. I get a few odd looks on the bus – I should have changed out of uniform – but no one challenges me. I carry the shopping up the hill to the house, and let myself in quietly. It's 10 am and Mum is still asleep.

I send a text to Ellie: 'Sorry can't train today. Mum sick.' And then I open all the windows again and spray everything with a strong air freshener. I clean the kitchen – that hasn't been done for a while – and then the bathroom. I check the front path, and mop it again because my night-time efforts didn't really do the job.

I make a cup of tea and some toast and take it upstairs. Mum's just beginning to wake up, so I dump it at her side and stomp back downstairs. Then I turn over the sofa cushion to hide the burned hole, lie down and watch a programme about house prices. And then another one, about cookery. And then I lose the plot completely and turn over to CBeebies.

When Mum finally makes it down the stairs I'm gazing at *Balamory*. I wish I had their problems, all the funny people living on an island in brightly coloured houses. She sits down next to me, and gently, nervously touches my shoulder. I pull away like she's hit me. 'Ty, darling,' she whispers. 'I'm watching,' I snarl, and turn my back.

'Why didn't you go to school?' she asks. I concentrate on Archie the Inventor who doesn't want to cross the road. 'I'm OK, Ty. You didn't have to bunk off.'

'I didn't bunk off. I phoned and said you were ill.'

'Oh.'

We sit and watch *Balamory*, just like when I was four, except then it'd have been *Thomas the Tank Engine* and we'd have snuggled up together. Today we're as far apart as one small sofa will allow. Archie is being helped across the road by PC Plum, two grown men hand in hand. It's possibly the silliest piece of television I've ever seen, but there's something about it that makes me want to cry. I'm definitely cracking up. Then she says, 'Ty, I called your gran last night. I know it was stupid.'

'You *were* stupid. How was she?'

'I didn't even get to speak to her. I just left a message.'

'Oh, great. You put us at risk so you can worry Gran by telling her what a crap time you're having.' And how it's all my fault – but I don't say that bit.

'Do you think we should tell Doug?'

I'd only spent all night thinking about this. 'No point. He gave us the phones didn't he? So he gets the itemised bills. He'll know all about it. '

'Oh. I'm so sorry.'

'Don't do it again.'

Then I go into the kitchen and I make us scrambled eggs for lunch and we sit and eat it without talking to each other. Afterwards I stand up, but her hand shoots out and grabs my wrist. 'Ow! Get off.'

Now we're both glaring. She says, 'You've got to stop sulking and listen to me, Tyler, or I swear I'll go crazy.'

'I don't have to do anything you tell me.'

She's shouting, 'You bloody well do. Sit down and listen to me. If it wasn't for you running after Arron when he didn't want you, we wouldn't be here in the first place.'

He did want me, I think. I don't say so though. I sit. I listen. But I don't look at her.

'This is really hard for both of us, Ty, but the main thing we've got going for us is that we've got each other. We can support each other through this. If we're fighting all the time, we've got nothing.'

Not true, I think. I am Joe, potential athlete. I have special training and an access card. I have a fan club of wannabe girlfriends and loads of boys on my team. It's you who's got nothing. Loser.

'This is really hard for me, Ty. I'm only thirty-one. I've got my own dreams – getting my law degree, qualifying as a solicitor, meeting someone special, maybe even getting married, maybe even having a brother or sister for you. How am I going to do that if we're getting a new identity every six months or so? What kind of life are we going to have? You've got school to go to every day, but I just sit here wondering if you're safe until you come home. If I go out, I spend the whole time looking behind me to see if anyone is following me.' Her voice is wavering, but she's managing not to cry.

'I don't know what's happened to you. You've got so tall and you look so different. It's not just the dark hair and eyes, it's everything about you. You used to tell me everything, Ty, and now we don't talk at all.'

Did she expect I'd be ickle baby boy Ty forever? Does she really believe I've been telling her everything for the last few years? I'm too angry to feel sorry for her, but there's a little bit of me that doesn't want this fight to dig any deeper.

'Get rid of your cigarettes,' I say. She looks shocked. 'I'll cut down, I promise, but I don't think I can get rid of them just like that.'

'Get rid of them, because if you don't I'll be thinking all day at school that you're going to burn the house down like you nearly did yesterday.'

She gets her bag and takes out the pack and throws it into the kitchen bin. Then, two seconds later, she plunges her hand into the bin and pulls it out. Pathetic.

'I promise I'll only smoke outside,' she says.

'Then you've got to go outside. You've got to go shopping and maybe find a job, or an exercise class, or a course or anything, Nicki. You can't sit in here all day long.'

'That's the first time you've called me Nicki for weeks,' she says, sounding happier.

'It's not going to happen again.'

'Oh yes it will.' She's smiling at me now.

'Look, we have to do this properly. We have to be new people, not just pretend.'

'How can we be new people when I have to dye your hair for you every two weeks? I don't want to be a new person. I'd worked bloody hard to get a life for us, move out of your gran's. I did that all on my own. For what?'

'You ain't got no choice,' I say, because I know this will really wind her up. My mum is obsessed with speaking English like they do on television. She says it's my passport to a better life, and if she can do it, so can I. Of course, when she loses her temper she cusses me like a normal person, but it's never a good idea to point out that she's setting a bad example.

When I told her that Urdu and Portuguese are going to be my passports to a better life she threatened to stop me talking to Mr Patel and particularly to Maria at the tattoo parlour. She just doesn't get me sometimes.

She reacts just as I expect. 'Speak proper English Ty, and don't be cheeky. Why did I send you to a good school like St Saviour's if you're going to talk like an ignorant chav?'

'You shouldn't have bothered,' I reply. I wish she hadn't sent me to St Saviour's. It was an ordinary state school pretending it was a private school and it had the boys and parents to match.

She sighs. 'Your dad went to St Saviour's, Ty, and I always said that you were going to go there, to get some of the advantages he had. He got a really good education there and went to university and you can still do all that. You don't have to be like me and ruin your life when you're just a teenager.'

'Thank you very much,' I say extremely politely in fluent BBC-News-at-Ten. 'It's nice to know that I ruined your life.'

'You didn't ruin my life. I did, because I was an idiot. You can still make something of yours.'

'So can you. You just have to get on with it.'

She rolls her eyes. 'I know I've been a waste of space. Tell you what, Ty, would you come shopping with me at the weekend? If I get some new clothes, maybe I'll feel more positive. There's probably stuff you need as well. It'll be nice to do something together.'

I have no choice but to nod. I'm still angry but I can't deny that I do love her really. And I feel achingly sorry for her, and I miss her happiness so much.

But I also know enough about my school to know that everyone goes to the shopping centre on a Saturday

morning, and I'm sure no one goes with their mum.
How can I get out of this? Joe Andrews is not about to
commit social suicide if I can help it.

CHAPTER 8
Full Report

It's 6.30 am and I'm getting ready to go to school to use the fitness suite before lessons start when there's a knock at the door. Who the hell's here so early? I pull back the curtain in the living room to get a look, and see Doug – a crumpled, unshaven, surly-looking version of Doug. I open the door reluctantly and stand there clutching school bag and PE kit, ready to leave right away.

'What do you want?' I ask. 'Mum's asleep and I'm going to school.'

'Bit keen, aren't you? It's only just got light.' I could say the same thing to him, except I can't be bothered. He gives a big yawn. 'Your granny gave me a ring. She told me you'd been leaving messages on her phone. That's the kind of problem I have to drive through the night to sort out.'

'It was Mum, not me, and it was one message.'

'Well, your granny's scared witless.' I don't believe him. Nothing scares Gran. 'I'm in charge of seeing that she's kept safe and sound too, and she's under strict instructions to let me know if anything happens to jeopardise anyone's safety. And unlike you and your mum, your granny knows what's what.'

'Oh.' Doug's in charge of looking after Gran as well as us. I don't feel exceptionally confident here. 'Well, what's going to happen? Are we in danger? Will we have to move?'

'That is for me to discuss with your mum. Can you wake her up?'

'No.' I say. I'm fed up with this. 'You can, or you can wait. I'm going to school.'

I push past him and run down the path. I deserve at least one day making use of this prized access card, even if tomorrow I might be on my way to . . . where?

I put Doug out of my mind and have a fantastic training session in the gym. I plug myself into my music – the iPod that was Arron's present to me on my fourteenth birthday, the birthday that has now been removed from history – and I let the beat fill my head. I throw myself so thoroughly into the exercise and the music that I clean out all the worry and memories and fill up with a sort of excited joy.

By the time I'm done I'm soaked with sweat, and there's only ten minutes to get ready before registration. As soon as I enter the changing room I crash down from that training high. Carl and the rest of the under-fourteen football team greet me with noisy abuse. I don't feel great in the circumstances about stripping off and making for the showers, so I sit down, start rooting around in my kit bag and hope they will leave soon.

Carl's a burly guy with hair so short that you can see the pink skin of his scalp gleaming through the bristles. He's got Manchester-City-blue eyes fringed with stubby near-white eyelashes, and a fertile crop of spots. He's about the only boy in year eight that's taller than me and he's twice as broad. He looks more like a rugby player than a footballer, although apparently he's like a brick wall in defence and has been scouted for some Championship team's academy. If he was in a film, he'd be played by Shrek.

He thrusts his face next to mine. 'You think you're so clever, don't you, getting your girlfriend to blag an access card for you?'

I'm not having this argument. 'Look, mate, it's not my decision. If it were up to me, you could all have them.'

'Nah, don't give me that. You think you're better than

us, coming here from London. Well, you better watch yourself, or you might find you don't look so clever after all, and all the girls won't think you're so great. We might have to reorganise that face of yours.'

God, this guy can't even come up with one decent insult. He can't even get the words right when he issues a threat.

The bell rings for registration – bugger – and they shuffle out. I dive in the showers and have the quickest wash ever, but I'm still buttoning my shirt with my tie flapping over my shoulders as I sprint to the classroom. Everyone else is filing down to assembly. Ashley Jenkins and her mates start whistling at me, but I just concentrate on the stupid buttons.

Our form tutor, Mr Hunt – you can imagine his nickname, and he does his best to live up to it – doesn't look pleased with me. 'Good of you to turn up today, Joe,' he says, very sarcastic, 'although we do prefer it when pupils get dressed before they come into the classroom.'

'Sorry, sir.' I'm tying my tie and trying to do up my cuffs at the same time.

'Can you explain yesterday's unauthorised absence? A domestic crisis I understand?'

If he knows, why is he asking? 'Yes, sir.'

'You don't have to call me sir, Joe; you're not in the cadet corps now.'

Eh? I can't be bothered with this. I have bigger worries than Mr Hunt understands, and I might not even be in his class by tomorrow. 'Shall I go to assembly, sir, or would you like me to explain about how my mum was ill?' I say, sounding as bored as I dare.

'Take a detention for turning up half-dressed and go to assembly,' he says, and I get there just in time to line up with my class, sitting down hurriedly next to mousey little Claire who goes pink when I lean over and whisper, 'I never knew you were Ellie's sister.'

'Silence!' shouts Mr Hunt, and we all sit catatonic while the head teacher lectures us about moral choices and how they are linked to school uniform. Making the right decisions becomes a habit, just like being smartly turned out – outward order, inner discipline – blah, blah, blah. It makes no sense to me at all.

At break, Brian in the next desk says, 'Wait a minute, Joe,' and pulls some papers out of his bag. 'It's the homework you missed from yesterday. I thought I'd better keep it for you. You have to do this and this by Monday, and on this one,' – he solemnly thumbs through a massive pile of Maths – 'pages four, five and six by Wednesday.'

Of course I could be anywhere by then. But it's nice of him to have kept it for me. Not the sort of thing Arron would have thought of. In fact, Brian, now I come to think of it, seems like an all-round good guy. Someone I can probably trust.

'Thanks Bri, that's excellent, really helpful.' I stuff the papers in my bag. 'Bri, can I ask your confidential advice about a few things?'

Brian's beaming. 'Of course.'

'Well . . . you know Carl and his lot? When they're trying to be threatening, what do you think they have in mind? Do I need to, you know, worry about them?'

Brian has no idea what I mean. I can see it in his innocent small-town, thirteen-year-old eyes. 'He's a bit of a bully, but it's probably mostly talk,' he says. 'He generally picks on people smaller than you.'

That sounds OK. I need to be sure though. 'So I don't need to be, you know . . . prepared?' He gapes. I spell it out. 'Weapons, blades, Bri. No one here uses them, do they?'

The penny drops. He shakes his head. 'Wow . . . no, I don't think so.' He looks curious, and impressed. 'Is that what you're used to?'

We're not going there. I change the subject, skilful as a Ronaldo step-over. 'You know how everyone goes down the shopping centre on a Saturday morning?'

'Yeah. . . Do you want to come with us?' asks Brian, half nervous, half hopeful. 'Well, yeah, but the thing is that my mum, it's her birthday, see, and she wants me to go shopping with her, but I'm not sure how it's going to look. . .' I trail off. It strikes me that I'm a lot clearer about knives and fights than I am about shopping etiquette.

'*You* can probably get away with it,' says Brian decisively, 'although I'd never live it down. Of course it all depends on your mum. Is she cool?'

The unsaid words 'like you' hang in the air, and suddenly I feel better about the whole shopping thing. Six months ago, when Mum was a lot cooler and I was not cool at all, this would not even have been an issue.

'She's OK. And maybe I can send her off somewhere and hang out with you guys.' I say, and Brian is obviously delighted. I can't help comparing his eager friendliness to Arron. Arron, who never seemed to have time for me any more. Arron, with his scary new friends. Arron, with his little jokey digs and put-downs that made me wonder if he really didn't want to be my friend . . . but then there was the iPod. . . I think back to Ty, patient and anxious, examining all the mixed messages that his friend was handing out and I just despise the poor sod – I mean me. It's getting harder to remember that I was Ty, that he really was the same person that I am now.

We go and play kick-about in the playground with Brian's friends and all is well until Carl and his cronies decide to join in. They smash the ball here and there, and then Carl launches himself at my shin in an assault dressed up as a tackle. 'Ow!' I crash to the ground. Carl and his mates are shouting with laughter. Good thing he wasn't wearing studs or I'd have a pulverised leg.

'Watch it,' I shout as I hobble off, wondering if I'll even be able to train with Ellie today. During the afternoon a huge bruise emerges, and it's quite painful as I jog to meet her on the running track. 'What's the matter?' she asks instantly, and I show her. 'Ouch, that looks bad. What happened there?'

'Oh, nothing. Just playing football in the playground and some ape crashed into me.'

'I can guess which one.'

'Yeah, yeah. It'll be OK.'

'What happened yesterday? Is your mum better now?'

'Yes, I think so,' I answer, then wonder how Mum has been today. What happened with Doug this morning? Has it set her off again? What will I find when I go home? I remember the packet of cigarettes retrieved from the rubbish bin.

'Ellie,' I say, 'sometimes my mum talks about, you know, moving on from here.'

'Going back to London?'

'Maybe,' I say, wondering how everyone seems to know that we even come from London. Did I say something? I don't think so. Maybe I just have an air of city sophistication. Maybe not. 'If I, you know, just leave all of a sudden, then don't worry about me. It'll be OK.'

She gives me a strange look. 'If you say so, Joe, but it'd be nice if you kept in touch though.'

I find myself making a promise I'll never be able to keep. Then we start warming up on the track and running races against the stopwatch. She seems pretty happy with the results, and there's something satisfying about running through the pain in my leg. I can cope. I can endure. It's got to be a useful skill.

We're nearly done when Mr Henderson comes out to join us. He looks a bit ticked off, and doesn't really cheer up when Ellie shows him her clipboard of times. 'Very good, well done,' he says, then, 'Joe, when you're done I need a serious word with you.'

'We should be finished in ten minutes. Is that OK?' asks Ellie.

'I'll be in my office,' he replies.

As I cool down and stretch I scan my brains for reasons why he might be cross with me. As far as I can see there's nothing that I've done, but who knows? Ellie seems puzzled too and says, 'It's probably nothing, don't worry about it. I had a chat with him yesterday and told him you were doing very well.'

Mr Henderson's office is a smelly muddle of sports equipment and sweaty kit. It's quite cosy though. There's a squashy armchair in the corner and he nods at it as I come in. I sit on the edge, feeling a bit nervous.

'Joe, why were you out on the running track when Mr Hunt tells me you had detention this afternoon?'

'Oh. I totally forgot.'

'Mr Hunt is none too happy with you. Says you were "bordering on the insolent" this morning and came into the classroom late and half dressed.'

To my surprise, I feel myself getting a bit upset. 'The thing is, he thinks I'm being rude when I say 'sir', but it's what I'm used to and I don't mean to be, and actually I'm really trying to be very polite and I didn't mean to be late and half dressed but when I finished training this morning the whole changing room was full of people and it wasn't really my fault, but he isn't interested and it isn't really very fair what he says. . .' I wind down. I sound like a whinging toddler.

'Two days ago I gave you the very big privilege of getting an access card to use the facilities out of hours. I don't have to tell you what an advantage this gives you and how many other people would like to have that card. I was somewhat surprised not to see you making use of it yesterday, and even more surprised when my wife told me that she'd seen a Parkview schoolboy down at Morrison's mid-morning. It wasn't hard to work out who it was from her description.'

Blimey. This little town has spies everywhere. I put my head in my hands. 'Mr Henderson, my mum was not very well yesterday. She . . . we . . . didn't have any food in the house at all. I needed to look after her. I really wanted to be at school and training and everything but I just couldn't. It's just Mum and me. We don't have anyone else to help us.

'I really do appreciate getting the access card and I did get up really early this morning and did a lot of training and I really like it and please don't take it away.' I plead.

I can see Mr Henderson is gagging to ask what was the matter with my mum, and I am desperate to spill it and say, 'She got drunk and nearly set the house on fire,' but we both hold back, which is good because the last thing I need is a visit from social services.

'Ellie tells me that you seem to be under some emotional stress, and she's worried that training is putting too much pressure on you.'

'No, no, no it's not. She never said that to me.'

'No, she likes working with you and she wants to continue. But she is only a student and she is being supervised and she was right to tell me of her concerns.'

She likes working with me! I have a warm, glowing,

happy feeling inside. But I also have an uncomfortable warm, glowing, embarrassed feeling turning my face red as I wonder what exactly she did tell Mr Henderson.

'I think you'd better go and apologise to Mr Hunt in the morning. Explain that you're new to the school and sometimes things are a bit difficult. '

'He knows that. . . What will happen about the detention?'

'You'll probably end up doing it tomorrow. Maybe he might hand out a double detention. You're already on full report, so he can't add that sanction.'

'What do you mean?'

He looks a bit sheepish. 'I think it's probably something you're not meant to know if you haven't been told. My mistake.'

'But you just told me. And I don't even know what it is.' It sounds bad though.

'It just means that the head teacher has requested regular reports on your behaviour and progress. It's what we do with people who are persistent troublemakers. When there's a full report request for a new pupil we usually find that it's someone who has had trouble in their old school, maybe an excluded pupil, something like that.'

I've never even met the head teacher. Could this be Doug's way of spying on me at school? Does my head teacher know the whole story? Mr Henderson says, 'This doesn't seem to be a big surprise, Joe.'

'No, I know why,' I say. 'I can't exactly explain but I'm not a troublemaker and I do want to make the best of this opportunity.'

He realises he's not going to get any more out of me and asks, 'Did you not have the chance to train at your last school? Did they not spot that you could run? Didn't your parents realise that you had a talent there?'

Athletics didn't really exist at St Saviour's. It was a voluntary option and you had to sign up for it and spend half an hour getting to a sports centre after school. I was quite interested but Arron said no way, and I wasn't going to go with all the posh boys and not him.

I did once go along to the local running club but when I got there everyone else was black, and although they were friendly enough, I felt a bit strange and never went back. Does that make me racist? I really hope not.

'I've never seen anything like this school,' I say. 'We didn't have these facilities. And my mum was more bothered about stuff like Maths.'

'Hmm,' he says. 'Look, on Sunday we're hosting the inter-schools athletics competition. You'll be able to have a go at racing. Maybe bring your mum with you, show her what you can do. I'm sure Ellie will think it's a good idea.'

Ellie might. I don't.

'Come along at 11 am,' he says, 'and I'll speak to Mr Hunt in the morning and try and sort things out for you. Feel free to come and talk any time you need to.'

Walking home, the fears I've been holding back all day suddenly come crowding back. How can I have abandoned my mum to face Doug on her own? Has she put us in danger? Is Gran OK? Are we going to have to move on? Is Joe about to disappear altogether?

The house is very quiet and dark. I wonder if Mum is even here, but then she comes to the top of the stairs. 'I'm in my bedroom,' she says, and I bound up the stairs and follow her into the room.

Her suitcase is on the bed. Her wardrobe is empty. I look from one to the other in despair. 'They're moving us, then? They think it's too dangerous?'

'No,' she says. 'They want us to stay. They think it's still safe. But I've had enough. I've told them that you're not going to testify after all. We're going home.'

CHAPTER 9
Lies

There's a danger here. The danger is that she's going to be the one who's cold and hard and determined and I'm going to be the one out of control, ranting and raving and shouting. I feel like shaking her. I feel like hitting something . . . someone. I can't. I mustn't.

I take a very deep breath and sit down on the bed. 'What do you mean? We can't go home.' I'm trying to sound calm and reasonable.

'Why not? You don't testify, no one's interested in us. We're not involved. They all know that. Why would they want to hurt us then?'

'But what about the court case?'

'None of our business. You did what you could at the time; nothing's going to change things now.' She's folding clothes furiously and adds, 'Who are you doing it for anyway? Arron? Too late, by a long time.'

'But there are other people too.'

'Yes. I know.' Her face is hard. 'But we have to think of ourselves first.'

'How can we go home? How can you think that we can just go back and everything be normal again? Our home got all burned up.'

'Doug told me they managed to put out the fire before it did much damage to our place upstairs.'

Well, thank you for telling me. I am filling up with silent fury.

'We can't go back,' I snarl, teeth clenched to prevent me shouting.

'We can. Why not? No one will be interested in us any more.'

All her determination is back, the energy that I thought had gone. I feel overwhelmed by her strength. We're back to normal – she leads, I follow.

I imagine life in our old flat, seeing my aunties, doing the paper round again. I think about being back at St Saviour's, short hair, tons of homework, the boys, the playground. No Arron though. Then I remember the smell of the petrol and hear the explosion and the way the flames crackled as they ate up the shop. She's wrong. She's mad.

'No they wouldn't.' I'm raising my voice now.

'They'd want to make absolutely sure we didn't change our minds. We'd be always looking out for them. And the police wouldn't be too happy either. What if they tried to . . . to say that I'd been involved?'

'They wouldn't do that.'

I feel about a hundred years older than my own mother.

'Yes they would. Why wouldn't they? I was there, wasn't I? I could easily have been one of them. And what if they find out I had a knife?'

As soon as I say it, I try and take it back. My voice kind of gobbles the word – I sound like a clucking chicken – and I bite my tongue. But I've said it. She heard me.

'You had a knife? What do you mean, Ty?' Her voice sounds a bit wobbly.

'I had a knife with me in the park.'

She's looking at me like I'm holding a blade to her throat right now. 'You had a knife? You carried a knife? You're lying to the police? You bloody stupid boy.' And she hits me, hard, on my cheek.

'Ow! Don't do that!'

It really hurts. I turn away so she can't see the tears in my eyes.

'What am I meant to do? You deserve it. Christ, Ty, I couldn't have done any more to help you get a better life, could I? I worked and worked to give us a home, to feed you and clothe you, give you – I thought – some values, good behaviour. When you got into St Saviour's I was so proud. And you're running round London with a knife in your back pocket. I didn't put all that effort in for you to end up with a criminal record.'

She lifts her hand and I know she's itching to belt me again, but she lets it drop. I want to hit her back. I hate it when she makes me feel guilty for needing food and clothes.

'I never used it,' I say, and remember how the blade felt heavy in my hand.

'What the hell did you think you were doing?'

I don't know what to say. Arron said it was pretty normal to carry a knife. We used to pretend that it was for wood tech or food tech or we'd just bought it for our mum, but really it was because we were sure that one day we would be mugged or beaten up or something and we wanted to be prepared. You didn't go to school in London without knowing someone who'd been mugged or beaten up or something. Knives are cheap and easy to get, and it was so normal to have one that I don't know why they didn't just list it as part of our school uniform. That's what Arron said, anyway.

'Everyone had knives,' I say. 'It was just one from the kitchen, not a real flick knife or anything. I started carrying it a few weeks ago after Arron got mugged.

He needed a knife for protection. He told me to carry one too.'

'You're talking complete crap,' she says. 'You don't always do what your friend tells you. Look what happened to Arron.'

I'm scared of the way she's looking at me. I'm scared of what she could do. She wouldn't grass me up to the police, would she? Not my own mother.

'Mum, I wasn't involved in the fight. I really did see what I said I saw. If you tell them I had a knife, they might not believe me about anything. I'd be in big trouble. And we really can't go home and be normal again. We could get killed.'

'No. . . Yes. . . I don't know. . . Maybe we could go abroad for a bit. Let it all blow over.'

That's more attractive. We could go to Portugal maybe, or Spain . . . anywhere they don't speak English and they produce international footballers. I draw up a fantasy list of countries in my head to suggest to the cops. Then I re-enter the real world.

'We haven't even got passports, have we?'

'No. But if we told the police that you won't testify but we need to go abroad, then surely they have to arrange something for us.'

'Why should they?'

She stops packing and looks at me. 'Why are you

arguing with me, Ty? This is for you as much as me. You can't be enjoying living here, missing everyone, watching me turn into a depressed lump.'

'I do like it here.' As you would know *if* you paid me any attention. 'It's OK at school. I'm doing lots of sport.'

'Sport?'

Maybe I can distract her by telling her about my amazing potential.

'Mum, was my dad any good at athletics?' That's how I find stuff out about my dad. Little questions that I sneak in when she's thinking about something else. She's never actually bothered to sit down and tell me about him.

She laughs, but it's not a warm sort of laugh. Perhaps today wasn't the best day to try that trick.

'Not really. Too lazy. He liked playing football but he couldn't cope with the chance that someone might beat him. Arrogant bastard, your dad, as I think I've mentioned before. No, it was me that was good at athletics.'

'Really, you?' Why did I never know this? 'How d'you mean, good?'

'Ran for the borough, I did. Came second in the London girls' under-sixteen 1500 metres.'

'Wow. . . Why did you stop?'

'Think about the timing. What happened to me

when I was sixteen? Try running when you've got a baby growing under your gym skirt,' she says grimly. 'Why are you asking, anyway?'

'Because they think I'm good at running. They've given me extra training.'

I didn't tell her before because I wanted her response to be just right. But she just sniffs.

'I'd prefer it if they gave you extra Maths.'

She's not interested. She changes the subject: 'Ty, are you saying you'd rather be here than at home?'

I shrug. She doesn't understand. She's not interested in what I want.

'I don't need to carry a knife here.' Maybe she'll care about my safety.

'You don't *need* to carry a knife anywhere. I can't believe you were so stupid.'

'It's safer here. And anyway, what would Gran say?'

'What do you mean, what would Gran say? She'd be overjoyed to see us again, to have us back, to have things normal. . .'

'No she wouldn't. She was the one who said go to the police. She was the one who said I have no choice, I have to do the right thing.'

'She didn't realise what it would mean. She can't have known this would happen.'

'Yes, but even so.' What was it Gran had said?

'A precious child has been lost, and Tyler has to do everything he can to make things right for that poor family.' I know she meant it.

'Ty, if we keep on like this, we're going to have a life based on lies.'

I'm feeling tired and angry and muddled and can't really express what I mean, but it seems to me that if I miss this one crucial chance to tell the truth when it matters, then my life will always be based on lies one way or the other.

'We can't run away, the lies won't go away,' I say, and I know I've said it all wrong.

I can't talk any more. I don't know if I can make her change her mind. I do what she wanted me to do the other day. I put my arms around her – God, she's so skinny, and she smells of stale smoke instead of flowers – and hug her and say, 'Please, please, Nic, let me stay here. Don't tell them about the knife, don't change anything. . .'

We sit there on the bed, heads together, not speaking, and then there's a knock on the front door. I jump, but she says, 'It'll be Doug. I told him we were leaving and he went off to make some phone calls.'

She goes downstairs and opens the door and I hear her say, 'I haven't changed my mind, you know.'

Then there's a mumble of voices and Doug calls out,

'Tyler, can you come downstairs now?' He's always made a big point of calling me Joe, and now I don't want him to stop. I can feel my Joe-ness fading away.

I walk down the stairs, head down, and it's only when I reach the hallway that I realise that DI Morris is there too. He's got his mate DC Bettany with him. They're not looking as friendly as they did last time. 'Hello, Ty,' says DI Morris, 'I think we need to have a chat.'

'I want to be there too,' says Mum. 'You shouldn't be talking to a minor on his own.'

I want to talk to DI Morris without her. I want to tell them that this isn't my idea. I want to ask what would happen if we go home – not just to me but to everyone involved. But she comes along, turning back at the living room door to say, 'Perhaps you can make us some tea, Doug.'

DI Morris sits himself down and pulls a file out of his briefcase. DC Bettany gets out his notebook. 'I know that Tyler's made a decision to withdraw his statement,' DI Morris says to Mum, 'but this is a fast-moving case, and new evidence is always emerging. We have some more questions to ask him, and this won't be the last time.'

I interrupt: 'I never decided to withdraw my statement. She decided. It's my statement, isn't it?

It's my choice whether I testify or not?'

'Yes, but of course your mother's co-operation and permission is vital if we are to maintain the witness protection programme.' He scratches his head.

'I suppose if you insisted you wanted to stick by your statement and testify and she didn't want to co-operate, we would have to find another person who could be what is known as an appropriate adult to safeguard your interests. Your mother could go home and you could remain in witness protection.'

An appropriate adult? Wouldn't that have to be Gran?

'Who. . . could that be?' I ask hopefully, not meeting Mum's eye.

'We'd possibly have to bring in a social worker and put you in foster care,' he says, watching both Mum and me very carefully. He can see she's twitching when he mentions a social worker. Those have to be two of her least favourite words.

I lose interest in the appropriate adult.

'Even if we did go home and I didn't testify, these people might still want to hurt us? Just in case?'

DI Morris sighs, 'It's hard to predict. But I wouldn't necessarily trust them to leave you alone. It's also been a very high-profile case. You might attract some general hostility if you return home.'

'What does that mean?' asks Mum. 'For all we know, you might be making this up just to get Ty to testify. You're not allowed to influence him.'

'Mum, it'd be easier for everyone if they hadn't had to take us into their protection. And how can they make up that petrol bomb?'

DI Morris sits and watches us. Then he says, 'Tyler Lewis, I have to say something to you. I am going to ask you some questions now that may lead to you being charged with an offence. You do not have to say anything. But it may harm your defence if you do not mention, when questioned, something which you later rely on in court. Anything you do say may be given in evidence.'

My mum gasps. I feel like I'm going to vomit. I know we're both thinking the same thing. Somehow he's found out about the knife.

'OK,' he says, 'I'm going to ask you about drugs at St Saviour's. Did you ever take money for drugs? We have reason to believe that you may know something about cannabis sales.'

All hell breaks out. Mum doesn't know which one of us to attack first. Luckily she decides on DI Morris. 'Are you accusing my son of drug dealing?' she demands. 'Because if you are, I think we need a lawyer here, right this minute.'

'I am simply asking Tyler some additional questions,' says DI Morris, very smooth. 'He knows he has the right to remain silent.'

'So you can blackmail him into testifying, is that it?'

'Not at all. You're making very serious allegations. If you're not happy with the way this investigation is being handled then I suggest you speak to the Independent Police Complaints Commission.'

'So what's happened? Someone's accused him? A druggy teenager's been found out with some hash and he's latched on to Ty and Arron because he knows they were involved with the fight in the park?' My mum's so angry that little bits of spit are coming out with her words.

While this is going on – and it is amazing to see Nicki back in full supersonic action again – I've been thinking fast. I'm pretty sure I know what he's on about. I'm dizzy with relief that we're not talking about knives.

'Was it Kenny Pritchard?' I ask.

'Shut *up*, Ty,' says Mum, shooting me a vicious I'll-deal-with-you-later look.

DI Morris says, 'What about Kenny Pritchard, Ty?' I can see from the smile lurking at the corners of his mouth that I've got the right name.

Mum says, 'This is outrageous. Don't say anything, Ty.' Then she hisses at DI Morris, 'How dare you.

Get him a lawyer.'

'He gave me an envelope once,' I say, 'and he said, "Give this to Mackenzie". I didn't know what it was and Arron didn't tell me. That's it.'

'See?' says Mum. 'That scumbag Arron. Nothing to do with Ty.'

DI Morris doesn't look convinced. 'Really, Tyler? Do you just want to think about that?'

Arron definitely never told me what was going on and I certainly never asked. So officially I know nothing. I had my suspicions, but they're just private thoughts, aren't they?

'I didn't know nothing,' I say, which makes DI Morris look even more thoughtful and Nicki wince at my English.

'Miss Lewis,' he says, 'If I promise you that Tyler will not be charged with any offence to do with drugs at St Saviour's, will you let us please talk to him on his own?'

She looks unsure. 'It's up to the Crown Prosecution Service to decide who gets prosecuted, isn't it?' she asks.

He looks a bit uncomfortable and she pounces and says, 'So if you're making promises like that, you obviously realise you haven't got a case against my son. Hah! Well you can talk to him for five minutes, but I'll be asking him what you've said and if it's anything out of order I'll be going to lawyers and the press and my MP and the European Court of Human Rights and you won't know what's hit you.' And she goes off to see what Doug's doing in the kitchen.

I'm left alone with DI Morris. I open my mouth to speak, but he puts his hand up to silence me. DC Bettany shuts his notebook. DI Morris says, 'Tyler Lewis, you're going to listen to me. Or do you prefer me to call you Joe?'

I shrug, but I'm pleased that he realises how hard it is to shift between names all the time. 'Whatever.'

'I'm beginning to get an idea about you, Tyler. The idea I have is that, yes, you tell the truth, but maybe not the whole truth. Is that correct?'

I squirm a little. Sometimes it is and obviously sometimes it's not. It seems a bit unfair though, when I've just coughed up the name Kenny Pritchard.

'Well, uh, it depends on what . . . and when . . . and what you mean by whole truth..'

He waits.

'I always try and be true.'

'But it's the bare minimum. And sometimes you're pretending to be careless about your answers when really you're being very careful indeed. Now I have no doubt at all that you knew very well what Arron was up to at school.'

'Umm . . . he never told me. But I did think . . . maybe. . .'

'And you knew he was getting into bad company.'

'Well, sort of. . .' It's all very well, but if you grow up on the estate where Arron lived, you can't avoid knowing dodgy people. It's a matter of how much time you spend with them.

'You need to tell the truth, Ty, because you're going to get cross-examined in court and believe me, three sets of defence lawyers aren't going to be gentle with you. Do you agree with your mother that you should go home and not testify?'

'No. I think she's mad. I want to go on being Joe. And I think I should testify'

'Why?'

'Because it's the right thing to do . . . I think. . .'

'OK. We will talk to her again. In the meantime, is there anything else you can tell me about Arron's delivery service? And is there anything else weighing on your mind that we haven't yet come up with a question for?'

Very reluctantly I nod my head. 'It's this,' and I go and get my PE kit bag and pull out my favourite thing. My iPod. The one Arron got me for my birthday.

DI Morris takes it and turns it over in his hands. 'Yours?' he asks, and I say, 'Arron gave it to me for my birthday. It was all ready to use with music and everything. I did wonder . . . he said it was an old one of Nathan's.'

He turns it on and twists the dial to show playlists. There's one I've noticed and worried about there – 'Rachel's faves' it's called, and I can't imagine Nathan listening to crap like Dido and Alanis Morissette. On the other hand there's lots of rap and hip hop on the iPod as well. 'You think this is stolen?' asks DI Morris.

'I don't know . . . maybe Nathan had a girlfriend or something . . . but I'm not sure.'

'I'm going to take this,' says DI Morris and looks surprised when I grab it from him and say firmly, 'No. I need it. Very urgently'

'You need it?'

'For training. I can't get another one and there's really good music on it, and it's so hard to concentrate without.'

'You could buy a new one.'

'But it wouldn't have any music on it, and we don't have a computer here, and I couldn't afford to fill it up anyway. Please don't take it.'

'I'll leave it with you for the moment. Now. Arron and the drugs.'

It's OK, I think, they know anyway. DC Bettany is writing in his notebook again. 'All I know is that he would sometimes give people stuff. You know Mikey? Mr Bling from the park? He might have been involved.'

'Why did you think that?'

'Because I once saw Mikey outside our flat and he gave Arron something. I'm not sure what but Arron was pleased and he bought me fish and chips. I thought it might be money.'

I have other reasons as well but he seems pleased enough with that one.

'Can you tell me some names of people you saw him giving packages to?'

'Umm . . . most of them were older. I didn't know them, but Kenny Pritchard definitely did give me something for Arron once and there was Cas O'Leary and Adam Comerford and that Polish boy in year ten.'

'And you never asked him what was going on?'

'Well . . . not really. . .'

'What does that mean?'

'I said once, "Are you getting money for that stuff," and he said, "Yeah, but not as much as you think."' I leave out Arron's sneering 'pretty boy'.

DI Morris sighs. He scratches his head again. He says to DC Bettany, as though I'm not even there, 'What I don't understand is why two bright boys were getting mixed up with all this. They were at a well-regarded school, a Catholic school, they had good hard-working mothers who cared about them.'

I don't think it's up to me to explain why Arron might have been doing whatever he was doing when I didn't officially know he was doing anything. And I was very careful not to get mixed up in anything at all.

DC Bettany is watching me: 'You know, Ty, if you'd blown the whistle on Arron when this all started, then just think what could have been avoided.'

It all gets a bit blurry after that. DI Morris goes off to talk to Mum in the kitchen, and, left alone in the living room, I lay my head down on the cushion. . .

. . . *I'm running and running and the person who's chasing me is going to hurt me, there's a knife in his hand, he's going to hurt me, but he looks just like me. . .*

Nicki is calling me, Nicki's going to save me. I wake with a shudder, and grab her hand. 'Nic . . . someone was chasing me. . .'

'It's OK, Ty, It was only a dream.' She's sitting by me on the sofa. 'The police have just gone. They're going to make an addition to your statement and come back with it another day for you to sign. Time for bed – you've got school in the morning.'

Slowly I remember what's just happened. 'Are we leaving? Are you angry?'

If she walloped me for the knife, what the hell's going to happen over the drugs?

She shakes her head. 'Let's talk tomorrow. But no, we're not leaving right away. They persuaded me. Said they'll arrange a holiday with the family and help with finding a job. They guilt-tripped me – asked me to think how I'd feel if it'd been you lying there dead in that park. It may not come to anything anyway. The prosecution lawyers have to look at the evidence before they decide whether it can even go to trial.'

All this for a trial that may never happen. 'I wasn't dealing drugs, honest, but I didn't ask Arron what he was up to.'

'That Arron,' she says. 'He's got a lot to answer for. Ty, you're not carrying a knife any more, are you?'

I shake my head, no. I'm not carrying a knife because I've seen what knives can do. But I need one for the same reason. It's a problem that nags at me all the time.

Lying in bed later, I can't get back to sleep. I'm feeling hot and cold, and like I'm going to be sick. I keep on hearing DC Bettany's words in my head. It's all my fault, I can see that now. I didn't do anything then, because Arron wouldn't have been my friend any more. But now I've lost my friend forever, and there's a death on my conscience.

CHAPTER 10
Top Shop

I struggle through the next day, yawning a lot and wishing I could just go home and sleep. Mr Hunt isn't in a forgiving mood so I have double detention, and even training on the track feels like a chore. I go through the motions but Ellie is disappointed. 'Get some rest this weekend,' she says, 'and I'll see you on Sunday at the inter-school race.'

Come Saturday morning, I'd be happy just to stay in bed. But Mum is definitely ready to leave the house. She's found her make-up and plucked her eyebrows, which makes her look younger and sharper. She's experimented with her hair – spiked it up and added red highlights from some dodgy spray. It's weird – she's always been blonde as long as I can remember – but it suits her. The word that my Auntie Emma would use is edgy. I tell her she looks great and she seems pleased.

'We're going to spend a bit of money on ourselves,' she says. 'You've grown so much that all your jeans are a bit short on you, and we could get some T-shirts too. I hate to see you in those awful hoodies all the time.'

Doesn't she remember that I'm wearing a hood up as much as possible on police orders? 'What I really need are good running shoes,' I say, and she agrees that I can get some.

We walk up to the bus stop, and I realise that I am actually taller than her. I can look down on her sprayed highlights. It's only an inch of difference, but it's massive. I was beginning to think I'd never grow and now it's really happened. After all the training of the last few weeks I'm stronger and fitter too. My whole body is different. Being Joe has turbocharged all the changes that they kept on promising in PSHE lessons. He's taller, he's hairier, he's got more muscles. His voice is almost always deep. He's managed to avoid getting spots though. Ty was a boy, but Joe is almost a man. I like it. I like it a lot.

Going through the shopping centre doors, I feel like a hundred eyes are on us. I turn to her hastily. 'Can I go and research trainers while you check out New Look?' And we arrange to meet outside Top Shop in half an hour.

'It's all very well in New Look,' she says, 'but I'm not doing proper shopping without your advice.'

The sports shop has good stuff – it's not one of those fashion shops in disguise – and I get busy checking out the trainers. Then I spy big bully-boy Carl buying football boots with his mum. She's making a huge fuss over getting him exactly the right thing and seems to have plenty of money to do so. I know he'd hate to be spotted, so I wait until his mum's busy with the assistant, wander past and say, 'Hey, Carl, how you doing?'

Carl snorts like a pig that's run out of swill.

'Shopping with your girlfriend?' I ask innocently.

Carl grunts angrily. His mum returns, carrying a pair of lurid orange boots which look like someone's vomited all over them, and asks, 'Oh Carl, sweetie, is this one of your team mates?'

'No,' growls Carl. She looks puzzled so he has to mumble, ' 's name's Joe. In my year.'

'Great boots,' I say helpfully. 'No one's going to miss you in those, eh, Carl?'

'That's just what I was saying,' says Carl's mum, and I'm loving the way that Carl glowers.

I've done enough. I have some ammunition to use against him just in case he mocks me with my mum later. I pick the shoes I want, and ask the guy behind the counter to keep them for me, Then, just as I'm leaving, I turn and mouth, 'Bye sweetie,' behind his mum's back. I hear her say, 'Seems like a nice boy.' And Carl splutters with fury.

Walking into the loud, bright jumble that is Top Shop makes me incredibly homesick for my Auntie Emma, who used to combine babysitting with shopping. My earliest memories involve glittering bangles and shiny shoes, playing peek-a-boo with the changing room mirrors and hide-and-seek amongst the clothes rails.

When I was nine, Emma's friends told her it was me or them, and Mum decided I was compromising my masculinity. Arron and I were packed off to Nathan's boxing club where we spent our Saturdays imitating the older boys and jabbing at a punch bag and hoping no one would make us actually fight. But I'm well known in my family as an ace style adviser. It's not a talent I tend to shout about.

I wander along behind Mum, as she picks things up and adds them to her huge pile of things to try on, and I realise I've stepped into the headquarters of the Joe Andrews fan club. I've seen about twenty girls from school, and every single one has waved, giggled or smiled at me. And, as we reach the changing room and the very welcome sofa placed outside for boyfriends, partners and unlucky sons, there she is. Ashley Jenkins. And she's not too happy.

'I'll come and show you the stuff I like,' says Mum

and she disappears behind the curtains. I sit down next to a big bloke reading *What Car?* and start sifting through the mags thoughtfully provided. But Ashley won't be ignored.

'Hey Joe,' she pouts, perching on the edge of the sofa's arm. 'What brings you here? I thought we were going to come shopping together?'

I have to admit she looks a lot better than she does in school uniform. Today she's wearing a tight yellow top and jeans that show off curves that usually look a bit lumpy under her tie and grey jumper. I can see the edge of a lacy black bra under the bright T-shirt. It's quite an attractive combination.

'Oh, yes. Sorry, Ashley, we must arrange it, but it's my mum's birthday soon and I said I'd go shopping with her today.'

Girls must read these things differently from boys. Ashley rubs my arm and purrs, 'Oh, that's so sweet.' Or maybe she's taking the piss? And Mum chooses this moment to pop out of the changing room, dressed in a short skirt and a revealing red top. She says hopefully, 'What do you think of this, Ty?'

Bugger. Why'd she have to call me Ty in front of Ashley? And what is she wearing? She's showing way too much cleavage. Mr *What Car?* is licking his lips.

'It's a bit much, *Mum*,' I say, trying to signal

enormous disapproval with my eyes. 'The colour's OK.'
I hope she'll get the message. She doesn't: 'Well I love it.
Hang on, I'll show you the jeans.'

Ashley is open-mouthed. 'That's never your mum?
She can't be old enough.'

I'm proud of having a mum who is young and pretty,
I really am. But, right now, I'm feeling extremely
anxious that she's forgetting everything that Maureen
the makeover lady said about looking anonymous.
'She's a whole load older than she looks,' I tell Ashley.

'Why did she call you . . . what was it?'

'She's half Turkish,' I lie. 'It's the Turkish word for
son.' If Ashley knows any Turkish at all, then I've made
a big mistake. But luckily she doesn't seem to.

'Can you speak Turkish, then?' says Ashley, and
I launch into a long complaint about the evil thieves
who short-change you at the cash and carry. She looks
a bit stunned, but I think she believes me.

Mum comes out again, this time dressed in tight-
cropped jeans and a white top. It suits her new dark hair,
but it's also indecent. See-through, in fact. I can see she's
feeling happier than she has for weeks, which is nice,
but right now I'd prefer to put her in a head-to-toe burka
like Imran's mum wore when we were at St Luke's.

'Mum,' I say firmly, 'it's OK, but you're beginning
to look too much like your friend.'

'What friend?' she says, admiring her denimed bum in the mirror. 'D'you know I'm a size eight now?' she adds, a little anxiously.

'There's no way you look fat,' I say firmly. These magic words are the key to successful clothes shopping with females. David Beckham probably says them to Posh all the time. Having softened her up, I go back on the attack. 'You know, your friend Nicki. You know . . . *Nicki*. You don't want to look like her. Why don't you find something more like your mate Maureen wears?'

'Maureen has no taste or style,' says my mum. '*Nicki* used to get a lot of compliments.' And she does a little twirl in front of the mirror.

'Mrs Andrews,' says Ashley, 'I'm Ashley. I'm in Joe's class at school. I really like those jeans. You look brilliant. Where did you find them?'

Mum laps all this up and starts chatting to Ashley about jeans and brands, and next thing I know they're going into the changing room together. As Ashley disappears, Mum turns around and makes a rude face at me, crossed eyes and everything. Clearly she doesn't appreciate my advice. Clearly she has no idea that she nearly blew our identities away. Just being in Top Shop is like three Bacardi and cokes to her. I bury myself in *Maxim* and hope for the best.

Two minutes later, I'm joined by two . . . three . . . no,

four of Ashley's friends. Mr *What Car?* looks pretty impressed. Lauren and Emily wedge themselves on to the sofa, Dani sits on the arm, Becca plonks herself on the pile of magazines. 'Where's Ashley?' demands Becca.

'In there, trying things on.'

'So are you two here, you know, *together*?' says Lauren. The way she says *together*, it sounds like Ashley and I are heading for a public snog in the main display window and she's all set to sell tickets.

'No, I'm here with my mum. She's picking new clothes for her birthday.'

'Aaah. . .' chorus the girls together. 'You're so nice,' says Emily. 'My mum would love a son like you,' says Dani. It's clearly not cool to crawl away and hide under a clothes rail as I would have done when I was nine – not really that long ago – so I shrug and say, 'It's no sweat.'

Mum emerges carrying a massive pile of clothes. 'Are you going to buy *all* those?' I ask. 'Are *all* these girls your friends?' she retorts. Ashley's close behind. 'Joe's very popular,' she says, making flicking motions with her hands at her friends, who ignore her.

'Is he?' asks Mum, clearly astounded.

'We think he's so nice to come shopping with you, Mrs Andrews,' says Emily.

Mum recovers. 'I mean, yes, isn't he great. I'm so lucky. Oh well, he's always been popular, haven't you, love? Always had all the girls running round him. Must be those big green . . . er, brown eyes. I'm just going to pay for these and then maybe I'll get changed into the jeans and we'll go and buy your trainers.'

I knew shopping with Mum would be bad but I hadn't realised that I'd have to give her a full CIA-style undercover briefing beforehand. First my name, then my eyes. . . Maybe it is safer if she's kept under house arrest.

'I'll meet you outside. 'Bye, girls,' I say and escape, thankfully bumping into Brian and his mates Max and Jamie who are hanging around at the top of the escalator.

'Oh, Christ,' I say, leaning on the balustrade. 'Ashley Jenkins just ambushed my mum in Top Shop.'

The boys whistle at Ashley's name and Brian asks, 'Were her mates with her? Emily and them?'

'Oh yeah, the full pack.'

'You could have your pick of those girls,' says Brian wistfully. 'If you hurry and make your mind up then some of us might get a chance to get a date before the end of term party.'

'What end of term party?' End of term is still weeks away.

'Arranged by the school, end of term, everyone under year ten. Usually good, and this year it's our main chance of, you know, getting some action.' He looks a bit uncomfortable, and I definitely get the impression that Brian's very new to even thinking about girls. Whereas I have thought about girls non-stop for at least a year – mainly Maria from the tattoo parlour – but never before felt I had the slightest chance of getting anywhere.

'Thing is, Joe, if you were to get off with Ashley , then you could put a word in with the others for us. . . Maybe set up some double dates, that kind of thing. . .'

Out of your league, mate, I'm thinking, but I say, 'Yeah, if I can, I will.'

I'm interrupted by Max whistling as he gazes down to the floor below, 'Who's that babe with Ashley?'

I look. Of course. It's my bloody mother, all done up in her new jeans and transparent top, and viewed from a distance she looks, well, not bad. I can't have young tossers like Max whistling at my mum. I have to put a stop to this right now.

I lean towards him, with a menacing glare, eyes narrowed, hands in fists. 'Doncha disrespec' my muvver,' I say slowly in my best and most aggressive gangsta voice.

It does the trick. 'That's your mum?' he squeaks. 'I'm really sorry Joe, I had no idea. . .' and the rest of the boys shuffle their feet and look a bit scared. I wonder if Brian told them about our supposedly confidential conversation.

I put my hands down. 'No problem, bro, easy mistake to make.' Especially when she's dressed as flipping Hannah Montana. 'I'd better go and rescue her from Ashley.'

When I reach them Mum's looking around for me. 'You don't look like a good Islamic girl,' I tell her in Turkish – Salik in the kebab shop was always saying it to his daughter – and it's an old joke between me and my mum because it's what I say when she's off to the pub. So she laughs and rolls her eyes at me and Ashley looks completely convinced, gives me a wave and blows me a kiss.

'Let's go and get your trainers,' Mum says, 'and then maybe some jeans and T-shirts for you. We can look wherever you want.' I'm secretly chuffed about this, as I steer her into the Nike store, because all Ty's clothes came from Asda or charity shops or down the market. Joe scores again. I wonder how often we can go shopping before Scotland Yard's cash runs out.

Several hours later we're leaving, laden with loads of really cool stuff, and I see Carl again. This time he's with the whole family – red-faced dad, plump harassed mum, and – yes! – Carl's pushing a double buggy with a bawling pair of snot-covered toddlers.

'See you, Carl,' I say, and I move my arm so it rests lightly on Mum's shoulders. Just as if she were my slightly older, but remarkably glamorous girlfriend. She looks a bit surprised, but it's worth it to see Carl's baby-blue eyes pop as we walk past. It's a good moment.

CHAPTER 11
Race

Today is the inter-schools athletics competition and I have no intention of telling my mum about it. She had her share of my time and attention yesterday. But when I go down for breakfast, she's sitting at the kitchen table all dressed up in her new jeans and red top. It seems a bit mean not to tell her the truth when she asks me where I'm going.

'Can I come?' she asks. 'I'd like to see you run. See what the fuss is about. I've been thinking it's good that you're getting into athletics. It'll keep you out of trouble.'

We both know what sort of trouble she means. Knife-carrying trouble. I say yes right away, to shut her up.

I make her change into something more decent though.

So here we are, out on the playing field, lining up at the desk to sign in. I'm hoping I can dump her somewhere because I've already seen that quite a few of my new friends are here. Max and Jamie definitely . . . and there aren't that many parents.

Ellie and Mr Henderson are at the registration desk and Ellie's face lights up when she sees my mum. 'Oh, I'm so pleased to meet you, Mrs Andrews,' she says. 'I'm Ellie. I'm sure Joe will have told you I'm supervising his training.'

My mum has just clocked the wheelchair and has put on her I'm-a-legal-secretary-and-nothing-surprises-me face. She shakes Ellie's hand and says, 'I'm Michelle. Thank you so much for the time you're giving Joe.'

Mr Henderson gives me a form to fill out. It's simple enough but I feel a bit bad when I have to put my fake birth date. I'm pretending to be ten months younger than I am. Isn't that cheating? I'm getting an unfair advantage. Isn't that as bad as taking performance-enhancing drugs?

Mr Henderson notices that I'm dithering and says, 'Is something bothering you Joe? It's all pretty straightforward, isn't it?'

'No . . . yes . . . I was just wondering which race to put down. . .'

'Well, it's quite simple, Joe. You are in year eight.

You are a boy. So you want the race for year eight boys.'

'Oh. OK. Umm . . . Mr Henderson?'

'Yes?'

'I don't suppose I could try running the race for year nine boys, could I? It might be more of a challenge.'

As soon as I've said this I realise I sound like a big-headed complete prat. Mr Henderson laughs, Ellie smirks and my mum rolls her eyes.

'Stick to your own age group,' says Mr Henderson. 'Although if you really want a challenge, there's a 1500 metres event later on which is open to any under-sixteens. I wouldn't normally enter a thirteen-year-old, but if you want a go. . .'

So of course I have to look keen and eager and say yes please. When I trail in last I am going to be totally humiliated.

Ellie checks with Mr Henderson that he can manage without her and offers to introduce my mum to her family. 'They're all here,' she says. 'We're going to have a wheelchair race. This event is really good for mixing in disabled events with the rest. And my little brother is running in the under-eleven 200 metres.'

Her parents are over by a row of benches for spectators. Two boys are chasing around in circles making a load of noise. Claire from my class – shy, tiny Claire – has the same approach to out-of-school clothes as she does to uniform I notice. She's wearing a huge shapeless navy shirt and baggy jeans, and she's sitting on one of the benches, hunched over a book. I'm standing right by her so I say hello, and she looks away from her book for a millisecond and then looks back again. She doesn't even say hello. I feel a slight prickle of irritation.

Ellie's mum is called Janet and she looks a bit like her – same warm smile and twinkly eyes – and Gareth, her dad, is a big red-headed guy. He's full of pride as he tells my mum about Ellie. 'It's amazing what she's been able to achieve in a wheelchair. You won't believe it when you see them race – there's such skill . . . so fast. I don't mind telling you Michelle, we thought the worst when she had her accident. She was a champion gymnast you know, tipped for the top – we were so proud of her. And then. . . But she's just got on and made the best of things and . . . well, she might be about to qualify for the Paralympics.'

'That's fantastic,' says Mum, and then Ellie tells me to go off and get changed and start warming up because the year eight boys' race will start in forty-five minutes.

I meet up with Max and Jamie in the changing room. The race is 800 metres, which is a good distance for me. 'There're four entrants from every school,' says Max. 'The main thing is to hack your way through the crowd.' I'll have to start fast and keep up the momentum,

I decide. I look at Max's short legs. I should be able to beat him at least.

They can't be bothered to do a proper warm up – 'It's not like I stand any chance of winning,' says Jamie, 'so why waste the effort?' – but I jog a bit and then do all the stretching exercises that Ellie's shown me. Then I check that my mum hasn't blown our cover. She's sitting next to Ellie who's raving on about my potential and what a great future I could have if I totally devote my whole life to athletics.

Ellie says, 'Joe, come here for a minute.'

I trot over obediently. 'Look,' says Ellie, 'look at his legs. They're long in proportion to the rest of his body. That gives him a great advantage before he even starts.' And she points out the length of my thigh, which means that her hand is brushing against my crotch. My mum's eyebrows are slightly raised and I think she's trying not to giggle.

Luckily they call the year eight boys' race and I can escape from this sexual harassment. I'm still bothered by the worry that I'm actually cheating. But then I decide it's not a problem. I'm year eight, aren't I? I'm definitely a boy. And some of the others lining up look pretty tall and big too.

Bang! The race starts and I sprint to the front of the pack. I'm breathing well, lengthening my stride, moving away from the other runners. There're about four of us jostling for front position and as we turn the curve we fall into place – first a big blond guy, me in second place, two others on my heels. I'm fine. I'm steady. This is going to be easy. . .

. . . And it is. I hang on for the final circuit and kick off. I overtake the blond. I see his scarlet, shocked face and then I'm out and away. It's not even hard. I'm not even pushing it. And then I speed up for the stopwatch and I'm getting to the final tape and – wow – it was easy, but it feels so good to win. So amazingly good.

Everyone is cheering and they're cheering for me. I punch my hand into the sky and then put it down again. After all, I've only won a poxy race for thirteen-year-olds. It's not exactly Olympic gold. Someone hands me a bottle of water and I gulp it down.

Mr Henderson slaps me on the back. 'Well done,' he says and he shows me my time. 'Excellent. Year nine are up next. See where that time would've got you.'

It's odd watching the year nine boys lining up. I ought to be one of them. In that group I wouldn't really stand out – I'd be average height, just another fourteen-year-old. Nothing special. Not like Joe. . . I watch them run, watch the winner celebrate – and then Mr Henderson shoves a piece of paper under my nose and I see that

I was faster by a full five seconds. I could've won that race too. I can't stop smiling.

Jamie and Max come and find me, and we high five. 'Knew you'd do it,' says Max. 'You're going to be an international athlete, aren't you? I overheard Mr Henderson talking to the head teacher and he said you had more potential than anyone else in the school.'

He's winding me up, I'm certain. 'Shut up,' I say, shoving him. 'Don't talk bollocks. Look what's next.' And we turn to gawp at the year eight girls, next on the track. Some of them look quite good in their PE kit.

I wonder how Ellie feels watching races like this. Does she feel bad that she has to use a wheelchair to race? Of course she must. She's so amazing, so positive, that it's easy to forget how difficult her life must be. She has to depend on other people all the time. I'd hate that.

What's worse: making the absolute best of a life which is so physically restricted, or having to accept that your life is always going to be dictated by fear and lies and uncertainty? I still think I'd prefer to be me – Ty or Joe or whoever – than be stuck in a wheelchair.

And then it occurs to me that if these people who like to intimidate witnesses get their hands on me, then I will be lucky even to be in a wheelchair.

My 1500 metres race isn't for another hour. I should really eat something now. I try and find Mum to get some money but she's disappeared. Claire is there though, still reading her book.

'Umm . . . Claire, did you see where my mum went?' I ask.

'No,' she says, eyes not moving from the book.

'Did she say if she was coming back?'

'No.'

'Umm . . . she was right here. Maybe I'll wait here for her.' I'm thinking aloud, but Claire slams her book shut and says, 'Suit yourself,' really huffily, stands up and walks off.

Eh?

I chase after her. 'Look, I didn't mean to upset you or anything. . . What did I do wrong?'

She's totally blushing and she looks like she's got tears in her eyes, except it's hard to see because her mousey hair is all over her face. What a freak. She needs a total new look.

'Nothing,' she says. 'Just leave me alone please. Your mum is over there, look.' And she points at the table where they're selling soft drinks, and when I turn to look she walks away fast.

Huh. Weird. Obviously I could catch her up but I can't see why I'd bother. It's strange though. Most of the girls in this school would take any excuse to talk to me. I know I sound full of myself, but it's true.

I find Mum, successfully extract a fiver and buy myself a sandwich and a can of Tango. Max, Jamie and I eat lunch together, lying on the grass and rating the year eleven girls on general fitness and potential for dating younger men. Mum seems quite happy hanging out with Ellie's family. They've met up with some of their friends and she seems fine, although they're all about twenty years older than her.

Fifteen hundred metres. OK. Humiliation time. As we line up at the start there's a buzz of chat among the spectators. I may be imagining it, but some people seem to be pointing at me, I think I hear my name. I shake my head. I must be getting paranoid. I'm looking at the other runners. They're all in year ten. OK, I'm only a year younger, not two, but even so. . .

Bang! We're off. And I'm taking it slowly, steadily, trying not to worry that I'm slipping to the back of the field, trying to believe that I can break through, accelerate when I need to. Trying to focus. All that matters is my step and my breath. I forget the crowd, forget everything. All the fear flies away.

And then gradually, gradually getting faster and faster, taking more air, lengthening the stride. And there's not long to go, and I'm up with the leaders and my lungs are bursting. I'm moving so fast and there's nothing to hold back . . . keep going, push it. . . Yes! I reach the tape a split second in front of the guy who's led all the way. I hear Jamie and Max shouting and cheering. I'm gulping, gasping, getting my breath back . . . and inside I'm just exploding with joy because I've actually proved that I'm really good at this. I can do it. I won!

Everyone from Parkview is slapping me on the back and telling me how great I am. Ellie wheels over to me – they all step back and away from the wheelchair – and grabs my hands and shrieks, 'Well done! That was brilliant!' And I can see my mum standing on the edge of the crowd. She's smiling. She's looking pretty shocked.

A man from the local newspaper comes up and wants to interview me but I say, 'No, sorry, got to go,' and manage to lose him in the crowd. The rest of the afternoon is a bit of a blur. There's Ellie's wheelchair race, which is amazing – like the chariot scene from that film Gran likes . . . *Ben Hur*, that's it – with the wheels whizzing round and Ellie's muscly arms going like crazy. It's a bit like a grand prix except without the hideous noise. She wins. She wins by a mile.

I'm standing with her whole family and we're all shouting and cheering, except for Claire who's still reading her book. Maybe she's jealous of Ellie because she's such a star. But how can you be jealous of someone who's stuck in a wheelchair?

Then it's presentation time and I get a trophy and

a little silver cup, and Mr Henderson takes them away from me and says my name will be engraved on them, and I feel a bit choked up because I kind of wish I could use my real name. Just because of my dad, that's all. I bet if he was around he'd be pretty impressed with me today.

And then I get changed and we walk to Ellie's house because her mum's invited us back for supper.

I thought she'd live in one of those houses you see on telly when they tell you how you can sell your house in London and buy something huge in the country, with a big garden and a driveway. I suppose I assumed that everything in her life had been perfect, then destroyed by a moment of terrible bad luck.

But actually she lives in an ordinary grey semi-detached little house, quite scruffy, with a blue door and a pile of rubbish in the tiny front garden. Janet leads us through to a big kitchen at the back, explaining that they had to extend and adapt the house when Ellie had her accident so that she could sleep downstairs.

'It was chaos then and it's a madhouse now,' she says cheerfully, 'But we all muddle through somehow.'

'You must be busy,' says my mum. 'Four kids – that's a lot of work,' and Janet says yes, she doesn't know how she gets through the day sometimes and she's glad she's got a job because it keeps her sane. And my mum says, 'Oh, I know just how you feel,' which is kind of insulting given that she's just got me.

Ellie's brothers ask if I want to play on the Wii with them. Of course I do. Mum never let me have anything like a Wii or a DS or a PlayStation – we couldn't afford it, she claimed, and it would distract me from schoolwork – so my entire life has been spent desperately wanting things that everyone else has got.

It's brilliant fun. We play tennis against each other and we're just doing the final battle between me and Ellie's brother Sam – I'm Nadal, my backhand is amazing, and he's Murray and he's got great fighting spirit – when Claire comes in and says, 'Supper.' She looks really narked to see me there. I'm more than a bit pissed off with her by now. How rude can you get?

I make sure to avoid her when we sit in the big kitchen and eat cold chicken and salad and boiled potatoes – absolutely the best meal I've had for ages, and I'm on to third helpings before anyone else has even finished their first.

Ellie's still banging on about my potential.

'You saw what he could do today,' she tells my mum. 'If he just commits himself he could go far.'

Good luck. She's talking to the woman who once took me on a bus for a day out in the City of London.

She showed me lots of huge skyscrapers and we watched people in suits rushing around and she said, 'This is where the rich people work. If you work hard at Numeracy and Literacy you can come and work here one day and make lots of money.' I was only six.

'I don't think there's much chance he could do all the travelling and everything,' says Mum. 'I remember there's a lot of going to competitions. All over the country. It's not very practical.'

'How do you mean, you remember?' asks Ellie. Here we go. Mum explains about getting pregnant at the peak of her schoolgirl athletics career. I concentrate very hard on shoving potatoes into my mouth. But I glimpse Ellie's mum's face and I think I spot a slight wariness behind the friendly smile.

Ellie is thrilled though. 'Oh, then you understand how he has to train.'

'I really want him to concentrate on doing well in his other subjects,' says Mum. 'He has to work hard at things like Maths and English as well as running. He'll be starting his GCSEs soon.'

'Not that soon, Mum,' I say swiftly. 'I'm only in year eight, remember. One more year to go.'

'But if you've got a real talent, then surely you have to put that first?' persists Ellie.

'Sometimes it's just not possible,' says Mum.

'He needs to think about his future career.'

'Well, just because it wasn't possible for you, I'd have thought you'd want to make absolutely sure that Joe makes the most of his potential.' Ellie's face is a bit pink and her voice is getting louder.

'Slow down, Ellie,' says her mum. She turns to my Mum. 'I'm sorry. Ellie tends to be a bit single-track. Sees what she wants and never mind about obstacles in her way.'

'It's good to be like that,' says Mum. 'That's what you need to get on. I wish Joe was more like that.'

I'm silently outraged because I am very dedicated to my future. It's just that it doesn't happen to be the career in investment banking or international law that she's picked out for me.

'Exactly, we agree then,' says Ellie triumphantly, and even Mum laughs.

'Well it's up to Joe,' she says, 'although if he lets his schoolwork suffer he'll have me to answer to. I wonder, though, whether he'll be as single-minded as you want him to be.'

Huh. Just because she wants to totally control my life. Ellie starts listing star athletes who've also got university degrees for Mum, and I'm exhausted just knowing these two bossy women have so many plans for me. Never mind. It doesn't bother me too much when

I've got a huge bowl of apple crumble and custard to take care of.

Afterwards I play football in the garden with Alex and Sam, Mum helps with the washing up and it's the most normal afternoon we've had for months.

Neither of us really want to leave. Mum says, 'Thank you so much. That was really lovely,' to Janet and they have a quick hug. The boys demand that I come again soon. Ellie waves at me and says, 'Training as usual tomorrow, no slacking.'

Only Claire is nowhere to be seen. But as we pull the front gate closed behind us she's waiting on the street, hidden by the overhanging hedge. She thrusts something into my hand without a word and runs back into the house.

'What was that all about?' asks Mum, watching her go. I shrug. 'No idea. She's a total weirdo.'

'Funny that,' says Mum, 'when the rest of the family are so nice.' Then she says, 'You know, Ty, I was proud of you today,' and my day is just about perfect.

Much later, after I've polished off my Maths homework and I'm safely alone in my bedroom, I retrieve the twist of paper from my back pocket. Claire's folded it about a hundred times and it's so creased it's hard to read the faint, pencilled words. 'Joe, I'm sorry I can't talk to you,' I make out.

'Please don't tell anyone you came to our house. And don't show them this note. Please. I trust you. Claire.'

I have no idea what it's all about. But here's someone who seems almost as scared as I am.

CHAPTER 12
What's Your Secret?

I have no idea what Claire's problem is. I suspect she's just a nutter. I refuse to believe that she's under threat in the same way as I am. How could she be? And why is she bothering me about it?

I'm still having problems sleeping. Alone in the dark it's hard to block out the churning thoughts that I keep under rigid control all day. I try and dodge the memories – the mud, the blood, the lifeless body – and I run right into the fears: hitmen and assassins, shadows and fire. I need a new direction, something to knock out everything. And I remember Ashley as she stroked my arm in Top Shop.

Despite myself I'm beginning to feel a bit excited by Ashley's interest in me. She did look pretty good in that T-shirt. She is very confident, and seems very . . . up for it, eager, experienced. . . She smells of cake, vanilla-flavour cake. I wonder what her skin would feel like to touch? I surrender mind and body to a fantasy Ashley. I've found the perfect distraction to help me relax.

Next morning, running on the treadmill, I decide to go for it. Ask her out. Try my luck. Why turn down something that's offered to you on a plate? If there's any danger that I'm going to die young, I don't want to go without at least a snog.

The only problem is that she's always surrounded by her posse of girlies, and I'm usually with Brian, Jamie, Max and a few hangers on. I can't quite face asking her out in front of all of them. In the end I write a note which says, 'Starbucks, today, 6 pm?' and pass it to her as we go into our French class, first period. She glances at it, smiles to herself, and when we start practical conversation, leans over my desk, giving me a distracting glimpse of flesh and whiff of vanilla, and whispers, *'Oui.'*

'C'est bon,' I reply, and then Brian cuts in with a stumbling question about the weather and Ashley gives her attention to Lauren.

Brian's trying to find out what's going on. *'Avez-vous un assignation avec cette jeune fille?'* he asks, although his accent is so terrible, it's like he's invented a whole new language.

'*Oui, c'est vrai,*' I reply, pleased with myself, and he says, '*Oo la la,*' and gives me the thumbs up. Of course, by break the entire year group seems to know about it. In the distance I see Claire staring at me, white-faced. I ignore her – that's what she wants, isn't it? She turns away. What is her problem?

Ellie gives me a really difficult training session after school. She's not satisfied with anything that I do, keeps telling me to go faster, be stronger. A few weeks ago I would have been slacking off. But I'm still on a high. I push myself harder than ever before.

Ellie's looking thoughtful when I finish my last circuit. 'You really enjoyed winning on Sunday, didn't you?' she says.

'Yes,' I answer honestly. 'More than I'd thought.'

I'm taken aback by how great this feels. I was never competitive before, never really felt I had anything to be competitive with. But this, this could be addictive. I don't care that if Joe Andrews wins an Olympic gold medal he'll probably get killed right afterwards. Right now, it almost feels worth it.

On the way back to the changing rooms I remember Claire's note. 'Ellie, thanks for inviting us for supper on Sunday. It was fun.'

'It was nice to meet your mum,' says Ellie. 'You should try and get her to join a running club or something, you know. She acts like she's too old but she's actually really young.'

'Yeah, right,' I say, meaning no, absolutely not, never ever. 'Ellie, is everything OK with Claire? She seemed to be acting a little, umm, strange.'

Ellie considers. 'As far as I know, she's fine. She never gives much away though. I had to really quiz her to get any information about you. She found moving from primary to secondary school a bit difficult last year, but I think she's settled down now. All her old friends from primary – Lauren, Emily, Ashley – are in your class, aren't they?'

Ashley! I'm meeting her in one hour. I nod, say goodbye and sprint to the changing rooms where I have a very thorough wash and get changed into the jeans and T-shirt that I packed this morning in my school bag. There's just enough time to go home, dump bag and kit and still get to the High Street for 6 pm. I'm more than a little scared of Ashley. It wouldn't do to be late.

At home, Doug's there and – excellent – he and Mum are looking at the local paper and picking out possible jobs. I rush in, say, 'I'm meeting some friends, see you later,' and run out again. I get to the High Street at five to six. And slow down to a walk as I approach Starbucks. I'm feeling a bit shy, as if she knows what I was imagining about her last night.

She's there already, sitting on a sofa, wearing a pale pink top and a denim skirt. She looks about a million times better than she does in uniform – softer, prettier, less make-up. 'D'you want a coffee?' I ask – I removed twenty quid from Mum's purse this morning – but she shakes her head. 'Let's go for a walk,' she says. 'It's too crowded here.'

We wander down the High Street looking in the shop windows – she's quite entertaining when she wants to be – and then she turns down a side road.

'Where are we going?' I ask.

'Let's go to the park,' she says. 'They keep it open until nine in the summer.'

Park? I never even knew there was a park in this town. Although, now I come to think of it, my school is called – duh, Ty – Parkview. But I'm not going there. 'No,' I say, instantly aware that I sound deranged, 'I don't want to go to a park.'

'Why not?'

'I can't tell you.'

We stand there uncertainly in the street. 'Come on,' she says. 'There's nothing to be scared of.'

And she takes me by the hand and leads me through the gates.

It's bigger than our park in London and there are several playgrounds and a wooded bit too. There're a few groups of hoodies and a clutch of girls drinking vodka down by the swings. Some old people walking dogs as well. It seems safe enough, but I'm very wary as we walk along. Ashley leads me to a bench that overlooks the lake. We're half hidden behind a bush and it's as private as you're going to get.

She sits down and pats the seat next to her. What do I do now? Put my arm around her?

'So, Joe Andrews,' she says. 'What next?'

I lean back, hands behind my head. I'm hoping that I look relaxed and sure of myself.

'It's your call, Ash. You always seem to know what you want.'

'Good answer,' she says, and she leans over and very, very gently kisses me on the mouth.

Wow! I have to say that that was one of the top experiences of my entire life so far. She tastes amazing. The whole feeling is amazing. My body is sizzling like a portion of *karahi* chicken. Or sausages in a pan. Assuming the chicken and the sausages are feeling the best they've ever felt, not that they can feel. . . She kisses me again.

I struggle to keep Joe's cool. Joe's probably been with hundreds of girls. My arm slips around her shoulders – very naturally done – and before long we're having the kind of deep-throat snog that Arron would boast about.

On and on, again and again. Luckily, I remember everything he said about breathing through your nose, relaxing your jaw, keeping your mind in neutral so you don't get over-excited. . .

My other arm is around her waist and my hand has slipped under the soft folds of her pink top. I can feel her silky skin and smell her cakey smell. . . It's incredible that right up to about twenty-four hours ago I thought this girl was just an annoying menace.

Eventually we surface for air. 'Wow,' I say, 'you're pretty direct.'

She laughs: 'No point hanging about and letting some other effing bitch get her hands on you,'

Oh, nice. But maybe Joe likes girls who talk like that. 'You'll just have to keep me busy,' I suggest.

She giggles, 'No problem. Talk to me in Turkish.'

I tell her in a soft, Istanbul-accented whisper that there are cockroaches in the kitchen and I'm worried about a visit from environmental health, and she sighs and says, 'That sounds so sexy.' I kiss her again and say in English, 'It's so dirty that I can't tell you what it means.' I wish I could tell Arron how un-gay languages are turning out to be.

I'm curious about her. How come she knows she can get whatever – or whoever – she wants? She's not the most attractive girl in the class – I mean, right now,

I think she's a love goddess – but Emily and Lauren are definitely prettier, and although she looks good now, school uniform doesn't really do it. If Ellie is right and I am catch of the season, then how come Ashley knew I'd go for her?

I touch her nose. 'What's your secret? How did you know I'd want to go out with you?'

She looks coy. 'Oh don't worry. I make very sure that I don't get any competition.'

'Oh yeah?'

'If I want a guy, I make sure no one else goes near him. Then I make my move first.'

'Oh yeah? And why me?'

She looks at me for a full minute: 'Well, first, because you are the fittest guy who has ever walked into that frigging school.'

What can I say?

'And second, because you are a bloody mystery man. Why did you move here from London? Why are the police asking about you? What are you on full report for? What's *your* secret, Joe?'

What the hell? I'm so shocked that I feel completely repelled, and I pull myself out of her arms and move away to the other end of the bench. 'What are you talking about?' I manage to say. I sound quite calm but my heart is beating like crazy and my hands have

144

bunched into fists.

'Oh, don't worry, only I know about this. I didn't tell anyone else.'

'What?' Now I begin to wonder what she does know and who she has told. I don't trust her. Is this how people seem to know we are from London?

I grip her shoulders. 'What are you talking about?' I'm not shaking her, but I'd like to, and she's beginning to look scared. 'Tell me, or . . . or. . .'

'My mum's the head-teacher's secretary,' she says sulkily. 'I know a lot of things about a lot of people.'

Bloody hell. I let her go. This could be a disaster. I'll have to talk to Doug, but if I talk to Doug then it could be the final whistle for life as Joe. And I like life as Joe. Just a few minutes ago it was the best life I'd ever had.

'Look, Ashley. I don't know exactly what you know but you're going to have to tell me what your mum said. Everything she said. This is very serious. She could lose her job over this.'

She rolls her eyes and says, 'I don't know why you're making such a fuss. She just said that you'd moved from London and there were special circumstances.'

'And what else?'

She pouts. 'And the police were involved and you were on full report and the head didn't really want to take you but had to for some reason, Mum didn't know why.'

Shit. The mother might as well work for the *Sun*. As the son of a secretary, I feel quite shocked. Mum worked for a firm of solicitors and was very, very strong on confidentiality – she'd never tell me anything.

'What else?'

'Oh, just about the full report. Most of the teachers say you're really bright but some think you're cheeky. And Mr Henderson thinks you're a future star.'

'Oh,' I sit and think. I can't decide what to do. I'm so angry that I feel like I'm going to be sick. And what to tell Ashley?

'Ashley,' I say, 'you mustn't tell anyone any of this. You haven't, have you?'

'No. . .' she says, but she doesn't sound very sure.

'Do you want to go out with me? Or not?'

'Yes. . .' she says, but she still doesn't sound very sure.

'Ok, then I'll do you a deal. You tell your mum she mustn't say anything about me. You don't say anything about me. And when I can explain, then I will.' And that'll be never, I add, but only to myself.

She nods, and there are tears in her eyes. 'I never meant to upset you, Joe. I didn't know you'd be angry.'

It's not her fault that she has a stupid, unprofessional mother. 'Don't cry. I'm not angry with you,' I say.

And somehow we're kissing again, and this time it's even better than before, and even more than before, and by the time we untangle ourselves it's getting dark and a bell is ringing to tell us that the park is about to close.

We walk to the High Street and then she says, 'That's my bus,' and I say I'll see her at school tomorrow. And then I run as fast as I can all the way home because I hate being out in the dark on my own.

I'm just rounding the corner into my street when a man steps out of the shadows and grabs my arm. I lash out wildly, yelling, 'Get off me,' and then recognise him. It's only Doug. What's he doing scaring me to death like that?

'What was that about?' I shout at him. 'I've got enough to worry about without you messing about.'

'Shush,' he says. 'I wanted to stop you before you get home.'

'Why?' I look at him, appalled. 'What's happened to my mum?'

'Just wait. . .' he says, but I've sprinted away from him and I'm flying towards our front door. I thunder into the hall and crash into the living room. Mum's there crying her eyes out in the arms of Maureen, the makeover lady. I shove Maureen out of the way and throw my arms around my mum. 'Nicki? Nic? What's happened? Has someone hurt you?'

'Not me,' she sobs. 'It's your gran. She's in intensive care. The bastards have attacked her.'

CHAPTER 13
Jelly Baby

I'm back in that no-emotions zone again, where everything is muffled and distant and you're so desperate to feel something – anything – that you want to bite your own tongue until it bleeds. Mum is crying and furious and raging at Doug, and I'm like a dead robot gutted of its circuit boards.

'You were meant to keep her safe. You let us down!' Mum screams, and Doug looks incredibly uncomfortable and can't really answer. Eventually Maureen pats Mum on the shoulder and says, 'Come on now, Nicki, let's put some things in a bag for you and we can get you to the hospital.'

'We're going to the hospital?' I ask and, despite everything, it's great to think we'll be seeing my aunties again. But no, Maureen shakes her head.

'I'm going to stay here with you, Ty, for the time

being, and Doug will take your Mum. It's too dangerous for you to go; we don't know who will be watching the hospital.'

I start shivering, suddenly imagining these people, these attackers, lurking in a hospital ward, ready to hurt, one by one, Mum, Louise and Emma. I'm wondering what Gran looks like.

'What actually happened?' I ask, 'What did they do to her?'

Doug can't even look me in the eye. 'We're not quite sure of all the details yet because your gran is still unconscious. She hasn't been able to tell us anything. But – I'm sorry – there was considerable violence involved.'

'They tortured her,' sobs Mum. 'They tortured her to get her to tell them where we are. And when she wouldn't tell them, they beat her up and left her for dead.'

'You can't actually be sure of that,' says Maureen soothingly, but Mum shakes her head and says, 'I know my own mother.'

'How did they find her?'

'Louise went over because she couldn't get through on any phone. If she hadn't. . .' Mum falls silent, and then suddenly runs out of the room. She just about makes it to the loo before she throws up.

Maureen looks after her and I'm left along with Doug.

He says, 'Try not to worry too much, Ty,'

'When can I see her? How long will my mum be gone?' As I ask I realise how pointless these questions are.

'We'll have to see how things go, how she recovers. It's your half-term holiday next week so that gives us more scope to move you around, but obviously our priority is to keep you safe.'

They wait until about midnight to leave. Mum hugs me and says, 'Take care, my darling.' As I watch her go I wonder if I'll ever see her again. It feels like she's disappearing into the black night forever.

Maureen sleeps in my Mum's room. I lie awake in mine. Eventually I give up trying to sleep and turn on my iPod. I remember my eleventh birthday when Arron and I went swimming, ate cake and ice cream, watched a *Star Wars* DVD. How did we get from there to here? What went so wrong?

In the morning, Maureen's asleep when I leave the house to go training. I write her a note and trudge down the hill. The empty streets spook me a little and I keep looking over my shoulder. It takes twenty minutes to get to school and by then, even a cat crossing the road is enough to freak me out. I walk through the school gate, jittering like I've drunk ten litres of coke.

The gym is my sanctuary. I train harder and faster

than Ellie has asked me to, as if I can do something for Gran by pushing myself to my limits. By the time I'm finished I'm wet with sweat and dizzy with effort. 'Take your time to cool down,' Ellie would say, but I have no time. I'm going to be late for registration. I run up to the changing room, pulling my shirt off as I go, push the door open and – what the – I'm flying though the air, landing in a heap at Carl's feet.

'Whoops,' he sneers, and pulls his foot back and kicks me in the ribs. I double up, swearing; he crows with laughter, and does it again. God knows what would have happened next, but the door opens and Mr Henderson appears.

'What idiot's left his kit bag here for people to crash into? Get a move on and get out of here,' he demands. Then he notices me. 'Stop messing around on the floor, Joe. Go and get changed right now.' I escape to the showers as Carl's gang file out.

I'm late again and that means yet another detention. Ashley's on the lookout as I come rushing into assembly and she's saved a seat for me. As I sit down I feel a sharp pain in the side where I was kicked. I wonder if the kit bag was left there on purpose.

It doesn't matter. Nothing seems to matter when I'm thinking about my gran all the time. I pay no attention during English and Geography and earn two demerits. I've forgotten my Maths homework, which makes detention a double. Ashley wants me to hang out with her mates at break but I've had enough. 'No,' I say, 'I'm not in the mood.'

She's disappointed. She wants to parade me in the playground like a prize poodle at Crufts. Then she says, 'Shall we go somewhere, just us?'

'Where?'

'I know. . .'

She knows everything, this girl. Right now, the way to a dark, dusty cupboard in the drama department. We squeeze in and there's just room for the two of us. My side is more and more painful where Carl kicked me, but it's amazing how much better I feel just slipping my arms around her. She seems to like the Turkish nonsense, so I'm saying random words in her ear – meat, vegetables, that kind of thing, trying to avoid obvious giveaways like shashlik and kebab. I can't even see her, but I can feel . . . and taste . . . and touch . . . and. . .

The bell's ringing for the end of break. I wonder wildly if she'd consider staying in here for the next lesson. For the rest of the day, in fact. Not only do I feel safe but I'm not thinking about anything scary at all. But she's tucking in her blouse and doing up her top button and saying; 'Come on Joe, we don't want to be late for PE.'

I'd forgotten it was PE today. Great. Another encounter with Carl. And all my kit is wet through with sweat. It's only as I get to the PE block and see the boys lining up at the door that I remember today is the first time we're going swimming in the school pool. And not only do I have no swimming things, but I am also wearing contact lenses which will float out of my eyes if I go underwater.

Mr Henderson takes the register and I raise my hand. 'I've forgotten my stuff,' I say. 'Never mind, I keep a spare set and a towel in my office. Go and find it, third shelf down in the cupboard.'

Damn. I will just have to keep my eyes closed or out of the water or something. Or maybe I can borrow some goggles? It's annoying because usually swimming would be one of my favourite things. We get changed and I hear Carl and his mates sniggering when they see my bruises. I don't care. They're pathetic.

We do a few lengths freestyle to warm up then stand in the shallow end while Mr Henderson explains what we'll be doing next. It's quickly clear that keeping my head out of the water isn't going to be an option. We have to dive off the side, swim underwater for *miles* and then swim through a polystyrene wall with a hole cut in it. Impossible. I will go in with brown eyes and come out with green.

I raise my hand. 'Mr Henderson, could I borrow some goggles?'

'No, Joe. If you had been listening you would know that this is survival swimming and thus has to be done unadorned with either goggles or flippers. The government in all its wisdom has decided that too many children are drowning and they want to make sure that you have the skills to survive any accidental falls off boats or into rivers. It's a new scheme and, as a Sports Academy, we've been asked to pilot it. So it has to be done properly.'

'I can't do it without. I'm sorry.'

Some of the boys laugh, not too nicely. Carl says, 'Got a problem getting your hair wet. have you? Think it'll spoil your looks? Think your mascara will smudge? Well we'll help you out.' Two of his gorilla gang grab my arms and Carl pushes my head under the water.

I'm fighting and struggling and kicking, and breathing in water through my nose and my mouth . . . and bubbles of air are escaping in great gulps, and my lungs are bursting . . . and I can only see sparkles and dots and . . . I'm dying. . . Then they let go their grip on my arms and I leap up to breathe again.

I'm coughing and gasping and I hear Mr Henderson yelling his head off: 'What the hell do you think—'

but I don't stop to listen. I launch myself at Carl, my arm goes back and – whack! – my fist crashes into his piggy face. He screams, hand flying to nose, and falls backwards, spraying a fountain of blood which stains my hand and clouds the water.

'Grab him, lift him out of the water,' shouts Mr Henderson, and Brian and Jamie fish Carl out. They haul him up to the edge where he quivers, snivelling, with blood streaming down his face, and then he spews up his breakfast all over the side of the pool.

'For God's sake,' says Mr Henderson. 'Go get a towel,' he barks to Brian. Brian goes running and comes back with Carl's towel, and is told to get changed as quickly as possible and go for the school nurse. 'And tell her she's probably going to have to call an ambulance. And then get Terry the caretaker to come and clean this up.'

I can't stop staring at the blood on my hand and the blood in the water. I'm starting to shake, like I did that time in the gym. The blood is dripping into the water and it's on me, and I'm going to drown in blood. It's only Mr Henderson's icy voice that pulls me into the present.

'All of you, get out of the water and go and get changed. You can then go to lunch. Joe, as quickly as you can to my office once you are changed.'

As soon as we're in the changing room Jamie and Max pat me on the back. 'You were totally within your rights,' says Max. 'He was trying to drown you.'

'Where did you learn to punch like that?' asks Jamie. 'Can you teach me?' Carl's lot, I notice, keep as far away from me as possible.

I shower – making sure that my hands are clean, that no blood remains – and dress as slowly as I dare, trying to put off the interview with Mr Henderson. Brian comes back into the changing room to get his stuff and finds me there alone apart from Jamie and Max who are asking if they should come with me. 'Because it's not fair,' says Max. 'You were only defending yourself, but he's let Jordan and Louis get away with it.'

Brian's flushed with excitement. 'Carl's gone off to hospital in an ambulance, still in his trunks, wrapped in a blanket, and the school nurse thinks his nose is definitely broken and they're worried he might have inhaled some blood and vomit into his lungs because he can't stop wheezing,' He too slaps me on the back. 'Great stuff, mate. Haven't had such an entertaining lesson for months. Not since Ashley slapped Kelvin's face in Geography for daring to ask her out.'

'I'd better go,' I say. 'He's going to be even more angry if I'm late.'

Brian offers to come as well but I think Mr Henderson might not appreciate a support party. 'OK,' says Max, 'but if he's really not fair and chucks you out, we're ready to go and protest for you. We'll make a petition or something.'

'Thanks,' I say, and I really mean it. I'm feeling very alone at the moment, and it's good to find people who are prepared to stick their necks out.

Mr Henderson is on the phone when I sidle into his office. He points at the armchair and I sit, head down, while he talks: 'Yes, yes indeed. Yes, yes, to casualty. No. No, nothing like this. Yes, indeed.' It's one of those conversations that sounds like it could go on forever and I'm almost surprised when eventually he puts the phone down.

'That was the headmaster,' he said, 'and you won't be surprised to hear that he wants to see you, with your parents, in his office on Friday morning. 10 am You will be suspended from school until then.'

My throat is very dry and it's hard even to speak. 'My mum's away and I don't know if she'll be back on Friday and she's all the parents I've got.'

'She's away and you're by yourself?'

'No, there's someone staying with me.'

'Then if she's not back, that person is in *loco parentis* and will have to come with you.'

I'm trying to imagine Makeover Maureen, who I have met all of twice, by my side as I am excluded from school, and the total global explosion that will take place when my mum finds out.

'Am I going to be excluded?'

'I have no idea, Joe. I would say you've made a pretty good attempt at it. What on earth did you think you were doing? You could have killed him.'

'Could I?'

'Knocking someone out in a swimming pool? What if he'd hit his head against the side? What if no one had brought him out of the water in time? He's probably suffering from concussion and a broken nose. Where on earth did you learn to punch like that?'

'Oh, I used to go to boxing club.' I'm actually amazed that I can punch so hard. I was the most useless boy in the club. All the training must have massively enhanced my strength.

'Boxing club. Lord deliver us.'

'What about him and his mates? They were drowning me.'

'There's no excuse for what they did, but you were actually under the water for less than a minute and they let you go as soon as I told them to. And there was absolutely no need for you to retaliate in the way that you did, whatever the provocation.'

I shrug. And again I feel that sharp pain in my side. I must have winced because Mr Henderson asks, 'What's the matter?'

'My side hurts. I got kicked this morning.'

'When you were messing around on the floor?'

'I wasn't messing around. I fell over someone's kit bag.'

'You fell over someone's kit bag and then someone kicked you?'

'Carl.'

'I see.'

'He didn't like me getting the access card. And he doesn't like me anyway.' There's no real need to mention mildly winding him up at the shopping centre.

Mr Henderson is looking puzzled. 'Joe – you look different. Is there something wrong with your eyes?'

He's spotted that the contact lenses have gone but he doesn't know what's different. He's never really clocked what colour my eyes are. What can I say?

'I have contact lenses and they shouldn't go in the water. Now they've gone. Maybe it makes me look a bit different.'

'So that's why you were making a fuss about swimming underwater! You should have brought a note from your mother. Joe, the fact remains that you punched and injured another student in the swimming pool.

I'm going to have to rescind your access card and I'm not sure that I can let you go on having special training with Ellie.'

Now I'm angry. This is really not fair. 'But it was him . . . he attacked me first. . . I had to defend myself. . . If you don't defend yourself you can end up dead.'

I'm so nearly crying that I have to shut up right away. Right away, before I start howling like a five year old. . . Oh no . . . I can't hold back the tears at all and I have to bite the back of my hand to stop sobbing out loud.

Mr Henderson shoves a box of tissues towards me. He sounds less angry and more disappointed. 'Joe, you know we think you're very promising and we've been very happy with your progress. I'll certainly be reporting good things about you to the head as well as this unfortunate incident.'

Now I've started crying, I really can't stop. The pain in my side is burning into me and I keep on imagining Gran's face, all swollen and cut, bleeding and mashed to a pulp. The thought of having no training, no Ellie as well, is too much.

Mr Henderson says, 'Joe, maybe I should call the person who's standing in for your mum and get them to come and pick you up? Who is it, a grandparent?'

'No . . . my gran's in hospital.' My voice is all over

the place. 'That's where my mum is. But they won't let me see her.'

The bell rings for the end of lunch. Mr Henderson sighs and says, 'I'm going to have to go and take 7P for rounders. Stay here and calm down a bit, and hopefully things will look a bit better on Friday. I'll try and make sure you're not disturbed. And when you're ready, then you can just go home.' He reaches into his pocket and pulls out a toffee. 'Try this. It might make you feel a bit better.'

He leaves me alone in the office and I force myself to take deep breaths and stop the crying. Chewing the toffee does help a bit. Eventually I'm able to dry the tears and the snot, and by then there are no tissues left in the box.

I've got to get out of here before the end of school when there will be hundreds of kids milling around. I've got to get out before anyone sees me and spots that my eyes are green and my nose is red and I've turned from cool hard Joe into jelly-baby Ty.

CHAPTER 14
Skeleton Soul

No one spots me sprinting across the playing fields and escaping through the side gate. I carry on running down the hill and into the High Street. The sensible thing is to go home right away, find my spare set of lenses and tell Maureen what's happened. I don't do the sensible thing. I cross the road and head for Ellie's house.

I have to explain. Maybe she can persuade them that I can go on with the training. I don't want her to think that I didn't value her training. I'm worried that she's going to despise my lack of focus, my lack of control, my basic weakness.

I ring the doorbell and Ellie's mum comes to the door. She looks surprised. 'Hello, Joe,' she says. 'Not in school today?'

I shake my head. 'Is Ellie here?'

'No, sorry, love. She's gone to a training camp for

Paralympic potentials. Her Dad's driven her and Magda, the new helper we're trying out. She won't be back until Sunday. I thought you knew she was away.'

She's right, I did know. I just didn't remember. I'm numb with disappointment. 'Sorry to bother you,' I say.

'It's no bother. I tell you what, why don't you come and have a cup of tea? You look like you could do with one.'

That's just what my gran would say. As I follow her into the kitchen, I realise that my eyes are filling up again. What the hell's happening to me? I bite my lip hard, but I can't speak at all as I slide into a seat at the big table.

Luckily, Ellie's mum doesn't seem to expect a lot of chat. She puts a mug of tea in front of me, and makes me a chicken sandwich. I can't remember the last time I ate anything and it doesn't last long. She follows it up with a slice of fruit cake.

Then she sits down next to me. 'That's better. It's good to see someone who likes his food.' She pats my hand: 'Joe, don't mind me asking but is everything OK? You seem a bit upset.'

I shake my head. Everything is not OK. Nothing is OK. Where to start?

'My gran is in the hospital. She's been hurt.

She's in intensive care. But I can't go and see her and I don't know what's happening.'

'But surely you can go with your mum, Joe? Maybe next week when you've got half term.'

'I don't think they'll let me.' I say hopelessly.

'They?'

'Er . . . the people in the hospital. I don't know.'

'Well, I'm sure they know what they're doing. They don't tend to like a lot of visitors in the ICU. Maybe things will look a lot brighter by next week.'

'Maybe. And I don't think school is going to let me go on working with Ellie.'

She laughs and says, 'I'd like to see them try and stop Ellie working with you,' which makes me feel a bit better. Then she asks, 'But why would they want to stop you? I thought everyone was very happy with the results?'

'I punched someone in the swimming pool. Mr Henderson said I could have killed him. I think perhaps they are going to exclude me permanently.'

'Why did you punch him?' She sounds pretty calm.

'He and his friends were trying to drown me . . . I thought . . . and he'd kicked me this morning.'

'Kicked you?'

'In the ribs.'

'Can I have a look? I'm a nurse, you know. I work three nights a week up at the General.'

Carefully I lift up my shirt and show her the two big bruises. She puts her hand on one and I jump away. 'Ow!' It's hurting like crazy now. Much to my shame I feel more tears running down my face. She tactfully hands me a tissue.

'Joe, you have to go to hospital and get that looked at. I think you might have broken a rib there.'

'But there's nothing they can do about that, is there?' It sounds like a big waste of time when I could easily take a few aspirin.

'Let me ring Michelle. You've not got a car, have you? I could run you two up there.'

'She's not here. She's gone to London to be with my gran.'

'So who is staying with you?'

I shrug and she gives me another tissue.

'Joe, she's not left you all by yourself, has she?'

'No, there's someone staying with me. Called Maureen.'

'Well, then. Get Maureen to take you to casualty for an X-ray. Joe, it's very important. A broken rib could puncture your lung, and that could kill you. Or at least bring your sporting career to an end.'

'Oh.'

'And if you have broken a rib, well, it's good for the head teacher to know that, isn't it? Fair's fair.

No good punishing you for violence if the other boy gets away with it. Look, I have to go and get the boys from school. Stay here, have some more tea, help yourself to cake and when I get back I'll take you home and talk to this Maureen.'

I'm not sure this is a good idea and it must show on my face. 'Really, Joe, you can't be too careful about things like this. You don't want permanent lung damage.'

Left alone in the kitchen, I go over and look at the many photos of Ellie on display alongside a shelf of her trophies. She looks so happy and determined. I wonder if there's another side to Ellie, full of rage at what life's done to her. I'm very tempted to sneak a look at her room but that would seem like I'm some sort of mad stalker, which wouldn't be a great idea.

I'm just cutting myself another piece of cake – OK, it's my third – when I hear a gasp, and a small voice says, 'Wh— what are you doing here?'

It's Claire, home from school. I turn around and suddenly I'm really fed up with her constant scared rabbit expression.

'I'm eating cake. What about you?' I say rudely, cramming it into my mouth.

'No, I mean why you are in my house? And why . . . how . . . have your eyes gone green?'

She noticed. Damn. Bugger. I'd totally forgotten

about the stupid lenses.

I stand there for a minute and then I put down the knife and walk towards her. My side is hurting so much that I feel dizzy but I put out my hands and grip her wrists. She looks absolutely terrified. Good.

I lean towards her and shift into gangsta. Menacing. Angry. Scary. 'You keep yer mouth shu' abou' my eyes. Forget you ever saw they was green.'

She's almost crying. I tighten my grip. She whispers, 'No, no . . . I won't say anything.'

'Not to Ashley or Lauren or Emily – none of dem, none of your mates.'

A blotchy red blush spreads over her face. 'They're not my friends. I'd have thought you'd know your girlfriend has no time for me. Hasn't she told you what a stupid freak I am?'

I let go and turn away. 'Who says she's my girlfriend?'

'She's told everyone you belong to her.'

'She doesn't own me. We're just messing around.'

'Whatever.'

'Whatever,' I echo. 'Anyway, keep it quiet.'

She's rubbing her wrists. I must have really hurt her. What am I turning into?

'Did you really punch Carl?' she asks in a whisper.

'Yup.'

'They say he's got to have plastic surgery.'

'Do they?' This strikes me as quite funny. Maybe Carl's porky features will be transformed by my efforts. Maybe he'll end up looking like a chimp. I can't help smiling.

Claire is looking at me like I'm a psychopathic maniac. Her voice is shaky. 'Joe, if I don't tell anyone about your eyes – and I won't, I really, really promise you – you won't tell Ashley that we talked, will you?'

Not this again. 'What is your problem with talking to me? Most people seem to like me.'

'Ashley doesn't like other girls talking to her boyfriend.'

I think back to Ashley telling me, 'If I want a guy I make sure no one else goes near him.' I think back to Claire's crumpled note. And I know, deep down, that Ashley, who I want like a kid wants candyfloss, is not a nice person at all.

But I still want her.

'Don't worry,' I say to Claire. 'I don't tell tales if you don't. But please don't treat me like I smell or something.' It feels crazy to say this when I've just been terrorising her, but I add, 'Right at the moment I could do with some friends.'

She gives me a little uncertain smile. 'I think a lot of people will be your friend now that you've smashed

Carl's nose. He used to pick on the year seven boys – they were chanting your name in the playground. And Max is organising a petition to go to the head to ask that you shouldn't be punished.'

Brilliant. I am the figurehead of a popular revolution. By Friday there will probably be riots in the dining hall and book burning in the library. I can't see this working in my favour with the head teacher. And what about when he tells keep-your-head-down Doug?

There's the sound of a key in the door and Sam and Alex erupt into the room, shouting and whooping when they see me. 'Boys, you stay here with Claire and I'll run Joe home,' says Janet. 'Claire, is that OK?'

'Yup.' I can sense her relief. What if she tells Ellie and her kind mum how I scared her? What have I done?

When we get to our house Maureen instantly spots my not-brown eyes and her own widen in alarm. I go upstairs to find the spare set of lenses while Janet suggests a trip to casualty. Maureen agrees right away: 'She's absolutely right, Joe – we've got to get this checked out, especially with your mum away.'

I don't protest. The pain is getting worse and my breathing is feeling a bit difficult. But I don't say so because that would be making a fuss.

By the time we've waited for a few hours at the hospital, Maureen knows the whole story. Well, everything except what I did to Claire. She's actually a nice lady – best police officer yet – and easy to talk to. She seems to think that I'll get away with punching Carl, although she doesn't really approve.

'In my opinion, schools should be a lot tougher about these incidents and then we wouldn't have the problems we do out on the streets,' she says. 'In the good old days it was zero tolerance. You and Carl, you'd have been out of that school. Nowadays it'll be a slapped wrist.'

They take the X-ray. I lie all alone on a table while a white machine clicks and whirrs above me. I wonder what it would be like if these machines could look inside your mind as well as your body and see the tangle of stories and lies and thoughts and problems inside; if they could make an image that captured the inner truth, the real person, the skeleton soul. Who would they see if they could look inside me?

We wait a bit longer and then a doctor comes and tells me that I've cracked two ribs and should take it easy for a bit. She prescribes painkillers and says, 'No rough sport because there is a danger of puncturing a lung if you have another impact. And no alcohol while you're taking these.'

'He's thirteen, for heaven's sake,' says Maureen, and the doctor asks, 'Have you been here on a Saturday night?'

'What about running?' I ask. 'That should be fine,' she replies, 'but if you have any trouble with your breathing, then stop right away and seek medical advice.'

We're about to leave when Carl and his mum emerge from another cubicle ahead of us. Carl's face is hideously swollen and he's holding an ice pack to his nose. His mum must have brought in some clothes because he's wearing a tracksuit. They've been here for hours.

I pull on Maureen's arm. 'It's him. Can we wait? I don't want him to see me.'

Carl doesn't look tough and strong any more, but like a little boy who's clinging to his mum for comfort. When I see how his mum has her arm around him, I long for my gran. She's the one I need right now.

'Come on, they're gone,' says Maureen and we walk to her car. Every step is painful and I'm sure I've screwed up my training schedule for the next few days, whether I can use the school gym or not.

Back at home, she makes me baked beans on toast. I switch on my mobile. I have eighteen texts and ten messages. Almost all the texts are from people at school sending their congratulations and pledging their support, like I'm the leader of a resistance movement under some oppressive regime. They must have got my number from

Ashley. She's sent me a text: *u r my hero. Cant w8 2 c u.*
park 2moro 4pm? Xxxxxx.

And then I listen to the messages and there's a
voicemail from Mum.

Maureen is buttering the toast. I go into the living
room and listen to the message. Mum sounds breathy
and anxious: 'Hello, Ty. I can't really talk but Gran is
stable and we're all here with her. I'm sending her lots
of love from you. Hope you're OK. Can't talk more.
Take care, sweetheart.'

I may be wrong. Maybe Doug told her she could ring.
But it doesn't seem right to me. Surely she's potentially
giving away where we are? Doug said no phone calls.
What if someone's monitoring calls or something?
I dither for about two seconds, then, as Maureen calls,
'Food's ready,' I make a decision.

I sit down at the table and hold out my phone.
'Maureen. My mum left me a message. I thought maybe
it wasn't such a clever thing to do.'

She takes the phone from me and listens. She shakes
her head. 'I'm not going to lie to you, Ty – I think she's
done this without telling Doug. It's understandable –
poor girl, she's under a lot of strain, but she shouldn't
have. I'm going to have to tell him.'

I nod, although I feel I've betrayed my mum.
'Eat up,' says Maureen. 'None of this is easy, I know.'

173

'Nope. . . Maureen, do you know a lot of families in witness protection?'

'Quite a few,' she says. 'I tend to get involved, as I did with you, in changing the way people look. You're unusual, though, because most of the people we deal with are criminals themselves. They're looking to escape prison by informing on their former colleagues. Complete low lives, to be honest. It's hard to be helping people you feel so little respect for. You two are different. I'm sorry it's been so hard for you.'

'It's not all hard. Some of it's been good.'

'I hope it stays that way,' she says, but she's being kind, I can see.

We sit and watch some stupid reality programme where two women change families and have to live in each other's houses. After about two minutes they are going crazy, shouting and sulking and threatening to leave. As I watch, I'm feeling older and older, like an ancient old man who's done it all and seen it all and all the adults are like children to me. I bet really old people feel incredibly lonely when everyone their age is dead.

I take a painkiller and go to bed. My ribs are still agony, though, and my head's full of violence – the real kind between me and Carl, and the infinitely worse sort that I'm imagining happening to Gran. But what I can't bear to think about is the way I tightened my grip on

Claire's wrists when I knew I didn't need to, and the terrified look on her face.

There's only one way to block it out. I grab my mobile and send a text: *OK 4 pm* And I shift on to my less painful side, close my eyes and start imagining – in fantastic exotic detail – what Ashley and I are going to get up to tomorrow.

But even that's not enough to bring sleep. I'm relaxed all right, but I can't get rid of the fear. I'm scared of the faceless people out there who want to hurt me like they hurt Gran. I'm terrified that Mum's phone call is going to lead them to me.

But the biggest fear is what I'm becoming inside.

CHAPTER 15
Old Habit

A shley's annoyed with me. I can tell the minute I spot her coming along the path, by the way she's frowning and flouncing and pouting.

It's a shame because she looks *fantastic*. She's in summer uniform, which means a really short skirt and a tight white polo shirt through which a purple bra kind of shines. I'm dimly aware that my aunties wouldn't have been so impressed – they'd use mean words like chav and tart – but I don't care what they'd think because to me she's really sexy, incredibly attractive.

'Hey Ash,' I say, as she sits down next to me. 'What's up?' I'm hoping that we can keep any talking to a minimum so I can explore this new look as thoroughly as possible. And I'm also worried that if I allow myself to dislike Ashley any more than I do now, I'll have to chuck her, which I'd rather not do quite yet.

We're just finely balanced right now.

'I thought you'd call or text or something yesterday or today and tell me exactly what happened – the whole story,' says Ashley in a huff. 'Everyone was asking me about you and I felt a right lemon not being able to tell anyone anything. You could have waited for me after school. And then you just texted '4 pm OK', no kisses nor nothing.'

Blah, blah, blah, blah. Loud and annoying, just as I thought. Me, me, me, me. And I suspect she's a bully. Why am I even here? 'I can give you kisses like this,' I say and lean in to do just that.

She's not having it though. 'But why didn't you call me yesterday? My mum knew more about what was going on than I did.'

'I was in the hospital for hours, Ash. Look.' I lift up my T-shirt to show her my bruises, which are nearly the same colour as her underwear. 'Two broken ribs from that thug Carl.'

Her hand goes to her mouth. 'Oh my God. You must be in agony.'

'Only you can make it feel better,' I lie, because today the painkillers are doing an excellent job and I was able to go out for a two-hour run this morning, no problem at all.

'Oh, I suppose I forgive you,' she says, and moves

in close for the kind of mouth-to-mouth resuscitation that Carl very nearly needed yesterday at the pool.

We're there for an hour, during which I discover that Ashley will let me go quite a bit further than Arron ever got with Shannon Travis, although – somewhat to my relief – there do seem to be limits. But one minute she's pushing my hand away and the next she's placing it right back where it was, which is kind of confusing.

And then we hear something. A rustling noise. . . We freeze. Nothing. 'It's OK,' I murmur and my hand creeps on to her thigh. And then muffled laughter, a bright light and – bugger– he's taken our photo on his mobile phone.

'Slag!' he yells at Ashley. 'Slapper. . . Wait till all the boys see these. . .'

It's Jordan. Carl's sidekick. And Louis is by his side. Ashley's never moved so fast in her life. She launches herself at them: 'Bastards! Delete them!'

They're laughing at her and at me, and they're taking the opportunity to feel her up a bit. Inside me there's cold fury. This is threatening. This is unacceptable. This is an emergency. And I reach into my back pocket and I pull out the knife that I took from the kitchen before I came out to meet her.

'Gimme da phone,' I say in my hardest gangsta

voice, slowly unwrapping the handkerchief I'd wound around it.

Now it's their turn to freeze. They look uncertainly at each other. 'Gimme da phone,' I repeat, except this time I throw in a bit more cussing. 'Den no one's gonna be hurt.'

'Oh my God, Joe,' says Ashley.

'You knows I can fight. And you knows I can run. And you see dis blade.' I wave the knife at them. 'So give. Me. Da. Fu'in'. Phone.'

Jordan throws it on the ground. I look at Louis. 'And you.'

'But I never took any.'

'Gimme da phone coz you is disrespectin' me and dis gel, and you is gonna pay for dat, muvverfu'er.'

He throws his phone down too and I say, 'Ash, get 'em.' She picks them up and I can see she's crying.

'Delete all their data and then give them back.'

She does it and I say, 'OK, now you're gonna apologise to the lady.'

They shuffle their feet. 'Sorry, Ashley. Sorry.'

'Get outta here.'

They stumble along the path, looking behind them every two seconds. Ashley and I follow – I don't want to let them out of my sight so they can ambush us halfway down. At the park gate I put the knife back in my pocket and make sure they've got on to a bus. Then I turn to Ashley, who has stopped crying but looks pretty upset. There's this little tiny bit of me that thinks it's not such a terrible thing for her to find out how she makes people like Claire feel.

'Are you OK?' I ask.

'Yes,' she whispers. Then, 'Joe, why did you have a knife?'

Because there are people out there who beat and tortured my gran to discover where to find me, and my mum may have stupidly given them my address. I shrug. 'Old habit.'

I wonder whether Jordan and Louis are going to go home and start looking in their kitchens to be ready for the next time they meet me. But most of all, I wonder what I'd have done if they hadn't thrown down their phones.

'How come you talked like that?'

It's just another language, I want to say, like Urdu or Turkish or Portuguese. We played around with the way we spoke all the time at primary school. And then at eleven some of us went to a school where you could go on doing that (St Jude's) and some of us went to a school where you spoke in gangsta and you wrote in text (Tollington) and two of us went miles across town to St Saviour's where it was, 'yes sir, no sir,' and the other boys laughed at you for coming from East London.

'Dat's da lingo in da hood, innit,' I tell her.

'You sound like another person altogether,' she says. I kiss her goodbye as her bus draws up, but her heart doesn't seem to be in it.

I lie low for the next few days. I don't answer anyone's texts – even Ashley's – and I don't go near the school. The only message I'd like to get would be one from Ellie but I don't hear anything from her. Maybe she's too disappointed with me to bother. Maybe Claire told how I hurt and scared her.

Maureen keeps me up to date with news from the hospital. Gran is still in a coma and although they say she's stable, they have no idea when she might wake up. Mum and my aunties are staying at the hospital. 'Are you guarding them properly?' I ask, and Maureen assures me that yes, there's a police guard there all the time. 'Have you found the people who did this?' I ask, but she shakes her head.

I watch a lot of daytime telly and I keep the curtains closed. It seems that one way or another I'm going to get permanently excluded from school. Jordan and Louis will report me for threatening them with a knife. Claire will tell someone that I bullied her. Carl will have suffered irreversible brain damage.

And then what? I won't be Joe any more and I'll

have to start all over again. I can't decide if that's a good thing or not. It seems that once Mum left, once no one knew me as Ty, then Joe turned into a monster. It's safest to stay at home and watch *Cash in the Attic*.

Friday morning, I come downstairs dressed in jeans and a T-shirt and Maureen sends me straight back again to change into uniform. She even cuts my hair a bit to make it tidier and combs it for me like I'm six. She drives us to school: 'Just remember, tell him you're sorry and promise it won't happen again. And look like you are sorry. No back chat, no arguing.'

Luckily everyone's in lessons and no one I know sees us as we walk through the corridors to the head's office. There's an outer office and Maureen knocks on the door and tells the woman, who answers, 'Joe Andrews and Maureen O'Reilly to see the head teacher.'

I get a horrible shock when I see this woman. It's like Ashley's aged thirty years overnight. Same dark hair, same spidery eyelashes, same pouty mouth, even the same strain on the buttons around the chest area. She makes me feel a bit sick. She looks at me like I'm a dung beetle – interesting but revolting. I remember how unprofessional she is and glare right back. I wonder if she knows about Ashley and me.

We wait for ten minutes, and then the door of the head teacher's office opens and Carl and his parents come out. Carl's nose is still swollen and there's a huge bruise that covers both eyes. I can't imagine that, having seen that, the head teacher is going to want me to stay in the school. To my surprise they come over to us, but only to sit down – it seems that they're not finished with the head. We all ignore each other, which is a lot of ignoring. I stare at the ceiling and in my head I rerun my 1500-metre triumph.

'Mr Naylor will see you now,' says Ashley's mum, and we walk into his office. I'm actually relieved that Mum isn't here. Maureen is a lot calmer than she would have been.

Mr Naylor is sitting at his desk and we sit down in front of him. He's quite old; grey hair, beard and specs, and I know from assemblies that he's nuts on order and discipline.

'Mrs Andrews,' he starts, and Maureen interrupts. 'Excuse me, but I'm not the boy's mother, Mr Naylor. She's away at the moment and I'm *in loco parentis*. The family is in severe crisis: Joe's grandmother has been the victim of an extremely violent crime,' – my stomach lurches – 'and is still unconscious. Although it in no way excuses Joe's behaviour, I think it may go some way towards explaining it.'

Mr Naylor and I are both a bit dazed by this opening speech. 'Ah,' he says. 'Well. I'm sorry to hear that,

Mrs . . . er. . .'

'Maureen O'Reilly,' says Maureen, offering him her hand to shake. 'Friend of the family.'

'Ah. Oh. Right.' Mr Naylor is trying not to look too nosy. 'Well, I was hoping we could hear from Joe his explanation of the event in the swimming pool.'

Event? That's a good one. Perhaps they'll add drowning and fighting to the next swimming gala. I give him a brief outline.

Mr Naylor reaches for a piece of paper on his desk. 'And Carl suffered a broken nose, concussion and severe bruising.'

Maureen says, 'Yes, but what Joe hasn't told you is that Carl broke two of his ribs earlier in the day. Show him, Joe.'

I unravel my uniform to display the bruises. It's kind of embarrassing stripping off in front of the head, but I suppose it's worth it.

'How did this happen?' asks Mr Naylor, peering over his specs at my torso.

'I fell over a kit bag in the changing room and Carl kicked me. I didn't realise anything was broken though.'

'I would suggest that any punishment you give Joe should apply equally to Carl,' says Maureen.

'Carl's parents are talking about taking the whole

matter to the police,' says Mr Naylor.

'That would be very foolish of them, unless they would like Joe's mother to press charges against their son as well,' counters Maureen with quick-fire speed.

'Joe, what are the roots of this argument between you and Carl? You've hardly been in the school any time at all, and I'm very disappointed to find you mixed up in what seems to be an escalating feud.'

'I . . . er . . . Mr Henderson gave me an access card to use the fitness suite and stuff out of hours and Carl was really angry, said the football team should have them too. That's the main reason, I think.'

'And there's nothing you've done to exacerbate matters?'

'No, I don't care if they have cards as well.'

'And over the last few days you've done nothing to stir up popular feeling in the school? This petition, for example,' – he points to a wodge of paper – 'and the protests that have been taking place?'

'I didn't know anything about that,' I say, and Maureen kicks into action again.

'Mr Naylor, over the last few days I've seen the very sad sight of a bright, athletic, sociable boy turn into a virtual recluse who sits and watches television all day and won't even open the curtains. He's had dozens of messages from supportive friends and he hasn't replied to one. Joe and his mother are new to this town and they came here not knowing a soul. He's had to find friends and get used to a very different atmosphere, and I think the school's let him down by failing to protect him from this sort of bullying behaviour.'

She pauses, but only to draw breath. 'At the hospital they told me that his breathing may have been affected all day, and that the supply of oxygen to his brain was obviously further restricted by being held under water. This could well have affected his judgement. Joe's come from a tough area and his mother sent him to boxing club to learn to protect himself. I'd ask you to consider that he was acting on instinct and in pure self defence.'

She ought to be a lawyer. That was brilliant! Mr Naylor opens his mouth to reply, but Maureen has more to say.

'He's been at home all week. Surely he's had his punishment.'

Mr Naylor clears his throat. 'I've certainly heard some good things about Joe and I have a letter here from Ellie Langley, the student responsible for his training. She makes a strong case for allowing him to keep on with the athletics programme. I'd like to hear Joe say he's sorry for his behaviour and make a commitment to behaving better in future.'

'He's certainly happy to do that,' says Maureen,

giving me a quick glance, 'but I'd also like to know what your strategy is for avoiding this kind of bullying in the future. I don't need to tell you what the consequences could have been if one of the broken ribs had punctured a lung.'

'Well,' says Mr Naylor, 'we're trialling a form of restorative justice at the school, which involves the two parties coming together to discuss the effect such an incident has had and jointly find a way forward. In this case, I was keen for Joe's mother to talk to Mr and Mrs Royston, as well as to try and avoid police involvement. So why don't I ask them to come in and we can see if Carl and Joe can, as it were, make peace?'

He gets up to go to the door, and Maureen rolls her eyes at me and mimes slapping her wrist. I'm so impressed at how she managed to turn me from villain to victim. But I wonder if a real court is also so open to twisting and turning the facts. Maybe there's no such thing as real truth, just lots and lots of different ways of explaining the same thing.

Carl and his family file in. We're all squashed into the space in front of Mr Naylor's desk and there aren't enough chairs, so Carl and I have to stand up.

His mum and dad make a lot of noise about how disgusting I am and how Carl's sporting career may be affected by the re-routing of his nasal passages.

Maureen counters with her poor-little-bullied-new-boy story, adding in some scare stuff about punctured lungs and a bright future in athletics that could have been blighted.

Everyone threatens to report both of us to the police. Everyone agrees that it's not necessary to involve outside bodies and criminalise two previously blameless teenagers.

Mr Naylor says, 'I'd like Carl and Joe to speak about how this incident has affected them and make a commitment to having a better relationship in the future. Carl, you go first, please.'

'You've smashed my entire face and I might not be able to play football for weeks,' says Carl. 'I might even have to have an operation on my nose. I only like playing football, so you've taken away the only thing I like.'

'Now, Joe,' says Mr Naylor.

'You set up that kit bag so I'd fall over and you could kick me, but I'd never done anything to you. I thought you and your mates were going to drown me in that pool. It wasn't my idea to give me an access card and not you, so none of this is my fault. And now it's been taken away from me.'

'Now, how sad it is to hear two of the school's most promising young sportsmen battling each other like this,' says Mr Naylor, sounding like we're all in church.

'Can we make a commitment to working together for the good of the school from now on? Perhaps there's a way that you two can find a joint project to work on?'

'I don't mind,' I say warily. I do feel a tiny bit sorry for Carl, if it's really true that he's got to have an operation.

'OK,' grunts Carl.

'So perhaps you two could apologise to each other, and then I'll ask Mr Henderson to work with you on finding a joint project to bring you together.'

'Sorry, Carl,' I mutter.

'Sorry, Joe,' he growls.

'Good,' says Mr Naylor. 'I shall expect to see a much more positive relationship in the future. You boys have great potential to bring glory to the school.'

We're dismissed. I'm not excluded. I'm no longer suspended. I suppose I might even get the access card back.

I ought to be happy, but I'm not. Joe's been given a second chance. I'm just not certain that he deserved one.

CHAPTER 16
Private

Half term is when they said I might be able to see my gran. But nothing seems to be happening. I keep on asking Maureen and she keeps on saying be patient, and I never hear anything from Mum. I'm beginning to feel she's forgotten me, even though I know she's not allowed to phone.

Ellie never contacts me either. I've been going for a run every day and do as much of the other training as I can with the few machines that they have at the local swimming pool – they have concessionary rates for under-sixteens, it turns out – but it hurts that she's not in touch. Maybe she feels that I've let her down and she can't be bothered any more.

Ashley's gone off to Spain for the week with her family. I texted her on the Friday night: *ddn't gt xcldd, hv a gd time, c u Jx*. I didn't hear anything back.

I'm almost sure that means she's chucked me.

Half way through the week Ellie's mum rings Maureen to find out how things are going and invites me over for lunch again. I think Maureen's relieved to get a few hours off – it can't be great fun being a permanent babysitter to a moping teenager. She drops me off at noon on the dot, although Janet had told her any time between twelve and one.

I'm really nervous. I'm worried about seeing Ellie again. Is she even going to talk to me? Have I mucked everything up? And I'm even more anxious about Claire. Ever since Mr Naylor made me apologise to Carl I've known I must say sorry to Claire for hurting her and scaring her. Only then will I be able to forgive Joe.

Alex lets me in. 'Come and play football in the garden!' he yells, and I follow him out to where Ellie's dad Gareth is setting up the barbeque. 'Hello, lad. How's it going?' he says, handing me a can of Coke. Ellie and her mum are out but will be back soon, he explains. The boys shout for me to play with them, but I ask, 'Where's Claire?'

'Upstairs, I suppose. Why don't you see if you can persuade her to come and get some sunshine for once?'

I creep upstairs as quietly as possible. Claire's room is up a second flight of stairs – it's a converted attic. There's a sign saying 'Private – Keep Out', but I don't even knock. I push the door open and for a moment I'm completely confused. The curtains are closed and it's totally dark in there.

I stay still and quiet while my eyes adjust. I don't think Claire's even in there; there's no sign of life. Then I see a slight movement and realise that she's sitting on the floor, half hidden behind the bed. She's got headphones on and her eyes are closed and she's got a strange look on her face, a look that reminds me of something, but I can't quite think what.

This is incredibly awkward. The only way I can attract her attention is to touch her arm, and I don't really want to scare her.

I'm frozen with indecision and about to give up and go downstairs again when I see it. A knife. In her hand.

It's a small, sharp knife, the type you use in art classes sometimes. What's she holding it for? As she holds out her arm and kind of strokes it with the knife I know what she reminds me of. Her face and her pose and the way her body relaxes as the blood oozes out are just like the junkies I've seen sometimes, shooting up in the park.

I feel as sick as I've ever felt, and I have to bite my tongue to make no noise. At the same time there's a tiny undercurrent of . . . I don't even want to say it . . . but there's something almost exciting about being there to see her gaze at the blood running down her arm. I feel like I'm watching something very private and very real.

She dabs at it with a tissue and pulls out a plaster and carefully sticks it over the cut. It's all planned I realise. She's got everything there ready. And then she unrolls her long sleeves and lies back against the bed.

I pull the door silently to try and escape. But she must have seen something out of the corner of her eye. She starts up and tugs the headphones from her ears. And shouts at me.

'What the hell are you doing in my room?'

I'm so amazed to hear her make a noise – quiet, mousey Claire – that I can't speak for a minute. I step forward and then sit down on her bed.

'I'm . . . uh . . . sorry. I mean I came to say I was sorry for the way I behaved the other day. I was out of order.'

'How long had you been standing there? No one is allowed in my room!'

It's very tempting to lie. It's very tempting to say, 'Only a minute,' and escape downstairs. What do I care anyway what she's up to? If she wants to hurt herself it's her business. But I say, 'Long enough to see what you did,' and after a moment's silence she whacks me in the mouth.

She's got the strength of a rag doll. 'Ouch,' I say unconvincingly, and I collapse backwards, lying on her bed. 'I'm sorry Claire. I could have said I didn't see anything. But I did and, to be honest, I don't think it's a great thing to be doing.'

'I s— suppose you and your g— girlfriend are going to tell the whole school about this are you? How dare you sneak up here and spy on me? I kept your stupid secret. You can just leave me alone!'

'I don't think Ashley wants to know me any more,' I say. 'I don't give her enough attention.'

'She's a cow. I hate her.'

'I thought you used to be friends?'

'Yeah, until the first day at Parkview when she and Emily and Lauren pretended they didn't know me, and they wouldn't talk to me and they didn't let me sit with them in class or at lunch and they told everyone that I was a dork.'

'I kind of know a bit how that feels,' I say, remembering the look on Arron's face when he realised that the rest of our gang would be going to St Jude's and he and I would spend two hours a day together just travelling to and from school.

'Oh, do you?' she asks, obviously not believing me.

'Yes. Look, Claire, I really won't tell anyone. After all, you never told anyone about my eyes and

I really appreciate that.'

'How did they change colour anyway?' she asked. 'Are they brown again now?'

I go and open her curtains. She blinks as the sunshine streams in. 'Look,' I say and I stare into her eyes. 'Now they're brown.' I flip one of the lenses out. 'And now one's green. I really trust you, and you can really trust me.' And I put the lens back.

'What the hell was that?' she says, but she's not so angry any more. She's still staring intently at my eyes. 'Is that your party trick?'

'No, no, really, Claire, no one must know. No one. Only you.'

'Not even Ashley?'

'Especially not Ashley. To be totally honest, I only went out with her because I was a little bit scared of her. And because she's quite . . . you know. . .'

'A slapper?'

'A twenty-first-century post-feminist,' I reply, a bit shocked, to be honest, by her unsisterly sexism. I was brought up by my aunties on a diet of *Cosmo* magazine and I know that you're not meant to disrespect women who want a full and active sex life. Especially if they want to have one with me.

She starts giggling and says, 'That's one way of putting it,' and I'm laughing too, and I know it's OK and we can trust each other. But there's a slight niggling doubt in my mind about keeping her secret. Maybe I should tell Ellie or her mum that she's hurting herself?

Ellie. What's going on there? 'Claire, is Ellie angry with me?'

'Oh I don't think so,' she says. 'She's just totally wound up about her preparations for this race at the weekend. When she's really focused, then she doesn't think about anything else. I think that's why mum arranged this barbeque, to take her mind off it. And also she's getting used to Magda, her new helper, and she hates that.'

'Hates what?'

'Ellie doesn't really like to admit she needs a helper, but mum and dad feel they can't always be there for her, so she has to have Magda, but she resents it. It's hard . . . for everyone. Ellie can get really cross sometimes.'

'Oh. Look, I really am very sorry about the other day. I was completely wrong to hurt you, I don't know why I did it.' I think about what Maureen said about my judgement being affected by lack of oxygen, but I don't think even that's really an excuse for hurting someone as delicate as Claire.

'I knew all the time you were scared,' she says. 'I just didn't know why you were scared of me. Why do you make your eyes brown when they're really green?'

For one crazy second I think I might tell her everything, this girl with a deep, scary secret of her own. This girl who understands that I'm scared. 'It's a long story,' I say, and I'm thinking how much I'd love it if someone my own age knew what's been going on. 'It's hard to know where to start.'

Bam! Alex and Sam crash through the door shouting their heads off. 'What are you doing? You're missing all the food! Mum says you've got to come downstairs right now.'

'Get out of my room, monsters,' yells Claire, and we chase them down the stairs. But as they disappear outside I ask, 'Can we talk more later?'

And she says, 'I'd like that.'

The garden is full of people. There's Janet and Ellie and Magda, who's blonde and Polish and seems sweet and shy. I say hello to her in Polish and you can see she's amazed that anyone's bothered to learn her language. Pity Doug cut off my lessons in the hotel. Maybe I can ask Magda to teach me more.

There's Alistair, who's Ellie's trainer and has one of those ludicrous, super-gelled, boy-band hairstyles; and there's Kieron who's another wheelchair racer with incredible pumped-up arms; and Tim and Sue who turn out to be the next-door neighbours. I can hardly get near Ellie. There're four small boys – two belong to Tim and

Sue – and they're nagging me to play football with them so, after I've swallowed a burger, that's what I do.

We play for about an hour and then we're all burning hot and sweaty and lying on the grass. 'We won! We won!' shrieks Alex, dancing around, and Janet comes out of the house with a bowl of cut-up watermelon. I look around and catch Ellie's eye. She doesn't look too unfriendly.

'Joe, come and tell me what's happening with your training,' she shouts.

'Yes, and Joe, you can tell us what Ellie's like as a trainer,' says Kieron. 'Is she as impossible to work with as she is with her teammates?'

'No, she's fantastic,' I say, and they all laugh. I don't know why.

Ellie says, 'Stop messing around. I really need to hear how Joe's getting on. And why on earth have you lost your access card? Did you know I had to write a letter to the head teacher to stop him kicking you out of school?'

'I'm sure that was never going to happen, Ellie,' says Janet.

'Oh it was,' says Ellie. 'Mr Henderson said you smashed another boy's face in and he nearly drowned.'

'That's not true at all,' says Claire angrily. 'Joe was nearly drowned by him.'

Everyone looks amazed to hear her speak. She's blushing again and looks like she wishes she hadn't bothered. I feel like everyone is looking at me, and I don't like it. 'I'm going to go,' I say. 'Thanks for lunch. Ellie, can you let me know when you want to do more training? Good luck for the weekend.'

'Oh, don't go, Joe,' says Ellie. 'Come and tell us all about it.' But I shake my head and make for the back door. I'm sure that as I go I hear one of her friends say something like, 'So that's your toy boy, Ellie.'

Claire follows me and we walk through the house together. 'Ellie gets a bit over-excited sometimes,' she says.

'Yeah, I'm just bored with talking about it now. And there's other stuff going on that's more important.'

'Oh. Look, Joe, don't go. Why don't we go upstairs again? Then we could talk.'

I'm not sure. I'm kind of disappointed with Ellie and I want to get away from all those laughing strangers. I want her to stay the perfect, golden girl that I can rely on, not someone who uses me to entertain her friends. I only really like it when Ellie's attention is focused on me.

But I follow Claire up the stairs because I've found someone that I can be as near to honest with as possible.

I'm really curious to know why she wants

to cut herself. And in my most secret, secret heart –
and I'm wondering how sick and twisted I really am –
I'd be quite interested in watching her do it again.

CHAPTER 17
Invisible

The first thing she does is draw the curtains so it's dark again. The next thing is to wedge a chair against the door so no one can come in. Then she sits down on the floor, as she did before. I can see she's got some cushions down there – it's her little nest.

I sit next to her. 'Why do you do it?' I ask.

'I try not to,' she says. 'I know it's a crazy thing to do. I'm really trying to stop.'

'When I saw you, I thought you looked like a junkie, you know, an addict, shooting up.'

'It feels like how I think an addiction must feel like,' she says. 'It builds up, and all I can think about is cutting myself, and then I do it and I'm OK again for a while.'

'How come no one's noticed?'

She shrugs: 'I'm not the sort of person that anyone notices much.'

I'm not having that. 'What about when you're in a T-shirt? What about swimming or PE?'

'I always wear long sleeves, for PE as well. I don't know what to do about swimming. We were going to have it for the first time last week and I was so worried. I'd made up a letter from my mum, but then you punched Carl and the pool was closed for cleaning.' She chuckles. 'I was very grateful to you.'

'Oh. Well, glad I could help you out.'

'That's OK.'

'But what builds up? Why do you do it? When did it even start?'

She considers, staring into space. It's like she's never asked herself these questions before. 'I started out just scratching myself. Then one day it wasn't enough, so I used my comb. I liked the feeling and I liked seeing the marks on my skin. But it was never quite enough. And then I cut myself by accident in art when we were lino printing and I knew that's what I'd been looking for.'

'But what is the feeling that builds up?'

She shrugs again. 'Could be anything. I might be feeling scared, or worried or upset. Sometimes I feel like I'm invisible, like I'm not as . . . as real as other people. But when I cut myself and see the blood and feel the pain I know I'm real. I can see . . . feel . . . myself better.

Does that make any sense? Probably not.'

It sort of does, in a funny way. I'm almost tempted to try it myself.

'But you're not invisible, you just hide yourself. I mean you're really quiet all the time, and you wear those long baggy clothes, and you've always got your hair all over your face. Even your school uniform is too big.' I have an idea. 'Why don't you stop hiding? Stop covering up who you are and what you're doing to yourself. Show me your arms.'

She blushes again, that red blotchy heat rushes into her face, and I realise what I'm suggesting. 'I don't mean . . . I mean, umm, put a T-shirt on or something. I won't look.'

But she's unbuttoning the top buttons of her shirt which is black and about five sizes too big for her. 'No, it's OK. . .' And she takes it off over her head.

She's sitting there in her jeans and little white bra, and all I can look at are her arms. Her poor arms. They're scratched and patched and scarred, and the new piece of plaster is already stained with blood. In between the wounds, old and new, I can see goosebumps standing up on her skin. The cuts are in a neat little line, like train tracks, with the oldest scars faded to white and the newer ones pink and shiny. It's the neatness that's the saddest thing, the way she's tried to be good and tidy while cutting herself till the blood pours out.

She reminds me of the assembly hall at St Saviour's, the crucifix with Our Lord hanging from it, bloodied and suffering. It's not that I'm at all religious, of course, but Gran used to take me to church with her sometimes and Mum and I had to go for a full year to get me into St Saviour's. I've always gone to Catholic schools and it's given me the idea at the back of my mind that pain is somehow more than just pain, that it's got supernatural power and meaning. What the meaning is though, I'm not too sure.

How could I ever have found the idea of her hurting herself exciting? I'm disgusted with myself.

She must have seen something of that in my face and she thinks it's directed at her. She's crying silently and trying to cover up her arms. As gently as possible I take her hand. 'No, it's OK. Look at them. Look at what you've done to yourself. Look at all that pain. You don't need to hide it from me.'

We sit there for a while, hand in hand in the near darkness. Far away I can hear the sound of people laughing and talking in the garden. Then she says, 'You won't tell anyone, will you?'

'I won't because I promised, but I think you should. I'm sure you can get help with this. Claire, there're enough bad people out there in the world who can hurt you without you hurting yourself.'

'Maybe,' she says.

'Yes,' I say.

She leans her head against my shoulder and I stroke her long hair away from her face. 'You can't hide away all the time, if this is what hiding does to you,' I say, and then wonder if I'm talking to her or me.

'Tell me your story now,' she says. 'Tell me why your eyes change colour.'

'Claire. . .' I hesitate. I know I can trust her. But what if someone threatens her?

'Yes?'

'What I'm going to tell you isn't just a bit secret. It's really secret. You can't tell anyone in your family or anyone at school. But if anyone really scary tries to make you tell them. . . '

'Yes?'

'Then tell. Don't protect me and don't put yourself in danger.'

'Danger?'

'Yes. Look, I'm not really called Joe. We didn't move here because my mum broke up with her boyfriend. We're here because I . . . I . . .'

'Because what? What is your name? Who are you?'

I've never seen Claire look like this. I mean apart

from the fact that she's hardly wearing anything. She's come alive, eyes shining bright blue, pink cheeks. Now I can see her face properly, she's so much prettier – but can I really tell her my story?

'I'm called Tyler. Most people call me Ty, but it's short for Tyler. Tyler Michael Lewis.'

It feels so strange to say my full name out loud, but what a fantastic relief. 'Tyler's after my dad and Michael's for my grandad.'

'Tyler,' she says. 'It's a nice name.'

'I saw something. I saw someone get killed. And when I told the police they said it wasn't safe to stay at home. We went home anyway but there was an attack . . . a petrol bomb. . . The shop underneath our flat got bombed, it all burned up. They had to give us new identities and send us away from London and they sent us here and that's how I became Joe and my mum became Michelle. Her name's Nicki really. They changed my eye colour with contact lenses and they dyed my hair – it's light brown, a bit like yours – and they put me down a year at school. I'm fourteen, not thirteen, and I should be finishing year nine.'

'Who did you see get killed?'

'A . . . a boy. They tried to mug him for his iPod and he had a knife too. It was a mess. Three against one.'

'Oh God, how terrible.'

I'm remembering the red, red blood on Arron's white shirt. 'And I ran to get help, and I managed to stop a bus and shout to the driver to call an ambulance, but it was too late by the time they got there. Much too late.'

I should have stayed. I should have been there when the ambulance got there. But instead . . . instead . . . there are some things I'm not ready to tell. Even Claire. Even now.

'Why wasn't it safe to stay at home?' she asks.

'Because someone wants to . . . to shut me up so I can't give evidence at the trial. And that person, those people, are really ruthless and they might even kill me I suppose.'

'Oh my God, Joe – oh, should I call you Tyler?'

I shake my head. 'Too confusing. And you might forget and get it wrong at school or something.'

She laughs. 'Oh, I'd never dare speak to you at school.'

'Bollocks to that, Claire, you're going to stop being invisible.' I laugh too. 'I'm meant to be being invisible and I'm doing really badly at it. But you don't have to be invisible at all.'

'I can't believe you ever could be invisible,' she says softly and I think – aha! – you *do* have a crush on me. Obviously someone like Joe would take advantage of the opportunity presenting itself. But I'm Ty right now.

'You're so wrong. I was completely invisible in London. My best friend thought I was babyish and no one at my school wanted to know me because I wasn't rich and I wasn't very . . . anything really. And I was short, and a bit podgy.'

'No!'

'It's true.'

She's laughing at me and I'm feeling incredibly happy to have found someone that I can tell all this stuff to. It occurs to me that no one knows all this – not Mum, not Gran – only Mr Patel in the shop downstairs had any idea of how difficult I was finding St Saviour's.

'When do you have to give evidence?' she asks.

'They said in the autumn, probably. I don't know for sure. The police come and ask questions sometimes but they don't tell me anything. And now my gran . . . she was beaten up because they wanted her to tell them where I was. Even though she didn't know. And she's in intensive care, and my mum's there with her and I don't know if I'm ever going to see her again.'

'That's terrible,' she says again. 'I don't know what to say. I feel such a wimp, making a fuss when you have real problems.'

'No, don't be daft, you have real problems too.'

I touch her arm, careful to avoid a scar. 'What will you do about this?'

'What can I do?'

'Here's my mobile number.' – I'm writing it down on a scrap of paper – 'You can call me if you feel it building up, if you feel like you're going to need to cut again.'

'But what if . . . if it's the middle of the night or something?'

'No problem. It's fine.'

'Have you got an email address?'

'I used to. . .' And I wonder if anyone's been emailing me any more on that address. How can I find out? Would it be safe to use the computers at school? But maybe it's better not to look.

'You need a new one. Shall I make one for you?'

'Yes, please.' I could do it myself easily but it's nice to think of Claire doing something to help me.

'Thanks, Joe. Thanks for trusting me.'

'Thanks for trusting me too.'

We're so close and so intent on each other, it's like the whole world's stopped. It's really easy to talk now. She tells me about the books and music she likes and I tell her about learning lots of different languages and being a football interpreter one day. She says, 'The first time I heard you speak French I thought you were French,' which is pretty nice to hear. There's no more noise coming from the garden and it's like we're in our own little dark cave. I lean towards her. . . Our lips brush together . . . and . . . crash! Someone's trying to open the door.

'What's going on?' calls her mum. 'Why have you blocked the door, Claire?'

Bugger. I was meant to have gone home hours ago and now she's going to find me barricaded into her half-naked daughter's bedroom. Maybe I can hide under the bed? Claire has the same idea and points to the floor while she whips her shirt back on.

'It's OK, Mum – just wanted some peace and quiet. The boys came in here earlier. You know they're not meant to.' Claire moves the chair out of the way and her mum opens the door.

'I don't know what's the matter with you, Claire. Why do you have to spend a nice sunny afternoon up here in the dark when we have guests and everything. I get no help from you at all.' Janet sounds completely fed up. 'You could at least let some light in.' She marches across to pull the curtains and almost falls over me. I scramble up quickly. 'Oh, sorry . . . I was just, er, having a rest on the floor.'

Janet is stunned, you can tell, and not sure whether to be angry or not. I can see her adding it all up – little Claire plus dark room plus chair against door, multiplied by violent boy (whose mother was obviously a teenage slag) – and failing to work out a satisfactory answer.

She obviously has the same opinion of Claire's pulling power as my mum had of mine. I'm sure that any minute she's going to notice that Claire's shirt is not done up to her chin as usual.

'Oh. You're still here, Joe? Maureen rang and asked where you were and I told her you'd gone home hours ago.'

'We were talking,' I say uncomfortably, and Claire says, 'Joe was just leaving, weren't you?'

Janet is still looking a bit suspicious. 'Thank you very much for lunch,' I say, and she says, 'You can stay for supper if you like. It's nearly six.'

'No, thanks, but I'd better get back if Maureen was looking for me.'

I sprint down the stairs and say goodbye as quickly as possible. Claire is looking pink and embarrassed, and I can hear her mum hissing at her, 'Claire, what was wrong with coming downstairs if you and Joe wanted to talk?' As I leave, I turn around and mouth, 'Call me.' And Claire nods and smiles.

Maureen's looking a bit annoyed when I get home. 'Where have you been? Janet said you left there at about three.'

'What's the big problem?' I don't really think it's any of Maureen's business where I've been. She's not my mother, after all.

'No problem, but I'd suggest you have a rest now. Doug's going to be here at midnight and we're taking you to see your gran.'

CHAPTER 18
Hail Mary

Maureen does a kind of reverse disguise on me before we go to the hospital. I have to take the contact lenses out and put on a black woolly hat, pulled down to cover up all of my hair – which looks pretty stupid and feels way too hot.

She wants me to wear shades too, but I tell her she has to choose between them and the hat because otherwise I will look like a total freak. Who wears shades at night? She pulls out some fake tan but I protest so strongly – after all, I'm due back at school on Monday – that she backs down. 'The main thing is not to draw any attention to yourself,' she says, which is pretty rich considering she was trying to turn me into a cut price Craig David.

And then Doug arrives and we drive and drive on nearly empty roads, and almost immediately we get in the car I fall asleep and I don't wake up for ages. And when I do, I lie quietly on the back seat and listen to their conversation without letting on that I'm awake.

'DI Morris seems to be happy to go with his evidence,' says Doug. 'He'll be interested in your input now you've spent a bit of time with the lad.'

'Oh, he's not talked to me about the evidence at all, sorry to say. He's very bound up in the here and now. Very upset he was when he thought he was going to be kicked out of school. It's good that the school scared him like that. He's learned a lesson. He's a good kid really, nothing like as hard as you made out.'

'Well that's your feminine intuition speaking, Mo, but I'm not so sure. Very manipulative, and the mum's no match for him. You know one of the defence teams is going to go on the line that he was involved? Went along with the whole thing, initiated it even, then ran off to get the ambulance. Pretty cool-headed if that's the case.'

'Don't believe it myself. That'd be a hell of a lot of lying for a young kid to sustain. And I thought there was no blood on him? That's what the bus witnesses say.'

'Took his time coming forward though, didn't he?'

'Hmm,' says Maureen, 'I can't see it. Why make up such a twisted story and come forward as a witness if it's going to make you a target for one of the biggest criminal families in London? These people have the money and the contacts to eliminate him like they're swatting a fly. He's pointing the finger at their son and they want him to disappear. Poor kid, I think he had no idea what he was getting into.'

'True enough,' says Doug.

They're quiet for a while – and I try not to let them hear that my breathing's gone a bit fast and shallow – but then I hear her say, 'So the sister's kicking off? Can't say I blame her.'

'She'll see sense,' says Doug, 'but it hasn't been plain sailing, believe me. Lots of aggro. Hard for our girl. Not in a great state.'

'Dear, oh dear. They'll go, though?'

'Have to. First Julie's got to be well enough to travel, and that's not so certain.'

Julie's my gran. Where are they sending her?

'Sooner the better, even if she's not well enough to go with them,' says Maureen. 'I wouldn't be happy having them hanging around that hospital. Not exactly secure, is it? How about our two? I think young Ty wants to stay where he is. I suspect there's a girlfriend in the picture somewhere.'

'Not decided what to do with them. That little stunt at school, bloody kid, made me think we'd better send them too. Crack down on him a bit, keep him out of trouble. But it's all expensive, you know. They'll be querying the costs on this one. If we can leave them be, all the better.'

They talk a bit softer and I'm desperate to hear what they are saying and make sense of it.

'No more news on . . . *mumble, mumble*?' asks Maureen.

'Not that I know of. Cliff's on surveillance. They're bloody clever, though. Know how to cover their tracks. We've not been able to prove any link.'

'Always the way. We switching cars on the way back?'

'Yes, it's all organised.'

'I wish we weren't doing it though,' she says. 'It's too bloody risky for the boy.'

'They think it'll help his granny,' says Doug. 'We don't want it turning into another murder investigation.'

'Exactly,' says Maureen. Then she looks around and says, 'Time to start waking up Ty. We're nearly there.'

I make a good act of stretching and yawning and Doug brings the car round to a side entrance of the hospital. I look at my watch. It's 3 am. Not exactly normal visiting hours.

He pulls out a police radio and talks into it for a while, and then a burly man approaches the car. Doug gets out and talks to him for a minute and then reappears.

216

'OK, Ty, you go with Dave here, and we'll see you later.'

'Aren't you coming with me?'

'No, we'll pick you up later. Don't worry. Dave will sort you out.'

What if Dave's some sort of a double agent? What if, when they're gone, he shoots me or something? I take a deep breath and get out of the car.

'Come with me,' says Dave, and we walk into the hospital. We walk up some stairs and along a corridor. He never speaks to me the whole time. Then through some double doors and up in a lift and we walk for a bit until we're in a corridor where there's a policeman in a uniform carrying a huge gun. Like a machine-gun sort of thing. Dave and he nod at each other.

'OK, this way,' says Dave and we walk into a ward. I wonder what the other families that come here make of the police guard. I wouldn't like it much if I had to worry about some sort of potential shoot-out at my relative's bedside. I feel incredibly guilty to have caused so much hassle to so many random people.

Dave opens a door to a side room, and says, 'Thirty minutes.' I don't really believe him. We've driven for three hours to stay for thirty minutes?

He stays outside. I walk through the door, nervous and jumpy. What am I going to see? Who's going to be there?

There's a bed and lots of bleeping machines and my gran in the middle. Just her and me. I thought Mum and my aunties would be here too. Where are they? Didn't they want to see me? It's so creepy being here by myself.

Gran's almost unrecognisable – she looks really old and her face is a kind of greeny-white colour, except for the bits which are purple and swollen. Her eyes have big blue-black bags underneath. She doesn't even smell nice, and her head is all bound up in bandages.

I'm only certain it's her because, in between the tubes coming out of her arm, I can see the little tattoo on her arm – the heart with Mick, my grandad's name, written inside. Gran had that tattoo done when they went on honeymoon. 'All the girls were getting them in those days,' she would tell me when I was little and wanted to know what it was.

It's only her heavy, rattling breaths that let me know she's even alive. She'd hate me to see her like this. I hate seeing her too. I take her hand. 'Gran, it's me, it's Ty,' I say. 'I'm really, really sorry, Gran. It's all my fault.'

She moans and her eyes flutter. My heart is beating really fast and my hands are sweating. I don't know what to say next. Then I remember Doug and Maureen's conversation in the car and I begin to wonder. Maybe this is some kind of trap? Maybe they've put me in here by myself because they think I'll tell Gran something that I've never told anyone else. Could they be secretly filming or recording me?

'Gran, I'm trying to do the right thing, like you said,' I say. 'I never hurt anyone. I just tried to keep Arron out of trouble. I didn't know what to do for the best.'

I tried and failed. I failed so badly. . .

The door opens and I spring round. Oh my God. It's my auntie Lou, but looking so pale and gaunt, and her roots are so dark that it's like the ends of her hair have been dipped in yellow paint. We hug, and it's amazing to be able to feel her and know that she's really here with me in this stuffy room.

'Ty, my love, what do you look like?' she says. 'You must be boiling in that ridiculous hat.'

'I am, but they said don't take it off,' I say nervously. Sweat prickles on my forehead and the hat feels really itchy.

'Idiot police,' she says, reaching over to hold Gran's hand. 'We think she's regaining consciousness, that's why we asked them to bring you here. She's opened her eyes a few times and even said a word or two, but she goes back again. We thought it might just nudge her in the right direction if she heard your voice. She adores you so much. We never thought they'd leave you in here on your own. You must have been terrified.'

'I'm OK.'

'Look at you, how you've grown,' she says. 'You're becoming a man.'

'Yeah, well... Where's Mum?'

Lou gives me a strange look. I suppose she's never heard me call Nicki 'Mum' before. 'Nic's in the waiting room with Emma. You'll see them later. They only want two or three of us in with your gran at any one time and they said that you and me and him' – she nods towards Dave, stationed outside the door – 'were more than enough. Talk a bit to her. She'd be so happy to see you again.'

I lean over the bed again. 'Gran, please will you wake up for me? I'm only here for a little while – they won't let me stay.' Again her eyes seem to flicker a little.

Lou coughs. 'Ty, you know what she's like. We've had the chaplain here every day. We thought if you said a prayer for her, it might just. . .'

'Oh bloody hell, Lou.' I'm not at all sure that I'm up for that.

'Just try it, Ty. It wouldn't work if any of us did it. She'd know we didn't mean it.'

And I would? 'Do I have to?' But I know I do. 'Where's her rosary?'

'It's still in her flat. The police won't let us go back in there and I asked them to bring it but they haven't yet, but the chaplain gave us this one.'

It's very simple – ivory plastic beads, nothing like Gran's beautiful olive-wood rosary which Grandad bought her when they went to Rome and is her most special possession. But I suppose it'll do.

I put the rosary in one of her hands and take hold of the other. I stick my head as near to Gran's as possible and reach across to hold the rosary too. I like the way the beads feel smooth and slippery, and they remind me of being a little boy when we still lived with Gran.

'Hail Mary, full of grace,' I say really slowly. I'm kind of hoping that my thirty minutes will be up before I have to get to the end. 'The Lord is with thee. Blessed art thou amongst women. . .'

Gran makes a kind of coughing noise and her eyes move again. Louise pinches my arm: 'It's working, keep going. . . I knew this would work.'

'. . . and blessed is the fruit of thy womb, Jesus.'

She opens her eyes. She opens her eyes! It's a flaming miracle.

'Holy Mary, mother of God . . .'

Gran's hand is clutching mine. Her eyes are open. She's mouthing the words with me. I'll have to finish.

'. . . pray for us sinners now and at the hour of our . . . our . . .'

'Death,' says Louise. Her eyes are full of tears and

221

she kisses me on the stupid woolly hat. 'Amen.'

'Amen,' echoes Gran in a really frail and wobbly voice. And then she says, 'Louise, is that you? Can you help me?'

After that, everything seems to move really quickly. Dave wants me to go after thirty minutes but I say no, it's too soon. The nurses and doctors need to see to Gran and Dave says I shouldn't be in there with them, so he takes me to the waiting room to see Mum and Emma. 'We'll give you fifteen minutes together and then fifteen minutes back with the old lady and then that's that.'

'She's not an old lady, she's only fifty-eight,' I say. Gran looked about a hundred and eight in that bed.

'Fair enough, son. Well done for bringing her round.'

The waiting room is just as hot as Gran's room. My mum's asleep on a sofa. She looks totally different – a bit like her old self again, because her hair is long and blonde. How did they manage that? Oh. It must be a wig. Emma's sitting in the dark, reading *Grazia* magazine with a little torch. She jumps up when she sees me. 'Ty! I can't believe it!'

It's so good to see her again. Emma's the easiest-going person in our family and she's the nearest thing

I've got to a big sister. 'Emma, Gran woke up!'

'I knew she'd wake up for you,' she said. 'They didn't want to bring you, you know, but it seemed like the only thing we could try to get to her. Ty, did you know they're going to send us abroad for a while? Me and Louise, and Mum, as soon as she's ready to leave hospital.'

'What about us?'

'Not you. I think, they think it's safer to keep us apart.'

'Yeah, well, they're experts at keeping people safe, aren't they?' She misses my sarcasm and answers, 'I certainly hope so.'

I think about Emma and her job in fashion and her boyfriend Paul. I think about Louise and her university degree and her flat in Hoxton and her job as head of English at a girls' school in Westminster. I have totally messed up their lives.

'I'm really sorry, Emma. It's all my fault.'

'No it's not, Ty, don't ever think that. You're just a witness. It's those boys on trial, they're the ones to blame. And whatever bastard threw that bomb into the shop.'

'Did you see it? Did you see Mr Patel?'

'I saw the shop,' she says, and she's looking the most serious I've ever seen Emma look. 'He was OK. Trying to sort out his insurance claim.'

'What . . . what does Lou think about going away?'

'Well, she's not very happy. She's giving up a lot. But no one is blaming you, darling, never think that.'

'Where will they send you?'

'I don't know, they won't tell us. It'll be a magical mystery tour until we get to the airport. I'm keen on Spain. Get a bit of sunshine.'

She gently shakes my mum's shoulder. 'Nicki, look who's here.'

She takes time to wake up and I'm shocked to see she's lost weight. Even the new red top, the one that looked so pretty before, is hanging loose on her. My mum is disappearing like a snowman when the sun comes out. She's blinking at me and says, 'Ty? Are you OK? What's been happening?' Her voice sounds like a little girl.

'I'm fine. Everything's fine. Gran woke up.'

'She did? Louise said she'd wake up for you.' She's not as happy as I'd have expected. In fact, she sounds a little bit pissed off.

'We can go back and see her in a minute. Nicki, when will you come home?'

She shrugs: 'When they say . . . I don't know. Maybe they think I should come now with you.'

She's lost it again, I can tell. She's back to how she was a few weeks ago, unable to make decisions, all her independence and fight and spirit drained away.

'What do you want to do?' Emma asks gently. 'Maybe it's time to be with Ty again? I'm sure Mum will understand.'

Nicki looks a bit confused. 'It's not really up to me. . .' she says.

'I'll talk to the police,' I say to Emma over her head. 'I'll work something out.'

She looks even more worried than before. 'Nicki, why don't you ask them to take you into Mum's room now? Then Ty and I will come along in a minute.'

My mum wanders out of the room and I hear her talking to Dave in the corridor. Emma puts her arm around me. 'Ty, sweetheart, I'm a bit worried about Nicki. She seems spacey, out of it, not really herself.'

'I know. . . She was getting a bit better but now she seems worse. Is she eating anything?'

'Not much, and she and Louise haven't been getting on very well. Nicki feels very sensitive and like she's being blamed, which isn't what Lou means at all. It's been difficult.'

'Why would she be blamed? It's down to me.'

'Well, she feels like Lou is saying she isn't a very good mother, which obviously doesn't go down very well.'

Well, obviously. So Louise does think it's all my fault.

Dave knocks at the door: 'I can give you another fifteen minutes with your gran, Ty, and then you really must go. They don't want to move you when it's light.'

I'm like an owl or a bat. A creature of the night. Or maybe a werewolf.

Gran is looking much more awake when they take us to see her again. She's not really up to talking though, and doesn't seem to know what's going on. 'Ty?' she says faintly and reaches out to touch me. 'What's that thing?' She's puzzled by the hat.

'Take it off,' hisses Mum, and I don't know what to do. So I whip it off really quickly, and Louise and Emma both gasp when they see my jet-black hair and Lou says, 'God, he looks exactly like his dad.'

Poor Gran is confused: 'Are you Ty?' I pull the hat back on and tuck my hair underneath. 'You've been ill for a while, Gran. My look's kind of changed.'

'Oh, that's it,' she says, and she seems happy again.

'Time's up,' says Dave, and I quickly hug them all. I lean over and kiss Gran. 'Gran, take care. Get yourself well again.'

'I'll see you soon, darling boy,' she says, and I wish it could be true.

'I'll be back with you soon,' says Mum, but she doesn't sound very sure.

Louise kisses me. 'It's so good to see you. Take care.'

'Take care,' echoes Emma, and Dave says, 'That's it, I'm afraid.'

He leads me away, through corridors, down in the lift and through an empty hallway. Out of a door into the cold. It's not so dark now and the birds have started singing. 'That all took far too long,' he says, and he lifts up his radio.

And then a car comes screeching around the corner and there's a loud cracking noise – bang! – and Dave shoves me back through the door before he stumbles and falls, blood seeping bright though his shirt.

CHAPTER 19
Under the Blanket

'Run!' he shouts at me. 'Run!' The blood is spreading out over his side.

'But . . . you. . .'

He points back along the corridor. 'Run, go . . . they might come after you. . .'

I'm backing off. I don't want to abandon him, but . . . he said. . . I run. I run away from the blood.

I run and run along the corridor and crash through two sets of double doors. The hospital is starting to wake up now and I nearly barge into some cleaners. 'There's a man back there,' I gasp, 'been shot. . .' And I run on past their gaping faces.

Hospitals are strange places. This one seems to be lots of buildings jumbled together. The floors have lots of different lines on them, blue, red, yellow, A, B, C. Very helpful if you know where you're going, but I don't. I'm just running, along echoing corridors, through tunnels, up stairs and past wards full of people who can't help me.

I'm trying to run as I would for Ellie, but I can't. I can't get my breathing under control. It's coming in short, sharp bursts, a jittering, terrified breath, a breath that slows me down and gives me a shooting pain in my side. What's the point of being a good runner if you can't run when you need to?

I need to pee. There's a loo and no one around and it seems like a good place to hide. Luckily there's no one in there. I find a cubicle, lock myself in, do the business, and climb up on to the toilet seat. I curl myself into a ball and try to think clearly. If I were watching this in a film it'd be really exciting, an action adventure. But when it's me on my own and I don't know what to do or where to go, it's not as exciting as you'd expect.

What if the gunman goes to the intensive care unit? What if he knows where to find my family? I'm going to have to get there first.

I hear a creak as the door opens. Someone's come in. I hold my breath, try not to make a sound, waiting to hear them use the loo, wash their hands, leave. Nothing. There's someone right outside the cubicle door just standing there. Oh Christ. . . Can bullets go through doors? I bet they can.

I'll have to do something. I stand up on the loo seat and kick the door open as fast and strong as I can. And kick again as I jump down. I can feel my foot crunch into some guy's groin – and he goes flying backwards into the urinals. I don't even look at him or wait to see if he's got a gun or not. I clatter through the door and leg it along the corridor.

Intensive Care. I need to go and warn them that he could be coming there. There's a signpost up ahead and I stop for a moment to search for the name. There it is . . . follow the red line . . . here and here and stairs or lift? I opt for the stairs and dash up three flights. At the top I'm gasping for breath but feeling triumphant. I'll get there, I'll save them. . .

The lift door opens and a large man steps out. 'Stop!' he yells at me and launches himself in a rugby tackle which I meet with another kick. Crash! My foot smashes against his teeth. I'm just about to follow through with a punch when I look at him properly for the first time.

Shit.

It's Doug.

'Sorry, sorry, really sorry, Doug. I didn't know it was you.'

He recovers slowly, blood dripping from his lips.

'What the hell did you think you were doing? First you kick me in the balls, then in the teeth.'

I'd have thought that was obvious. 'I didn't realise it was you. I was trying to escape. I thought you were the guy who shot Dave. . . Did you know? He needs help. . .'

'Don't worry about him. He's OK. We need to concentrate on you.'

'How did you find me?'

'We put a trace on you before you went in, just in case anything happened. To be honest, I was worried you might do a runner. You're an unpredictable little bugger.'

'What do you mean, a trace?'

'Electronic tagging device. Useful when someone goes AWOL.'

'Dave said to run. . . I didn't want to leave him. . .'

He pulls out his mobile. 'Got him. Main entrance in ten.'

'Main entrance? Isn't that a bit dangerous?' I'm like a suicide bomber. Anywhere I go, I could bring death and destruction to innocent people.

'It's the only place they won't be expecting us. Walk slowly, try and look normal.'

We walk back down the corridor. My breathing is still coming in painful bursts and I'm constantly looking behind and around me. 'What about Mum and

Gran. . .?' I ask, and Doug says, 'Lots of people to look after them.'

We're nearly there. 'Stay calm,' mutters Doug. 'Once we're with other people, don't do anything to bring attention to yourself.'

I can hear police sirens and hope that means that someone's got to Dave in time. What about the guy that shot him? Is he going to be lying in wait for us?

We're at the main entrance. There are people here. They look normal – some old men, a woman with a baby, but what do I know? They might have guns, they might be about to shoot us. Suddenly I don't feel so brave any more. I can't do this. 'It's OK,' says Doug, but what does he know?

And we're walking through the door and out into bright sunlight and there's a big black car, and Doug opens the door and pushes me in, a bit more roughly than necessary, in my opinion. Maureen's sitting there and gestures for me to crouch down on the floor, and I scrunch myself down as low as possible. Doug gets in the front, next to the driver, and Maureen covers me with a blanket. 'It's just for a little while, just to get out of here.'

It's stiflingly hot under the thick scratchy blanket, and I'm getting cramp and I'm desperately hungry and thirsty. The motion of the car is making me feel sick too, and I retch a bit, but there's nothing there to be sick with, just a foul taste in my mouth.

But worst of all is sitting in the dark feeling more and more panicky about what nearly happened to me, and what could be happening right now. I'm seeing the gunman standing in that little room and blasting them all away. My family turned into little scraps of blood and bone and hair and flesh.

I'm wedged against Maureen's legs, and after we've been driving for a bit, she leans down and rests her hand on my shoulder and whispers, 'Don't worry. Try not to worry.'

Eventually, after what feels like hours, they stop and Maureen pulls off the blanket and says, 'Oh dear,' when she sees me. I am so hot that I can feel my whole body burning up and my hair and shirt are completely wet with sweat, and I suppose I might look a little bit like perhaps I've been crying.

'OK, quickly now, out of the car and over to that one.' I kind of groan because I was really hoping that we were going to stop driving for a bit and my legs are so cramped that I can hardly walk, but I half hop, half stumble to the other car. Doug's already transferred to the driver's seat, and he's not looking too sympathetic.

'Just lie down on the back seat,' says Maureen. 'Try and relax.' Doug reverses and then speeds along the little country lane we're parked in. 'Here, have some water,' says Maureen, and I prop myself up on my elbow and gulp it down gratefully. She says, 'You're looking a bit green. Take one of these,' and passes over a little white pill which I assume must be for travel sickness.

I must have gone to sleep then, a blissful sleep with no dreams, because it's nearly night when I wake up again. We're pulling in at a service station and Maureen shakes my shoulder and says, 'You could do with some food, I should think.'

'Wh— what time is it?'

'It's nine at night. You've slept almost all day,' says Doug.

'I gave you a sedative. Thought you could do with it,' says Maureen.

'Why are we still driving?' I have a sudden horrible thought. 'You're not taking me to a new place to live, are you?'

They both laugh. 'No, even we can't work that quickly,' says Maureen. 'Let's just say we thought it was best to bring you back by the scenic route and get back after dark. We can have some food here, then we'll go to the house around midnight. Doug'll have to stay over.'

'I'm really sorry, Doug, about what happened.'

'Attacked me not once but twice, you little bastard,' says Doug, but he sounds OK about it. 'Given that you thought I was a vicious gunman, I'd say you were pretty brave. Of course, if you didn't think that, I'd have to take it personally. And now I'm going to have to stay over. Don't think the missus'll be too happy with me but needs must.'

It's never occurred to me before that Doug and Maureen both have lives of their own which they've put on hold to look after me.

'I didn't know you had a missus.'

They laugh again. 'Oh yes, he most certainly does,' says Maureen. 'Keeps you on a very short leash, doesn't she, Doug.'

'A fine woman,' says Doug, and Maureen winks at me.

We go into the service station. I'm still a bit nervy, but the sedative seems to have slowed me down. My body feels heavy and my eyes keep trying to close. I'm so stiff and cramped that Maureen has to help me walk from the car to the cafe. I'm hobbling like an old man and I don't feel like someone who fought off a police officer twice. Even if it was only Doug.

They both want sausage and chips, and Maureen realises that I can't make a decision and chooses fish and chips and a cup of tea for me. We sit down and I start mushing up the fish with my fork. 'Have you got a husband, Maureen?' I ask.

'No chance. Married to my work I am. Luckily for you, eh?'

I nod, and she says, 'Try and stop messing with the food and eat some of it. It's no good to you if all you're going to do is play with it.'

Maureen really reminds me of my gran. She's about the same age and she's got the same sort of friendly face. 'Maureen, did you know my gran woke up? She did it when I was there.'

'I do know, and I'm really pleased for you. Why don't you tell me about it?'

So I tell her what happened, and she ruffles my hair like I'm a baby and says, 'I think you did a fine job there.' Then she pauses and says, 'I didn't realise you were a church-going family. Should I find you one for Sunday?'

'Not me and Mum, just Gran.' I wish I did have the comfort that Gran gets from prayers and church and stuff. But it's never seemed to connect with me, and Mum would have kicked up big time if I'd gone holy on her.

'Oh, shame,' says Maureen, which I think is a bit odd. 'The jury would like to hear about you going to church,' she adds, which is even weirder.

'How did you think your mum was looking?' asks Doug.

'Crap.'

'Yes, we're a bit concerned about her. We can't contact

236

the hospital right now. We want to get back first with no risk of anyone making any connection between us and them. But I'm pretty sure that they'll move everyone right away. Your mum will be back with you very soon.'

'So . . . will you go away then, Maureen?'

She hesitates, and I'm desperate for her to say no, she's going to stay and look after both of us. She can see it in my face, I think, because she says briskly, 'Let's cross that bridge when we come to it.' And then, 'Right, you're going to eat something if I have to pick up that fork and feed you,' which makes me try a chip and find it surprisingly tasty.

I'm asleep again as soon as we get back into the car and I don't wake up until we're back at the house. Joe's house. For the first time it feels like home. My anonymous beige room is so peaceful. A safe place, our safe house. I need to believe it, so I do. I collapse on to the bed and it's incredibly comfortable.

Downstairs I can hear the television. Doug's switched on Sky News. I hear snatches of headlines drifting up the stairs . . . 'shooting . . . hospital. . .'

Shooting? Hospital? I pull myself up and stumble down the stairs. There's an aerial shot of the hospital, and then the reporter standing by the main entrance. 'The policeman who was shot was an armed officer protecting a woman who had been injured in a violent assault. Questions are being asked about security in the hospital, with families of patients complaining that their loved ones were put at risk.'

'The woman at the centre of this incident has now been moved to an undisclosed location. The injured policeman is recovering and his condition is said to be stable.'

'They've moved Gran?'

'Sounds like it.'

'It's a good thing,' says Maureen. 'Now you won't have to worry about her.' She gets up. 'I'm going to run you a bath, and then see if you can sleep some more.'

I do sleep, but it's not the easy, empty sleep I slept in the car. I'm back in the hospital running along the maze of corridors, but this time I go through some double doors and I'm in my gran's room, with all the bleeping machines and the smell and the bandages . . . and in the bed it's not Gran, but Claire, and it's not her arms that have been cut, but her throat, and there's blood everywhere, on the walls and the bed and dripping on to the floor, and there's a screaming noise – and it's coming from me. . .

And Maureen's sitting on my bed in her dressing gown and handing me another little white pill. 'Better take another one,' she says. 'No good sleeping if it just gives you nightmares.'

I take it and as I swallow, I wonder whether my life – awake or asleep – will ever just be normal again.

CHAPTER 20
Sharon and the Pope

In the morning I try to go running. I put on my kit. I lace up my shoes. I open the door and I think about how I'm going to warm up, then stretch, then run for at least an hour.

And then a car comes along the road and I shut the door again.

Three times I open the door and three times I close it again. In the end I sit down on the step and just watch the road for a bit, hoping that if I see what a boring, quiet street it is, then I'll be able to jog down it.

What I see is Ashley Jenkins walking up the hill towards me.

She's tanned and wearing skimpy shorts and a crop top, and I'm surprised that I don't feel more than a flicker of interest. Maybe Maureen's sedatives have shut me down, switched me off. I bloody well hope it's not

240

forever. I'd have to sue the police, which would be totally embarrassing.

It can't be coincidence that Ashley's walking along my street. But how could she know where I live? Of course, I'm so stupid. Her motor-mouth mother must have fished my address out of the school records.

'Hello, Joe,' she says. 'Are you going to invite me in?'

'OK,' I say, not quite sure what's going on. Am I meant to take her up to my bedroom, where I haven't even picked up my sweat-stained clothes from yesterday? Is Ashley about to take things to a new, fantastic but terrifying level? Am I capable right now? Are we even together any more? 'Do you want a coffee?'

We go into the kitchen where Maureen and Doug are sitting at the table and looking very interested in my visitor. I try and ignore them while I fill the kettle, which just makes me look really stupid because Maureen immediately says, 'Hello, my name's Maureen and this is Doug,' and Ashley says, 'Hi, I'm Ashley,' and then everyone looks at me and I don't say anything.

I make coffee and say, 'We're going upstairs,' to see if they object, but she spoils it by saying, 'Actually, Joe, maybe we'd better stay in the lounge if no one's in there.' I can see Doug and Maureen exchanging knowing glances and I feel like a complete prat.

It's clear to everyone that I am about to go through the ritual of being officially chucked. Doug and Maureen will probably listen at the door and then have a good laugh about it.

We go into the lounge and I shut the door behind us. 'Where's your mum?' asks Ashley. 'Or are they your real parents and you were just pretending that your big sister was your mum?'

'No, she's away right now and they're staying here with me. They're just friends.'

'Oh.'

'How was your holiday?'

'It was good.'

I'm not going to ask her why she's here if she's not going to say. We can go on having this sort of conversation for hours if she wants.

'Nice weather?'

'Yes, very sunny.'

'Nice hotel?'

'Yes, lovely.' She sighs. 'Look, Joe, I didn't want to go upstairs because I thought we needed to talk.'

'Oh, yeah?'

'It's just... Look, I think maybe we should stop seeing each other.'

There are two things I can say. I can say, 'Yes, fine, OK, it was good for the two weeks that it lasted, especially when you were in Spain,' and show her out. Or I can ask why. Stupidly I go for option two.

She looks uncomfortable. 'It's just. . . Thing is, Joe, I don't know if you know but I didn't grow up round here. My family came here when I was nine from Catford – you know where that is?'

Of course I do. She's a South Londoner. If you're from north of the river like me, then South London is somewhere you know about but have never been to. Most of the things you've heard aren't good.

'And the reason we left was to get my brother away from that area. My brother Callum, he's six years older than me, and he was getting involved in gangs and carrying a knife and one day he got stabbed.'

'Was he . . . was he killed?'

'No, of course not. I said we moved here to get him away from London, duh. Anyway when I saw you with that knife the other day, I knew . . . I knew I couldn't be with you.' Her lip trembles and I think she's about to cry. 'I saw a different side of you.'

This is totally unfair: 'But I only did it for you. They were touching you, and they had those pictures. . .'

'I know, and they're sick bastards, but you know what, Joe, we might have been embarrassed by those pictures, and it wouldn't have been nice, but it wouldn't have been the absolute end of the world. But say you'd stabbed one of those boys. . .' Her voice trails off.

She's not altogether wrong and I know it. 'I'm sorry, Ash. I never meant to scare you.'

She's crying now, and the sedatives seem to be wearing off because I really would like to try and cheer her up a bit. I go and sit on the sofa next to her and tentatively snake my arm around her almost-bare shoulders. She doesn't object, and my other arm manages to rest itself against the bit of her back between the shorts and crop top. And then I'm kissing her tears away and we're lying down on the sofa, and I'm hoping very much that Doug and Maureen will have the sense to leave us alone while I find out whether she was doing any topless sunbathing in Spain.

She pulls away. Eventually. Half-heartedly. 'And that's the other thing,' she says.

'What?' I'm still stroking her bare stomach and the other hand is doing some really successful exploration.

'You and me. It's too much, too soon.'

'Mmm . . . I don't see you complaining. . .' I'm nibbling her neck and she smells all coconutty.

'That's the problem.'

'What do you mean?'

'I know everyone thinks I'm a slag who'll do anything, but I'm really not, Joe.'

That's just not fair. 'I never thought anything like

that. I think you're amazing and sexy and . . .' I kiss her glossy lips, '. . . very sophisticated.'

'Yes but the thing is that I don't seem to be able to say no to you, Joe, like I can to other boys. The boys I've been out with before, they knew that they couldn't . . . you know . . . go too far. I made sure they knew. But I keep on forgetting to tell you to stop, and I'm getting a bit scared. I mean if we'd gone up to your bedroom, I can imagine, you know, one thing leading to another. And I don't want to end up like. . .' She hesitates, but I can see this one coming a mile off.

'Like my mum.'

I very deliberately remove my hands, wipe them on my jeans as if I'm cleaning off something dirty and move away like she's giving off a bad smell.

'I don't mean— '

'I know what you mean. I know *exactly* what you mean. But you know what? My mum was happy to have me. She wanted to have me. And we've never scrounged off the state. She's got qualifications, and she's worked and worked to look after me.'

I'm so furious I can hardly speak. It's incredible how much shit you take in life just because your mother happens to be a teenager when you're born, and your dad can't be arsed to know you.

Ashley says, 'Joe, don't take this the wrong way.

I don't mean anything against your mum. I think she's really cool, but she must have been ever so young when she had you. Not much older than us. And I just wouldn't want to have to make those choices.'

I can't stand looking at her. 'Oh yeah, Ashley, I bet you say this to all the boys.'

'No really, Joe, it's really true.'

'I bet you found yourself some waiter in Spain and you've been at it with him all week.'

'No . . . no. . . I've really thought about this a lot.'

'Why come here dressed like a tart, then?'

Her face falls. My aunties would kill me if they heard me speak to a girl like that. But I don't care. I only want to hurt her like she's hurting me.

'I'm not. . .'

'Yeah, yeah. . . Well, you've done what you came for, Ashley. What are you going to tell everyone? "He was so hot I couldn't trust myself with his body, so I chucked him"? Or "I thought he was a psycho with a knife"?'

'I don't know,'

'Maybe I'll tell everyone I chucked you because you're just a slag.'

She stands up and I can see I've made her angry. Good. 'Go on then,' she says. 'See if I care. It's what they all think anyway.'

'No, I won't do that.' Her unexpected dignity has shamed me. 'I'm sorry, Ashley. I thought you were disrespecting my mum and I've had enough of that for a lifetime.'

'I'll tell people we broke up because my parents told me I had to chuck you after you punched Carl. That's true, by the way. And all the girls'll be after you whatever I say.'

'Yeah, but they're too scared of you to speak to me.'

She shrugs: 'It's OK. I'll tell them they can talk to you.'

'All of them?'

She looks suspicious. 'Why . . . who were you thinking of?'

'Oh, no one. . .'

'Hmmm.' She's not quite sure what to think, but I hope I've made things safe to talk to Claire at school.

She leaves then, and I lie down on the sofa and I feel quite upset, although it's not being chucked by Ashley that's bothering me, but the memories she's stirred, the days and days and years and years of being told that there's something wrong with you because your mum is young and poor and had a baby when she wasn't much more than a child herself.

It's not just stuff like Father's Day when you've got no one to make a card for, and politicians on the telly saying that single mothers cause lots of problems in society. It's not just Vicky Pollard on *Little Britain* and the word pramface and the word bastard as well.

It was the way everyone looked that first parents' evening at St Saviour's, when I realised with a horrible grinding feeling in my stomach that all the other parents came in pairs – even Arron's, although his dad wasn't the one he used to have – and Mum was at least ten years younger than anyone else's, and she didn't dress the same way as the other mums who were either suits or frumps.

And in the playground, the voices, the voices that I pretended not to hear. Your mum's a slut. Your mum's a whore. Will your mum do it with me?

No one I tried to talk to really understood. Auntie Emma said I was making a big fuss about nothing and she was sure that loads of kids at school had single mothers, and when I explained that most of them had dads as well, she said, 'From what I hear, you're better off without yours.' Mr Patel said every woman needed a good man and perhaps I should come with him to the mosque some time, learn a more traditional way of life.

Arron said, 'The problem, mate, is that she's too fit. She's nothing like a normal mother. She looks like she had you when she was eight.'

And then he said, 'You just have to pick one of them to fight and they won't do it any more. Come on, bro, remember the stuff we learned at boxing club.'

And I shook my head because there were so many of them and they were all bigger than me, and I thought if I fight one I'll have to fight them all. And I could see he despised me. And later he started with the 'pretty boy'. And the 'girl'. And the 'gay'. And I had to take it because he was my only friend. But I worried that if I took it, it made it true.

And none of this would have mattered so much if I hadn't worked out a conversation that had bothered me for years; since I was about eight or nine and Nicki and I were watching *East Enders*, and Sharon was weeping and wailing about a baby she'd been pregnant with and hadn't had. Had somehow decided not to have.

And I turned to Nicki and said, 'I didn't know you could quit a baby.'

And she said, 'Well, sometimes you can.'

And I said, 'Could you have?'

And she laughed and said, 'What a question! Not with your gran and the Pope on my case!' And when I looked puzzled she kissed me and said, 'I wouldn't ever want to be without my lovely boy.'

But it nagged away at me for ages, as things do that you don't really understand but you think might be important, and I stored it away until the day before I was due to start at St Saviour's. I was trying on my new blazer and Nicki said, 'You know Ty, at this new school they're going to be much heavier with the God stuff. It's all very well, and I'm so proud you're going there, but remember you've got a mind of your own. Don't let them fill you up with Jesus and Mary and the Pope until you can't make your own decisions.'

And I saw sadness in her eyes and I pulled that old conversation out of my memory and I kind of realised that if it hadn't been for Gran and the Pope then Nicki would have decided to be like Sharon on *East Enders*. And just then I still didn't really understand how or why but a bit of my inner certainty, my basic happiness, died that day. Which wasn't a great way to start a new school.

I'm still lying on the sofa, feeling a bit sorry for myself, going over it all again and again when there's a knock at the door and Maureen comes in. 'Doug's gone,' she says. 'He's going to find out what's happening, and maybe he'll be collecting your mum.'

She's trying not to look too nosy. 'Your friend gone too?' she asks, although quite where she thinks Ashley is hiding I'm not sure.

'Yup.'

'All well?'

'She chucked me, if that's what you want to know.'

'Sorry to hear that. Long relationship?'

'Two weeks, but we had some amazing moments,' I say gloomily, and then I realise how stupid that sounds and I start to laugh because actually I'm kind of bubbling with happiness inside to be able to be Claire's friend. I'm thinking I can go shopping with her and help her chose nicer clothes, and take her long rippling hair and tie it back with a silky ribbon, and have someone to talk to that I can trust and feel close to. A real friend.

Maureen laughs too and says, 'You must be absolutely devastated. Why don't I make you a cup of tea?'

'Yes, OK. Thanks.'

We sit at the kitchen table and I tell her about not being able to go running. She says, 'Look, Ty, that was a very frightening experience yesterday. Don't kid yourself. Some evil bastard tried to kill you and that's a big thing to cope with.'

'Yeah,' I say and she says, 'You know, Ty, what doesn't kill you makes you stronger,' which is pretty amazing because I would have thought that Maureen'd be way too old to have even heard of Kanye West.

'Anyway,' she goes on, 'We're happy that your identity as Joe is very secure, and no one can connect you here with Ty. It's possible we might be able to arrange some counselling for you in the future, but right now you're going to have to take a bit of advice from me.'

'What's that?'

'Keep calm and carry on. It was a poster during the Second World War – no, I'm not that old, cheeky bugger – and I've always thought it was a good motto.'

It's a good one for a runner, I think, and I wonder about giving it another try. Maureen seems to read my mind. 'Go on,' she says. 'Maybe you can do it this time.'

I hesitate a bit on the step, then I fiddle with my iPod until I find the Kanye West song she was talking about, and I walk down the garden path. I almost turn around and come back when I get to the garden gate. But with Maureen watching me and Kanye in my head telling me to be strong, I manage to jog down the street and around the corner and I'm running again. And maybe, just maybe, I can take her advice.

CHAPTER 21
Lost Property

My mum arrives back at about 9 pm on Sunday, just as I'm ironing a shirt for school the next day. She's pale and dazed, blinking like she's just woken up. I put the iron down and come and hug her. 'Hi, Nic. How was Gran?'

'I don't know,' she says in a faraway little voice. 'They took her away from us. And then they put us in some hotel place. . . And then we were there, and now we're here, except Emma and Lou are somewhere else. I don't know where.'

I wonder if it was a hotel at all. She's acting like she's been in a loony bin. 'It was because of the shooting,' I say impatiently. 'They had to move you in a hurry.'

'Oh God, yes, the shooting,' says Nicki, like she's a TV and someone's turned her on. 'You could have been killed. Are you all right? Oh, God, Ty.'

'Yes, yes, would I be doing the ironing if I'd been shot?'

The screen goes blank. 'Oh. I don't know. They didn't tell me anything.'

'They must have told you that I was OK.'

'I suppose so.' She's doubtful. 'They talk to Louise mostly and she doesn't tell me anything.'

Maureen has been listening to this, standing tactfully by the door and she comes over and puts her arm around my mum. 'Nicki, love, you have a good sleep now and you'll feel more like yourself in the morning. I was wondering, would you like me to see if I can stay on a few days? Just to help you get back on your feet again, and tell you how Ty's been doing while you've been away.'

Nicki looks like there's no one there at all. 'Yes, whatever you want,' she says. 'Whatever. . .' and her voice trails off and she wanders out of the room.

'Blimey,' says Maureen, 'what is she on? I'd better go and help her get ready for bed. She's so away with the fairies that I don't think she can even do that. Don't you worry, Ty, whatever my boss says, I'm not going anywhere in a hurry.'

I just bend my head over the ironing and concentrate very, very hard on getting all the creases out. I iron six shirts, five handkerchiefs, ten T-shirts and two pairs of trousers. I move on to tea towels, underpants and even socks. When there's nothing left in the house that I could possibly iron, I gather together all the books I'm going to need for the morning. And then I find an episode of *The Simpsons* on telly and I watch it without laughing once.

Doug and Maureen come and sit either side of me. 'OK, Ty, I am definitely going to stay,' says Maureen. 'Doug thinks your mum may just be a bit out of it because she had a sleeping pill in the car, so you should see a great change in her in the next few days.'

'She was a bit like this in the hospital,' I say doubtfully.

'She's been under a lot of stress,' says Doug. 'She just needs some recovery time.'

Why can't she just keep calm and carry on like me? It's not as though she was the one who was shot at, or the one who's going to have to get up in court and tell her story, or even the main person involved here anyway. Stress . . . it's just an excuse really. An excuse for being useless.

I get up and collect my pile of ironing to take upstairs.

'I'm going to bed.'

Maureen follows me up the stairs. 'I'm going to

put half a sleeping pill and a glass of water by the bed, just in case you have nightmares again.'

'Thanks, Maureen. Thanks for staying.'

She looks at me and says, 'It'll get better, Ty. This'll pass, you know.'

She's great, Maureen, but she's also police. And the police told me that Gran would be safe in her flat, and that I should go into the hospital with Dave. So I don't altogether believe what she has to say.

Mum's still asleep when I get up in the morning. Maureen makes me some toast and wishes me luck, and I trudge off down the hill. It occurs to me that last time I was properly at school – apart from my date with the head teacher, of course – I was in floods of girly tears, sobbing my heart out in Mr Henderson's smelly office. What if somehow everyone knows about that? What if there's some secret CCTV footage that has been sent to everyone's mobiles? I very nearly turn back a few times before I reach the school gate.

Brian, Jamie and Max pounce on me the minute I walk through the gates. 'Hey, Joe, good to see you back, mate.' We do a bit of high-fiving, and Brian asks, 'So, what's the story? Did they throw the book at you?'

'Nah. Carl and I have to work on a joint project together.'

Everyone has different ideas. Jamie thinks we'll be

running cricket club for year seven. Brian reckons we might be sent to some sort of boot camp for delinquent youth.

'Or maybe you'll have to scrub out the swimming pool,' suggests Max.

'With our toothbrushes?' I suggest.

The boys go silent, nudge each other and look at me. Ashley's directly ahead of us in the playground, at the centre of her group. They're all looking over at us and several have supportive arms round Ashley who is wiping away a tear.

'We heard the news, mate,' says Brian. 'What a bummer. But her parents are very strict, I hear.'

'It's always the ones with the strictest parents who are the real goers,' says Max.

'Maybe she'll be up for a secret affair?' asks Jamie. I shake my head: 'Nah, time to move on. There'll be plenty of other opportunities in this school.'

Brian sighs: 'For you, maybe, but it's a desert for some of us.'

As the bell goes for registration, I'm vaguely aware that I'm attracting quite a bit of attention. People are looking my way, pointing me out, and there's a general murmur that seems to be directed towards me. Girls are smiling, some year seven boys start clapping and cheering before being shushed by the playground supervisor.

I'm trying to ignore all the attention and just look out for Claire.

She's quite easy to spot because there're only about three girls still wearing winter uniform. Her hair is still all over her face. She looks as scared and lonely as ever, like I used to feel at St Saviour's, although I hope I wasn't such an obvious loser.

I can't imagine how I'm ever going to get people to accept that Joe could be friendly with this girl – especially when really fit girls like Lauren and Emily and Zoe from 8P are giving me a lot of glances and winks and secret smiles whenever Ashley's back is turned. I'm pathetically concerned that Joe's image shouldn't be tainted. But is Joe cool enough to give Claire a boost?

I try and catch her eye but she completely blanks me. Maybe she's not aware of my official status as Ashley's ex. When we sit down in assembly we're so close that I could almost reach out and touch her hand. I'm inching towards her, little by little, trying to make a tiny bit of skin to skin contact which no one else need see – but she moves her hand away and puts it in her pocket.

I'm almost snubbed, but, OK, it's best to be cautious. And then I remember. Ellie's race, Ellie's big, important, qualifying race was yesterday. And I didn't wish her luck and I didn't ask how it went. I've blown it.

I've totally blown it. This nice supportive family who've only been good to me must think I'm a selfish scumbag. Claire is obviously furious on her sister's behalf. And Ellie will never want to train with me again.

Assembly passes in a blur as I try and think of plausible excuses. As we leave, Claire casually takes her handkerchief out of her pocket and as she does a scrumpled piece of paper falls out. She glances at me, and I reach down and pick it up. I shove it in my pocket but I know what it's going to say. It's going to tell me that she wants nothing to do with me, and nor does Ellie.

Geography and Science pass me by. I know it all anyway. I'm trying to think what I can do, how I can make some sort of excuse. I can't think of anything.

As the bell goes for break I jump up to try and find a quiet place to face the worst and read Claire's angry words. But the science teacher says, 'Joe, you're to go straight to Mr Henderson's office.' Carl is already there, looking a lot less mutilated than he did last time I saw him. Mr Henderson keeps us waiting outside for an awkward five minutes, then calls us in. He doesn't suggest that we sit down, so we don't.

'Well,' he says. 'I appear to have been left picking up the pieces.'

I study my shoes. Carl gazes at the ceiling.

'The head teacher has some idea about you two

learning to work together. Some sort of joint project. Something that will help the school and also use your undoubted talents. He was thinking of . . . he suggested . . . something like helping with the annual five-a-side tournament that we run for local primary schools.'

That could be a laugh. Carl looks enthusiastic too.

'But that's not the sort of thing I have in mind at all,' says Mr Henderson. He opens the door to the corridor and points out a large cupboard. 'See this? Every piece of lost property we've acquired over the last three years is in here.' He opens the door to show us mounds of mouldering clothing. The stench is overwhelming. 'Your job is to sort all this out, return every bit of labelled clothing to its owner, then wash the rest so that it can be used by those disorganised creatures who forget their kit.'

Oh, for God's sake. I can see that Carl's equally unimpressed. 'You can do this while the rest of your class are having swimming lessons because I am not having either of you use the pool for the rest of the term. And when it's finished, you can tidy the equipment cupboard for me.'

That's it. I wonder if it's worth mentioning the access card, given that Ellie's never going to speak to me again.

'Um, Mr Henderson?'

'Joe?'

'I was wondering,' – I glance nervously at Carl – 'about my access card.'

'Ah yes, the famous access card. The start of all this trouble.'

He goes to his desk drawer. 'Joe, you are having your access card back, but you are specifically barred from the pool. Ellie has said that she will not continue working with you. . .'

Oh no.

'. . .unless you have the card back. She wants you to enter for some more competitions during the summer – I think she's going to talk to you about it, and now that she's all but qualified for the Paralympics next year she needs you to be able to work intensively on your own. I hardly need tell you that if there is any breach of any school rule – and that includes the most minor uniform regulations – then you will have the card taken away.'

'What about me?' asks Carl.

'What about you?'

'Can't I have one too?'

'We've been through this, Carl. If I give one to the football team, then there are so many others that I will have to give them to that the whole system will become unworkable.'

'Yes, but you don't have to give one to the rest

of the team. Just to me. And then Joe and I could train together.'

I'm quite impressed by Carl's cheek in making a case for himself.

'So the two of you get rewarded for your appalling behaviour, is that it?'

'No, we get to improve our sports performance. Joe, wouldn't you like to be on the football team?'

I nod. Actually I'd love to be on the football team. I've always wanted to be good at football. It was a real disappointment to me to find when I went to primary school that I was so crap compared to the boys who had dads and brothers to play with, and even though I nagged Nicki to let me join a football club it never really happened. I'm good at the stuff you can practise by yourself – keepie uppies, that sort of thing – and obviously I'm fast, but I go to pieces a bit when I play in a team.

'Well, we can work together, get you skilled up, on the team.'

Mr Henderson looks extremely unconvinced but says, 'We'll try it for a fortnight. If you two genuinely work together then we'll make it permanent – and we'll send you out to make peace in the Middle East.' Carl gawps. 'It's a joke, boy. Joe, I'm going to give you a key to the lost property cupboard – guard it with your life.'

We're just leaving the PE block and I'm wondering whether I can ask Carl if his offer was genuine, when I hear someone calling me. 'Joe! Come over here a minute!'

It's Ellie. She's heading for the running track, clipboard in hand, and Magda, her Polish helper, is standing by her side looking a bit gloomy. Ellie hands the clipboard to Magda and says, 'Can you just go and tell them that I'll be five minutes?'

Magda looks blank. 'I . . . tell?'

Ellie rolls her eyes. 'The girls' group – over there. I'll . . . be . . . five . . . minutes.'

I can just about do this in Polish. 'Girls must wait a little,' I say, and Magda flashes me a grateful smile. She walks off in the direction of a clutch of girls who must be the young sportswomen that Ellie mentors. Zoe from 8P is among them and she gives me a wave. She won the girls year eight race at the inter-schools competition, and she actually looks great in shorts. But I've got other things on my mind.

'God, that girl is annoying,' says Ellie, eyes still on Magda.

'Ellie, I'm really sorry,'

'Sorry? It's not your fault that yet again I have a useless helper. In fact, it's really helpful that you can speak her language.'

'I never wished you luck . . . or asked how you did. . .'

She grins: 'Too busy with your love life, eh? I hope it was because you were too busy training.'

I wonder what she'd say if she knew the truth. 'I have done my best with the training.'

'Anyway, I won, which is great, so I forgive you,' she says airily. 'Start training again with me tomorrow? We're celebrating at home tonight. You can come if you want.'

'Oh, great, thanks, I'd like that.' Then I remember. 'But I might not be able to. My mum's a bit . . . not very well. . .'

'Oh well, if she's feeling better then bring her along. Anyone can come. Just a little party to celebrate.'

'Thanks, Ellie.' Her shining happiness is the sort that swallows up all your worries and concerns. She's like a kind of superperson, a celebrity. Everything about her is *more*, somehow, than ordinary people. It's strange that Claire isn't like that – in fact, Claire is the opposite, somehow smaller, quieter and less of a person than everyone else.

'Oh, but one thing, Joe,' says Ellie. 'I'm going to ask you because no one else will. What on earth were you doing locked in my little sister's room for three hours?'

'I . . . er. . .'

'Claire won't tell us, and my mum is completely confused about what you might have been up to, and she's all worried that you've got bad intentions. I said I thought you had plenty of girls to choose from so it'd be pretty unlikely you'd be after Claire like that, but Mum seems to think different. Says you were in the dark.'

'We were just talking and then I was feeling a bit tired so I had a lie down on the floor. . .'

Ellie looks pretty unconvinced. 'I can't think what you were talking about. She never speaks. Or are you saying she bored you to sleep?'

'No, we were talking about school and that. She's OK to talk to. Maybe you should try talking to her a bit more often.'

I'm feeling a bit annoyed on Claire's behalf. After all, Claire seems to care so much about Ellie's feelings that she won't even speak to me, even though Ellie doesn't seem bothered at all that I forgot her race.

Ellie shrugs. 'Whatever. See you later. . .' And I have to run all the way to Maths while she goes off to the running track.

It's only as I walk home that I'm able to pull out Claire's note. There's an email address and a password, and that's it. She's kept her promise and made me an account. We can communicate wherever I am, whatever happens, whatever my name is. With Mum crumbling and Gran ill and my aunties disappeared abroad – where in the world are they? – it's a promise of continuity, of support, of friendship. I decide I am definitely going to Ellie's party tonight.

CHAPTER 22
Claire

Nicki's in the kitchen when I get home. Maureen doesn't seem to be there and I wonder nervously if she's left already. But Nic certainly seems a lot better. I can even cope with calling her Mum again. She's put on some make-up, and the radio's on for the first time since we moved into this house.

'Come and have a cup of tea,' she calls. I sit down at the kitchen table: 'Are you feeling OK?' I ask.

'Ty, darling, I'm so sorry. Did I scare you?'

I have a whole new concept of being scared. Things like horror films and getting told off at school, things that used to scare me a bit, wouldn't even register now. I'd hardly describe last night with Mum as scary compared to, say, being shot at. But the idea that I was going to be left alone with a zombie – that was pretty worrying.

'No, but you were really out of it.'

'They gave me a tablet and I hadn't eaten all day, and hospitals do my head in at the best of times. Ty, Maureen told me about what's been happening at school.'

'It's all OK now. You don't have to worry about it.'

'But I do worry about you, I do. . . I'm so sorry I've not been here for you.'

'You had to be with Gran.'

'That's not what I mean, and you know it. I've been useless since we left London.'

I'm not going to disagree. 'So you're not angry about the swimming pool thing?' She shakes her head: 'Don't make a habit of it. But Maureen explained it all to me and it does sound like these boys were being very nasty to you. Are they still? Are you being bullied?'

It's so ironic that she never asked me this when I was at St Saviour's, when I was bloody miserable every single day and she was so busy with work and everything and so happy that I was at a good school that we never talked properly at all unless it was about homework.

'No, it's fine. Everyone likes me except these few boys and it's because they're jealous.'

'And Maureen said you've been seeing a girl? But you split up?'

'Ashley. The one you liked at Top Shop. We went out a few times, but her parents said she had to chuck me because I punched Carl.'

'Are you upset?'

'No, she wasn't really my type.'

Mum looks like she's trying not to laugh. She pats my hand. 'You don't want to get too serious, anyway.'

'Not with her, anyway.'

'Not with anyone – you're only fourteen, for heaven's sake. You're still my baby.'

Huh. Outrageous. I could point out what she and my dad were doing when they were fifteen. But I won't.

'Mum, there's a party at Ellie's tonight, to celebrate because she won her big race. I'm going to go . . . you can come too if you want, and Maureen, I suppose.'

'Maureen's gone to see her boss and talk about how we're coping,' says Mum, frowning. 'I get the impression that she's worried about us.'

'Maureen's really nice – she'd only be helpful.' Christ. Am I about to be taken into care? Would Maureen do that to us?

'Sat me down and said I had to be more supportive of you, look after you better. Louise was saying the same thing, that you wouldn't have been running around the park getting involved in fights if I'd been more on the case, talked to you more, not left you so much to Gran.'

'Oh well, Lou's always like that,' I say soothingly.

In our family no one ever holds back when it comes to telling people how they could be doing things better.

Her eyes fill with tears: 'I just can't believe that there are people out there who want to kill you, Ty. You're a kid, not a gangster. What would I do without you? I love you so much.'

'I'm not going anywhere,' I say uncomfortably. She's been really together so far but she's probably not up to talking about the shooting business. Also, I suspect she might not think it was so clever to kick someone who could have had a gun twice.

'What about the party, then? Do you want to come with me?'

'It's a school night. I don't know if you should be going,' she says, which is such an Auntie Lou thing to say that I don't take it seriously.

'It won't be late. It's just a few friends round.'

'Oh, well. OK. They are a lovely family. She's fantastic, isn't she, Ellie, really inspiring.'

'She thinks you ought to get running again. Join a club or something,' I say.

'Oh. Well. I do think about it sometimes.'

I get up. 'I'm going to get changed.' And she decides she will come, and at 7.30 we're knocking on Ellie and Claire's door again.

Ellie's mum looks happy to see my mum and gives

her a hug and asks about Gran. She's obviously not so sure about me, although she asks about my ribs. I can't wait to see Claire in her dark little den again. But we're going to have to be clever about it.

When I get out into the garden I think it'll be possible to disappear in this crowd. There are tons of people here, and kids running around all over the place. People are drinking beer, the barbeque is sizzling and someone's set up a karaoke machine in the kitchen. It's a proper party. Mum looks a bit nervous, but Janet introduces her to some of Ellie's mates from the gym and I can see the old Nicki, the flirty, funny, have-a-laugh girl coming out again. Give her an hour and a few drinks and she'll be belting out 'Dancing Queen'.

It's hard to spot Claire. She seems to fade into the background so easily, like a lizard or a moth. It takes a good ten minutes to find her, sitting in the garden being talked at by an old lady. I wait patiently until the old lady trots off and then Claire looks over and smiles and says, 'Hi, you.'

'Can we go and talk?' I ask. She shakes her head: 'My mum said I should stay down here.'

'Oh. It's too noisy. Where can we go?'

She thinks, then says, 'There's always Ellie's room. That's not upstairs. She only said not upstairs.'

It's funny. With Ashley, I knew where I was. I didn't

like her, but I did fancy her. The evidence was completely unarguable.

But with Claire, I don't know. I care about her. I think about her . . . but not in, you know, the sort of way I'd think about Ashley in bed at night. I daydream about looking after Claire, and her looking after me, about being close and talking and sharing and soppy stuff like that.

If I see her at school, I don't fancy her at all – she's too much of a freak – and I try not to remember that time she was cutting herself because being turned on by that is just wrong. I know it's wrong. I'm not some sort of perv. I just thought for a misguided second that it was kind of interesting.

But sometimes, when I remember that day she took off her shirt, I feel a bit stirred up, and right now, looking at her big blue eyes, the prospect of being alone with her is very attractive indeed. I wish I could just be consistent.

'We'll have to be really quiet,' she says.

We wander out to the hallway and miraculously there's no one there. Claire pushes the door to Ellie's room and we slip inside. But it's hopeless. It's noisy, boiling hot, even when I peel off my hoodie; there's the constant sound of people passing through the front door and, worst of all, anyone in the front garden can see us through the window. I'm beginning to feel breathless. 'We can't talk here,' I say, 'it's no good.'

So we scuttle up the stairs, hoping that no one notices. Once in her room Claire wedges the chair against the door again. I pull the curtains. And we sit in the dark on her cushions and I put my arm around her and I feel about as happy as I've ever felt.

'So, thank you for making the email address,' I say.

'It's nothing. You could have done it for yourself.'

'I thought you were upset with me because I forgot Ellie's race.'

She snorts: 'I wish I could have forgotten about it. We've had nothing but race, race, race for weeks. And now she's won and now Magda's quit, we'll hear nothing but Paralympic training for the next year, and Mum and Dad will always be going away, and everyone will be running around Ellie as usual.'

'Magda's quit?'

She chuckles: 'They always do. Couldn't take being bossed around.'

I like being bossed around by Ellie, but I can see that it might not be great if you aren't being trained by her.

'Aren't you pleased she won?'

'Pleased for her, but not for me.'

I touch her arm as softly as possible. 'Are you OK? No more . . . you know. . .'

'No . . . but it's not always easy. I did try and ring you the other day but there was no answer.'

She's wearing a kind of floaty tunic thing and leggings – it's nicer than her usual over-sized shirts but it still swamps her. I push her sleeves up and look at her arms. At least there are no new plasters, although the latest cut, the one I saw her do, looks pink and sore. I stroke her arm with my finger. 'I'm sorry. I was away.'

And I tell her about Gran and the hospital and Gran waking up and coming out of the door with Dave. And the blood, and the corridors, and kicking Doug twice. And how the worst bit was afterwards, alone under the blanket.

And she listens, and she takes my hand and she asks, 'Who are they, these people who want to kill you?'

I've been thinking a lot about that myself in the last few days. 'It's the family of one of the guys that was in the park that day. I think they are professional criminals, you know, real gangsters. I don't know who they are.'

'And they want to kill you because you saw their son do the killing?'

'I suppose. . .' I think about what I actually did see. 'I think he must have been the leader, the one who started it all. I mean, I don't actually know which one it was that's threatening me. Unless. . .'

'Unless what?'

'Well, Nathan. He's the brother of my friend Arron. It was Arron that I followed to the park. And Nathan told me to keep quiet or else. But I don't think Nathan's part of a family of criminals. I mean, I know the family, I'd know if they were criminals, wouldn't I?'

And if they were, they'd be living in a big house somewhere, not in a flat on an estate in Hackney. And you'd have thought Nathan would want me to be a witness because I'm doing it for Arron. I mean, I'm doing it for Gran and I'm doing it for me and I'm doing it for other people too, but if it wasn't for Arron I wouldn't be doing it at all.

But I remember the smell of Nathan, the sour-sweet smell of sweat and fear as he pushed his face into mine, and I'm not sure. Maybe Nathan would know a hitman. He certainly knew where my gran lived.

Claire says, 'Can't the police tell you more? Now that this has happened? It doesn't seem fair that they know more than you.'

'None of it is fair. . .'

I'm not all that sure I want to know any more. 'Let's talk about something else, Claire.'

Claire leans against me: 'Is it true you've finished with Ashley?'

'She finished with me.'

'Is it true her parents told her to chuck you?'

I'm torn. I don't want to tell Claire about the knife. I don't want to tell her about what Ashley said. It's really embarrassing, and it might put her off me if she knows what I've nearly been up to with her enemy. She's probably going to think I'm some sort of opportunistic sex maniac, which wouldn't be totally inaccurate. And it is true about the parents. It just isn't the whole truth. But I need to practise this whole truth thing, and Claire's my best listener. So I tell her everything.

She's shocked, eyes wide, but laughing as well: 'I can't believe she said that to you. Do you think she says that every time to every boy she goes out with?'

'No. . .' Of course not. 'Well, maybe.'

'Pathetic. She's pathetic. What a fake. Although she's not wrong about the knife.'

'No, I was stupid and wrong to carry one again. But I did feel less scared.'

'Again?' she asks.

'I used to carry one in London. Lots of people do there.'

'Yeah, and lots of people get stabbed. Do you watch the news?' she says. Then she says, 'It's a deal: I don't cut myself, you don't carry a knife.'

'No knives for anyone,' I say, and wonder if I can keep this deal.

'The thing is, you can fight to defend yourself,

and you can run away. You didn't need a knife in that hospital, did you?'

'If I'd had one I might have killed the wrong guy.'

'There you go.'

I'm feeling so much better and so fond of her that, as I stroke her hair away from her forehead, I want to kiss her, but I don't think I should. It's so unclear what sort of a friendship we have, and I'm worried that she's only about twelve. But she leans over to me and says soft and shy, 'Let's seal it with a kiss,' and the next thing I know we're in the tightest hug possible, and my heart's done a massive flip.

'I think you're incredibly nice,' I say, and realise immediately that I've picked the wrong word.

'Nice?' she says. I don't think she's very impressed. I'm flustered and all confused because I've never felt like this before – so close, so equal, so caring and cared about. Tenderness kind of sums it up, but I feel shy just thinking about it. Arron never gave me instructions for this.

'I think you're great,' I say. And then, because it's bothering me, 'How old are you, anyway?'

'I'll be fourteen on November fifth.' She's exactly a year younger than me. That's fine.

'That's amazing . . . it's my birthday too, except I'll be fifteen. But the police have changed it to the fifth of September.'

'It must be horrible to have even your birthday changed.'

Mum always used to take me to see the fireworks for my birthday. Gran would never come because she thought Guy Fawkes night was an anti-Catholic celebration, but Mum said it was all about anti-terrorism and just a bit of fun anyway. I suppose we can go to the fireworks this year, but it won't be the same.

I clutch at her hand. 'Will you talk to me at school now it's OK with Ashley?'

'I suppose so, but people will think it's very strange. No one's friends with me, and everyone wants to be your friend. And Ashley's such a bitch . . . you have no idea, Joe, she's so horrible. She likes to control all the girls. She told them that I was a freak and they all started to be mean to me.'

I don't like to tell Claire that the way she looked and acted might have contributed a little to her freak status. I believe her when she says that Ashley bullies her.

'I don't care what anyone says,' I say, and I hope I'm telling the truth. I kiss her again, really slowly, just to make sure. She smells of soap and she tastes sweet and minty. She's lovely. 'You're very special,' I say, but I say it in Portuguese, so she just laughs at me.

And then – damn and blast – there's a pounding on

her door. Her mother's come to check up on her and she's found just what she'd forbidden. Claire's blushing and panicky as she dislodges the chair from the door, and I'm totally embarrassed.

'Claire!' says Janet. She's not happy. Her lips are pursed together. 'What's going on?'

'Nothing,' I say, jumping away from Claire, who goes pink and says, 'We just wanted to talk.' She's so unconvincing that even I don't believe her.

'You could have talked downstairs. . . I don't think it's very suitable to be sitting here in the dark,' Janet says.

I get up. 'It was just very noisy, Mrs Langley. We didn't mean to cause any problems. . . I'm going to go. Ummm . . . thank you for inviting me.' And I take to the stairs without looking back.

I head for the garden. I need to find Mum and get home before it gets too late – I'm still nervy about walking around when it's dark. It's chilly when I get out there and I remember my hoodie, still in Ellie's room. I'd better get it.

But when I open the door to her room, there's someone in there. Two people, sitting on Ellie's bed. One's a bloke . . . I think it's Alistair, Ellie's trainer, the one who looks like he should be in Boyzone. And he's kissing my mum.

CHAPTER 23
It'll Do For Now

Of course this isn't the first time. I've met an unexpected visitor at the breakfast table once or twice, and when she's seeing someone I spend even more time than usual staying with Gran or downstairs with Mr Patel or in my room. It's not like I've never seen her kiss anyone, obviously.

But she's never got off with anyone at a party that I've been at before, probably because the only kind of parties we've been to together were things like Great-Aunt Edith's funeral, or trampolining at the leisure centre for someone's seventh birthday.

'Don't mind me,' I say, reaching for my hoodie while they jump apart. Alistair obviously thinks I'm a complete clod and says, 'Look, mate, could you just give us a minute?' And Mum pretends we're all at some polite tea party and says, 'Oh, Alistair, I don't know if you've met my son T— Joe.'

'Son? Cho?' says Alistair.

'No, Joe,' she says.

I can see him looking from her to me and back again and trying to do some quick maths in his head so I say, 'It's OK, she is about the age that she looks,' adding meanly, 'which still makes her about five years older than you.'

'Joe!' says Mum. I can see she's wishing we still had our cosy Nicki 'n' Ty relationship when she'd quite often pass me off as her little brother.

'I'm going,' I say. 'Will I see you later? Or not?'

'Can I give you a lift?' asks Alistair. I can see my mum doesn't know what to do, but she doesn't want to send me home alone on a bus while she's swanning around on the back of Alistair's flash motorbike or whatever, and she says, 'That's so kind of you, Alistair – we'd both like a lift, wouldn't we, Joe?'

So I scrunch up in the back of Alistair's motor, which turns out to be a grotty Ford Fiesta, and they sit in the front talking about Ellie's training and Ellie's gym and how Michelle used to love running until she unfortunately got pregnant and blah, blah, blah, blah, blah, blah. Both of them pretend I'm not there and so do I.

By the time we get home I'm in the foulest of foul moods, and I stomp into the house and slam the door while Mum takes her time saying goodbye to Alistair at the front gate.

Maureen's back and she looks a bit startled when she sees the expression on my face.

'Are you OK?' she asks. 'Where have you been?'

'None of your business,' I say rudely and crash on up to my bedroom. I'm expecting Mum to follow me right away so I can tell her what I think of her, but she stays downstairs for about an hour and I can hear her and Maureen chatting and laughing together, probably about me.

I get ready for bed, do my Maths homework with the book propped up on my knees, then lie in the dark and remember how it felt to hold Claire in my arms. She doesn't seem too young and small any more. She's not a freak at all. She's pretty and delicate and her lips felt so soft and her skin was warm and smooth. I'm just moving on to imagine what might happen next time . . . and then my mum barges into my room and switches the light on.

'Oi! Go away! This room is private!' I protest.

'You've got no secrets from me,' she says. Huh. That's what she thinks. I don't bother to reply.

'Are you OK, darling? I'm sorry about what happened.'

She doesn't sound sorry at all.

'You should be ashamed of yourself,' I say.

'Well, I was a bit embarrassed. But he's a really nice guy, and guess what, Ty? I think I've got a job!'

'What job?' I ask suspiciously.

'Well, Ellie asked if I'd think about being her helper because she's fed up with the sort of girls she gets usually and she'd like someone a bit more on her wavelength. And Alistair thought it was a good idea too.'

'And that was him giving you your final interview, I suppose?'

'Oh come on, Ty, it was a party and we were just getting to know each other. We were having a chat and then he gave me a quick kiss. It was just unfortunate that you walked in just then. He's asked me out for a drink tomorrow night. Where were you anyway? I couldn't see you anywhere.'

Huh. That is classified information. I'm thinking about this idea of her helping Ellie. Mum'd be hanging around my school all the time. She'd get to know Mr Henderson. She'd be there when I was doing my training. It's a terrible idea.

Also it's totally wrong for my Mum. A helper has to look after the other person, doesn't she – help with things like showers and getting changed and so on? I would say I'm uniquely placed to judge that she'll be unsuited to that kind of role.

'What do you mean, you could be Ellie's helper? That's not what you do. You're a qualified legal secretary and you want to be a solicitor.'

'Yes, but it'll do for now, won't it? And it could be interesting, and I like Ellie a lot.'

There's something incredibly sad about my ambitious, hard-working, clever mother saying, 'It'll do for now.'

'She'll boss you around all the time.'

'No, she won't.'

'And you'll have to go away with her when she has training camps and competitions and then I'll be left here on my own.'

'Janet said you could stay with them. She really loved the idea, thought it would take a big strain off their family.'

I think she means Janet loved the idea of Ellie having Mum as a helper. I can't see her being thrilled about me as a house guest. Presumably this invitation was issued before she discovered me in Claire's room. But if she would have me to stay, it'd be fantastic to spend more time with Claire, not to mention the excellent food in that house . . . and the Wii. . .

'Do what you want. But you're not coming to my training sessions.' And I cover my head with the duvet to indicate that I've had enough of her today.

'It's not all about you, you know,' she says as she switches off the light and shuts the door.

In the morning, Carl's there when I get to the fitness suite. "Hello, mate," he says, sounding a bit nervous. Neither of us is quite sure how to play this, but both of us want to hang on to the access cards. So we work out a programme for him based on the one Ellie did for me. As we're getting changed afterwards, he suggests that I play football with his mates at lunchtime so he can give me some tips. I'm not sure though, because I'm wary of Jordan and Louis, and because my ribs may not be ready for football yet.

'Don't worry about Jordan and Louis, they'll behave themselves,' he says. And then he adds, 'And they'll keep their distance from you anyway because of you-know-what.'

'What?' I ask.

'What?' he echoes.

'What's you-know-what?' I ask.

'Your . . . you know . . . knife.'

'What knife?'

'They said you threatened them with a knife at the park one day.'

My heart is racing but my face is calm.

'You what? Christ, dem boys have been watching too much telly,' I say. My voice seems to be sliding back to East London.

'They said it.'

'Nah . . . I didn't need no knife to scare them off. You know, Carl, they act all brave but they ain't got no bottle.' *Bo'ul*, I pronounce it, and it gives me a flash of Arron's face as I say it, Arron saying, 'He ain't got no bo'ul,' and meaning me – 'They made it up to make themselves sound like big men but, you know, I just had to show them this . . .' I turn my hand into a fist, 'and they ran off, peein' their pants.'

He laughs a bit nervously and I think I've got away with it.

'Don't worry about it,' he says. 'See you at lunchtime.'

But I do worry about it. If this story gets to the head teacher then Joe Andrews will be excluded from school and exterminated by Doug. Then Tyler Lewis will probably be charged with murder. Because if they think I'm regularly waving a knife around, then they'll believe the people who say I was involved that day in another park far, far away. I think and think about what I can do to stop anyone talking, but I can't come up with an answer short of mass murder and obviously that's not the way to go.

Claire and I manage to pair up in Science and I forget all my worries. She's very serious about the work, and it's sweet the way she scrunches her face up when she looks at the test tube to read measurements out for me to write down. She's clipped her hair back from her face and she's wearing summer uniform, her arms covered with a cardigan. She's beginning to look normal. I scribble a note in faint pencil on my table of measurements: *I like your hair like that*, and she blushes and spends ages rubbing it out.

I whisper to her, 'Was your mum very cross?' and she nods and then writes another pencil note which says, *It's OK, I think*.

When we've finished and are clearing up, I tell her about Mum's plan to be Ellie's helper. She says, 'I know, they were talking about it last night. Ellie's really pleased. She thinks your mum will be great.'

'I don't know . . . it's not really her sort of thing.'

She looks at the test tube she's drying and says, 'Mum said you'll come and stay sometimes.' And when she looks up, we've both got silly grins on our faces.

'No talking,' shouts the teacher, and we get ready

for Maths. It's the first time I've ever been sad to finish a Science lesson.

Playing football with Carl's lot goes well at lunchtime. I take Brian and his mates along with me and they join in too. Carl mixes up the teams so we're not obliterated. He offers some good tips – 'You're faster than anyone on the pitch but you need to think about passing the ball. Your problem, mate, is that you forget you've got anyone else on your team.' – and I even score a goal, so I'm feeling pretty pleased with myself when we hear the bell go for the end of lunch.

But Ashley is waiting for me as I come off the football pitch. 'Walk with me?' she says, and I know it's an order.

'OK.' I can see people all around us noticing that we're together and nudging each other.

'How are you?' she asks.

'I'm fine.'

'Not missing me then?'

'I didn't say that.'

She's got her full warpaint on today and I don't fancy her at all, thank goodness.

'So . . . are you seeing anyone else then?'

'Give me a chance, Ash, we've not been split up for five minutes.' And anyway, what business is it of yours?

'Because I saw you with that retard Claire in Science.'

What? I can't believe it. 'I . . . you . . . what?'

'I saw you. Smiling at her . . . touching her hand. . .'

Bloody hell. 'And so? Your point is?' I say, cold and distant.

'Well, it doesn't look good for me, does it, if you split up with me and immediately start going out with the dorkiest girl in the year. I want you to keep away from that minger.'

I stop still and say, 'You can't talk about her like that. You shouldn't talk about anyone like that.' People are jostling all around us and I'm sure some of them are listening.

'Oooh,' she says, 'so you do like her? I didn't really believe it.'

'She's my friend. And you don't have any right to tell me who to be friends with.'

'I can tell you that she's a weirdo. And I can tell you that if she ever took her cardigan off, you wouldn't like what you'd see underneath.' And she laughs, a really nasty, sneery laugh.

'You bitch!' I say. I want to hit her. My hand flies up and I'm ready to lash out.

Then Brian bashes into me and says, 'Steady, mate.' And I come to my senses and lower my hand.

And there's a crowd of people all around and Ashley's laughing and saying, 'If you want to know any more about your little friend, just come and ask me, any time.' And I hear a squeaking sob and Claire's running away, pushing through the crowd to escape into the playground.

CHAPTER 24
Finding Claire

Should I run after her? I'm tempted to go off to my next lesson, let her recover on her own and not give the gossips anything more to chew on. But when do I ever do the right thing? Instead, I push my way through the crowds streaming into their classrooms then sprint after her and, being pretty fast, I catch up with her in the middle of the playground.

That's the middle of the deserted playground, overlooked by about fifty classrooms all packed with people.

'Come on, we can still get to PE,' I shout.

I thought she'd be crying but she isn't. She's white-faced and her fists are pressing to her mouth. She's looking from side to side, like a mouse cornered by a cat, desperate to escape. She gasps, 'Go away,' in what would be a fierce whisper if it hadn't had a hiccup in the middle that sounded like another sob.

'I'm not going away. Tell you what, I'll take you to the nurse. But we need to go inside right now.' And I jerk my head towards the watching windows, grab her elbow and pull her towards the door.

She gives a little yelp. And then she follows me inside and I can see the tears coming so I search my pockets for a handkerchief, but of course I haven't got one. I nobly offer my tie instead. She shakes her head and pulls a tissue out of her cardigan pocket.

A teacher comes out into the corridor and asks us what we think we're doing. 'Claire isn't feeling very well so I'm taking her to the nurse,' I say.

'Do you even know where the nurse's office is? Because it's not along here,' she says, looking curiously at Claire.

'Yes, we're just going.' And we walk along the corridor to the flight of stairs that leads to the sick room.

'Look, it's OK, it's OK,' I say as we get there. 'Ashley's only shown herself up as a complete bitch. No one knows anything about you. You have nothing to worry about.'

'I. . .' but she can't say anything.

I knock on the door and tell the nurse that Claire

has a migraine. She takes one look and puts her arm around Claire. 'I'll come and see you later,' I say. 'I hope you're feeling better soon.'

I sprint to the PE department. I should be swimming but I'm actually going to be sorting vile-smelling lost property. Carl's already knee-deep in ancient knickers and crusty shorts.

'Blimey,' he says, 'what was all that about in the playground? You looked like you were fighting her.'

"What? You couldn't see us from here."

"Mate, the whole school was watching," he says. "We were all late for PE. What's the story?"

'Women,' I say. 'You know what they're like.'

'Too right,' says Carl, and we sort the smelly piles into labelled and non-labelled while discussing Man Utd's prospects for the next season which, frankly, is exactly the kind of conversation I need right now, and by the end of the period I feel like Carl's my main man.

I want to make a swift exit, but they're all waiting for me. Lauren, Emily, Dani and Becca. Only Ashley's nowhere to be seen.

'What happened?' asked Becca. 'What happened to Claire? What were you doing in the playground? Had she had . . . you know . . . some kind of mental breakdown?'

I shrug. 'She wasn't feeling well. Had to go to the nurse. Migraine.'

'Yes, but what was it all about?' says Becca. 'Why were you shouting at her?'

'You're not seeing her, are you?' asks Lauren in a way that suggests that only someone very strange would have anything to do with Claire.

'Maybe she's got some sort of weird crush on you?' suggests Dani.

'What was Ashley going on about?' says Emily.

'Look, it's not for me to say what's going on in Ashley's mind. First she chucks me, and then she bitches about Claire because we happen to be friends.'

'Friends?' says Emily, like she can't believe her ears.

'Yup. Friends. I do athletics training with her sister, right. I know the whole family.'

'Yes, but *Claire*. . .'

I'm worried that I'm going to start blushing. 'There's nothing wrong with Claire. She's just a bit shy.'

As soon as I can shake them off I go back to the nurse's room. But Claire's not there. 'She left about five minutes ago,' says the nurse. 'What a shame, she could have done with someone to see her home. She was in a bit of a state.'

'You didn't ring her mum?'

'At work. Claire said she was OK to walk home.'

I don't think this is a good idea. What if Ashley's lying in wait for her? I'd follow her right away but I have to meet Ellie at the running track. As I walk there my mind's on Claire. She'll go home, no one will be there and . . . oh, my God.

I sprint up to Ellie, yelling, 'Keys, Ellie, keys. I need your house keys.'

'What on earth. . .?' says Ellie, but she fishes her keys out of her bag and gives them to me.

'I'm going to run to your house. Can you get there really quickly too? It's Claire . . . she's in danger. . . '

'You what?' says Ellie, but I'm running. I'm running down the High Street and around the corner. I'm bashing into people and swearing, and running across roads without looking properly so cars screech to a stop and swerve to avoid me.

And I'm at the top of their road and I'm running down and I'm praying – to Jesus, to Mary, whoever – that I'm going to get there in time.

And I run up Ellie's wheelchair ramp and I fumble with her set of keys and then I leave the door open so she can get in.

And I run up the stairs, two at a time and I get to Claire's door. Of course she's blocked it with a chair, so I kick and push and shout, 'Claire! It's me! Let me in!'

But she's done it really well and it takes an

almighty kick to finally topple the chair away.

I slam into the room and fall over the chair – damn – it's so bloody dark in here. But I know where to find Claire. I drag myself up and feel my way round her bed, while my eyes adjust to the darkness.

'Claire? Are you here? Are you OK?' Far, far away I hear Ellie calling me. 'Joe? What's going on?'

But I've found what I'm looking for. Claire is sitting propped up against the bed but she's fallen forward so her nose is touching her knees. She's not speaking – is she even conscious? – and when I touch her arm my hand feels wet and sticky.

I leap for the curtains and tug them apart so fiercely that the whole lot clatters to the ground. And I can see then that I feared right – she's cut herself, but it's not a neat, tidy little cut like usual, it's a big angry slash which is pumping blood over her skin and shirt.

'Ellie! Call an ambulance!' I yell.

Christ almighty. I need to do something fast. I take the knife from the floor and grab the sheet from her bed. I cut a strip of fabric from the sheet and loop it around her arm, just under and then over the wound, lifting her arm up as high as I can. I need a stick – the only thing I can find is a pencil which isn't really long enough, but I wind the sheet around it and then turn it around and around so the sheet tightens on her arm. I'm so scared that she's going to die. I'm screaming, 'Claire, wake up, Claire, wake up,' and her eyes flicker open and she stares at me as if I'm a stranger. And we sit there like that, waiting for help, with me concentrating all my effort on winding the sheet as tight as possible.

Ambulances come quicker here than they do in London. The door crashes open again and there're two paramedics, a man and a woman, who run over to Claire and push me out of the way. One takes the pencil from my hand. And I can't bear to look any more and I stumble down the stairs to Ellie, who gasps when she sees that my shirt's soaked in blood.

'Oh my God, what's happened? Did someone attack her? How did you know?'

I shake my head. 'No one attacked her. She did it herself. She cuts herself when she's upset, and she was very upset.'

'She does what? Oh, my God. Is she all right?'

'I don't know. She opened her eyes.'

One of the paramedics comes downstairs and says, 'Who put on the tourniquet? Was it you?'

'Yes.'

'Good job. When did you do it?'

'About ten minutes before you arrived.'

'Well done. We'll bring her downstairs now and we'll take her to hospital. Can one of you come with us?'

It should be Ellie really, but I'm not sure how it'll work with the wheelchair. She says, 'You go Joe, and I'll ring my dad and see what's happening about the boys. Mum's at the hospital already – that's where she works – general surgical.'

They bring Claire down the stairs on a stretcher and we get into the ambulance. Ellie shoves a jacket of her dad's into my hands and I put it on – it's a huge, smelly fleece thing but it covers the blood and it warms me up because although it's a hot summer's day I'm feeling cold and shivery.

We speed through the streets with the siren blaring and I'm remembering the ambulance I called to the park that day. The ambulance I never saw. The ambulance I didn't wait for. And I'm holding Claire's hand and I'm saying the Hail Mary in my head, because if it worked a miracle for Gran it might work one for Claire as well.

And we're in casualty, and Ellie must have got hold of her mum already because she's waiting there for us in her nurse's uniform, which reminds me a bit of Arron's mum, and she doesn't even speak to me, but she grabs Claire's hand and says, 'It's all right, darling, it's all right. Mum's here now, it's all right.'

They disappear down the corridor and I don't really know what to do, so I just sit down in a corner and wait.

And I see Ellie and her dad arrive, but they go straight past without seeing me and get taken off somewhere.

I suppose I should just go home but I don't seem to be able to move. I wish I could call up my gran to come and look after me. After a bit I think about Mum saying, 'It'll do for now,' and I think, well, sometimes you have to compromise. And I send her a text: *pls Nic cm n gt me, at hsptl, a&e Ty.*

Her first text says, *wtf*? And then she sends another, *omg r u OK*? And then she sends another, *on way*. She and Alistair arrive about twenty minutes later – I must have interrupted their big date. She spots me right away.

'Are you OK? What happened? Did someone attack you?'

Alistair looks a bit bemused, given that I am pretty obviously unharmed.

I shake my head. 'No, I'm fine. It's Claire, you know. Ellie's sister.'

'What happened to her?'

But I can't say. And Mum sees it and she gives me a hug, and we just sit there for a bit with her arms around me until Alistair says, 'There's Ellie. Hey, Ellie, over here.'

Ellie comes over and she's obviously a bit surprised to see Alistair, and she's looking from Mum to him and back again and working out what he's doing there. I don't think she's all that delighted.

She leans forward: 'Joe, Claire's all right. They stopped the bleeding. They're stitching it up. She's got to stay overnight, but she'll recover. They say you might have saved her life with that tourniquet.'

'Oh,' I say. 'Good. Is she awake? Will you say hi from me?'

But Ellie shakes her head and says, 'She's asleep and they'll keep her asleep for some time. You might be able to come and see her tomorrow.'

So Alistair takes us home in his Ford Fiesta, and when we're in the car, Mum asks me, 'However did you know how to make a tourniquet? You've never even done a first aid course.'

I answer, 'I watched Arron's mum do it once.'

She's satisfied with that because Arron's mum is a nurse and I did spend a lot of time at their house. And it was true what I said.

But if I'd been telling the whole truth I would have said a bit more. And this is what I would have said: 'I watched Arron's mum do it once. I watched her that day after we ran out of the park. I watched her that day I stabbed Arron.'

CHAPTER 25
Ashley's Story

Alistair isn't the complete waste of space he looks. At home, he makes me a cup of horribly sweet tea and says I have to drink it for shock. Then he looks in our fridge, which is empty as usual, and drives to Tesco to stock up. When he comes back, he cooks stir-fry chicken and noodles and opens a bottle of wine for him and Mum. I'm feeling a lot more friendly towards him as I eat, although he should realise that the way to my Mum's heart isn't through feeding her.

She's already run me a bath and I'm having supper in my pyjamas. Maureen's not here – there's a note which says, 'Had to go, called out on urgent job elsewhere. Your gran is doing well. See you soon.' I'm kind of grateful she didn't see me covered in blood.

Mum pushes the noodles around on her plate and then goes and looks at my school uniform. She's got a look on her face like she's going to throw up.

'God, what on earth happened? There's so much blood here – what the hell did she look like?' I don't want to think about that, and I think she realises because she doesn't ask me any more.

'Ellie never talks about her sister,' says Alistair. 'She comes along to training sometimes. Just sits there in the corner reading, never gets involved. Poor kid, she must have been in a terrible state.'

Mum's still looking at the clothes. 'The shirt doesn't matter, you've got plenty, and I think the stains will come out of the blazer if we put it in to wash now – good thing it's black – but the tie is ruined.' She holds it up – the grey and blue stripes are splattered with dark brown. 'We'll get a new one tomorrow. You may as well take the day off school, get over the shock and tell me what happened properly.' And I nod and say, 'Yeah,' and duck when she tries to give me a kiss. Luckily there's still a sleeping pill by my bed, so I know I can avoid bad dreams.

But I'm up early as usual and get ready for my gym session. I'm not giving anyone a chance to take my access card away; I'd rather not wait and see if Alistair is still here to cook us breakfast, and I'm not up for a heart-to-heart with Mum about Claire. I'll go to school, I reckon, and then I'll swing by the hospital and hopefully Mum will be out with Alistair again tonight. And maybe she'll overlook that I skipped the debrief.

The blazer looks fine, I have a clean shirt, but the tie is no good. I finger the key to the lost property cupboard – there are plenty of old, unlabelled ties there. I sneak one out on the way to the changing room. Now no one will know a thing about what happened yesterday.

Carl and I have a good training session. We're competitive and we set targets which push us both further. It's working well, I think, this restorative justice scheme. I'm really feeling OK, considering what happened yesterday. In fact, when I think about Ellie telling me that I might have saved Claire's life I feel really chuffed with myself. Surely, saving someone's life is such a great thing to have done that it counts against other bad stuff? I can't be such a bad person after all; sometimes I get it just right.

This good feeling lasts all the way to registration. I'm there on time, properly dressed, ready for the day ahead. I'm talking to Brian about our football match, getting my books together for French. Ashley ignores me and no one else asks about Claire. They don't know. Maybe no one will ever find out. I hope not – Claire would find it so humiliating to be gossiped about. For a moment I feel sick when I think about what it would be like if all the bitchy girls knew that she was cutting herself.

Then Mr Hunt comes into the classroom, looks around the room and says, 'Joe Andrews, Ashley Jenkins, straight to the head teacher.'

We walk there together in silence. She's looking nervous, thoughtful. I don't feel I have anything to worry about. I'm the hero of this particular episode and she's the villain. I saved Claire's life. I did something good. We reach the door of her mother's office.

And then she turns to me and says, 'You better back up everything I say.'

'What?'

'Don't contradict me. Don't tell Mr Naylor what I said about Claire. Or I'll have Jordan and Louis down here quicker than you can say . . .' she gives me a flickering smile, 'knife.'

Oh, my God. Oh, Jesus. And we go into the office and she says, 'Hi Mum, we're here to see the head teacher.'

Mr Naylor is seated at his desk and gestures for us to sit down opposite him. I'm keeping a wary eye on Ashley. 'Good morning, Mr Naylor,' she says, all demure. I mumble something.

'I'm sure you both know why you're here,' says Mr Naylor. 'The very shocking news about Claire Langley in your class.'

'I don't know, I'm sorry, Mr Naylor,' says Ashley. She lies like an expert. I close my eyes and pray that he will be discreet. But no.

'Claire slashed her wrist yesterday afternoon. She lost a lot of blood and had to be rushed to hospital. Thankfully she is now making a good recovery.'

He makes it sound like she was trying to kill herself. I have to say something.

'She didn't slash her wrist . . . she just cut herself.'

Mr Naylor and Ashley both look at me like I'm mad. I shut up.

'Claire's parents spoke to me this morning and I want to find out exactly what was happening in the lunch break and afterwards yesterday – the period, Joe, when you were seen acting aggressively towards Ashley here, and then straight afterwards were witnessed by half the school shouting at Claire and manhandling her in the playground.'

Eh? 'No . . . it wasn't like that,' I say, but I don't sound very convincing, even to myself.

Ashley says, 'Mr Naylor, I've known Claire for years. She's a really sweet girl, not very confident . . . you know . . . she's quite young. I noticed Joe had his eye on her and I thought that was totally wrong. I know him and what he's like. I wanted to protect Claire from him . . . from what he gets up to. So I told him to stay away from her . . . from my friend. And he didn't like it and he called me a bitch and I thought he was going to hit me.'

'I . . . I . . . never hit you. . .'

'Only because Brian told you not to. Anyway, I think Claire overheard and got a bit upset. She's never had a boy interested in her before. I think she was really easy prey for Joe. Joe was angry with me and I was scared. And she ran away and he chased her. I don't know what happened after that. I felt a bit upset and I went to the girls' loo to . . . to recover. . .'

She should get an Oscar. Even I am beginning to be taken in by her. I don't know what to do. . . She's twisting everything, she's lying, but I can't risk Jordan and Louis telling about the knife.

Mr Naylor says, 'What do you mean, Ashley, what Joe gets up to? I know it's embarrassing, but it's important to get these things out in the open.'

Old perv. I know what he's hoping for, and Ashley gives it all she's got.

'We went out for a bit and at first I thought he was great but. . .' she wipes away a tear, 'he wanted too much. Too much, too soon. And he's very forceful – pushy – in getting his own way. I had to finish with him. I was a bit scared.'

Oh my God. What is she accusing me of? Forceful? Pushy?

'Is this true, Joe?'

Is what true? 'I . . . I . . . I didn't think I was doing

306

anything wrong. Ashley . . . she said her parents made her chuck me because of what happened in the swimming pool. . .'

Now why did I have to remind him of that?

'Ah, yes. You haven't had a very happy start at Parkview, have you? It's probably very different from what you're used to,' says Mr Naylor, like I'm a Neanderthal caveman or something. 'Now, Claire's mother backs up what Ashley's been saying here. She tells me she's been very worried because you've spent hours on end locked in Claire's bedroom in the dark with her, and she's also worried that you might have been trying to pressurise her into something she wasn't ready for.'

Ashley's glaring at me.

'Claire's my friend,' I say. 'A really good friend. My best friend. I wasn't pressurising her . . . I saved her life yesterday. Didn't her mum mention that?'

'She was very perturbed that you seemed to know that Claire had been regularly cutting herself yet had not sought help for her. She even suggested that you might have been involved somehow with this . . . this mutilation.'

'I saved her life. . . I would never do anything bad to her.'

'Joe, half the school saw you shouting at her and

307

pushing her around in the playground. I have a report here from the deputy head. She says Claire seemed terrified of you.'

'No . . . really . . . I was just trying to help her. . . I took her to the nurse. Ask her . . . she'll say I was being nice. . .'

Mr Naylor turns to Ashley. 'Ashley, thank you very much for coming here today. I am sorry if this has been difficult for you and I can assure you that we will do everything possible to protect you from aggressive behaviour in the future.'

This doesn't sound good. I try again.

'Why don't you talk to Claire?' I plead. 'She'll tell you I wasn't doing anything bad to her.'

'In due course I will, I am sure. Now Ashley, if you go back to class I will talk to Joe alone.'

As Ashley leaves she shoots me a glance that makes it very obvious that the news that I've been spending time with Claire while officially still with her did not go unnoticed.

'Joe,' says Mr Naylor, 'bullying girls, bullying girls for sex, that is really the lowest of the low. Boys who don't understand that no means no are a danger to society.'

'But I didn't. . .'

'I am going to have to think very hard about how to deal with this. I shall need to speak to Ashley's parents and also Claire's. I am going to suspend you for the rest of the day and . . . is your mother now returned?'

'Yes.'

'I would like to see both of you tomorrow morning, eleven o'clock. Now leave. And try not to get into any trouble between now and tomorrow. Do you think you can manage that?'

I nod – yes, you sarcastic old tosser – but I'm beginning to wonder. Maybe I'm destined to get into trouble again and again and again, and it's going to get worse and worse until fate or God or whatever has severely punished me for everything I'm getting away with.

CHAPTER 26
The Wolf

Joe Andrews can't survive this. This is beyond bad. Sexual harassment? Or was Ashley suggesting something even worse? But what the hell can I do?

Claire's mum and dad. I need to talk to them, explain, make them understand. Maybe they can explain to Mr Naylor that I'm actually a hero. I need to go to the hospital and find them. I need to go now. But I really don't feel up to telling Mum I've been suspended again.

I go to the nurse's office. 'Hello again,' she says. I tell her that I think I'm about to vomit. It's not altogether untrue. 'You are looking pale,' she says. She calls home and I can hear Mum's voice at the end of the line saying, 'I don't even know why he went in today. I told him last night he wouldn't be up to it.'

Twenty minutes later Mum and I are walking out

310

of the school gates. Alistair's Ford Fiesta is parked outside – so he *did* stay the night. I decide I don't care. I have enough to worry about. 'Can you take me to the hospital?' I ask.

'I didn't know you were feeling that ill, darling,' says Mum, all concerned, and I say, 'No, I'm not, but I want to see Claire. I need to see her now.'

So they drive me to the hospital and insist on coming in with me, which I'm not happy about, but then we find out that Claire's just been discharged and so it's good, really, that they are there to drive me to her house.

'Look, I'll leave you here,' says Alistair. 'I think it'd be a bit much for everyone if I come too.'

'Mum, you go with him,' I say, but she replies, 'D'you know what, I'm a bit fed up with taking orders from you. I think I should know what's been going on.' As I walk slowly to Claire's front door she gives Alistair a kiss, a long lingering kiss – this is so *not* the moment – and he says, 'I'll call you later.'

She catches me up and rings the doorbell. Claire's dad comes to the door. He looks tired and annoyed. 'We've only just got back from the hospital,' he says. 'It'd be better if you could come back later.'

'Please,' I say, 'I really need to talk to you, to you and Janet. I don't have to bother Claire if you don't want me to.'

'If you'd be kind enough to give him some time,' says Mum. 'He's very upset over what happened.'

He scratches his head and says, 'Look, son, we owe you because she could have been dead if you hadn't helped her out when you did. Come in and we'll have a chat.'

He takes us through to the kitchen and we sit down at the big table. Then he disappears upstairs for a long time. As we wait I look around. There are so many pictures of Ellie, so much stuff that belongs to the boys, but you'd never know Claire lived in this house. But what made her so invisible – was it her, or did the rest of her family just not leave her enough space? What would Claire be like if she was an only child like me?

Eventually they come and sit at the table with us. Janet and Gareth. Two nice people who look about ten years older than they did last time I saw them. Janet has little red puffy eyes and the tip of her nose is scarlet. Gareth's face is white under his freckles. And now they are here, I don't know what to say. Lucky that my Mum tagged along.

'Janet, Gareth, we're just so sorry about Claire,' she says. 'I'm sorry to intrude, but Joe was anxious to find out how she was. He had quite a shock.'

'Did he now?' says Janet in a cold voice that you wouldn't think could come from such a kind person.

'Well, we'd like to talk to him, find out what's really been going on.'

They all look at me. I don't know where to begin. It's hard when you suspect people are thinking bad things about you but they haven't said them yet.

'I knew she was cutting herself, but she said she would stop,' I say. 'I was trying to help her . . . she's my friend. . .' I fade to silence. I can feel massive hostility radiating from the other side of the table.

'How did you know this about Claire?' says Janet. 'What have you been doing to her, locked in her room? We trusted you, Joe, invited you into our home . . . made you feel welcome. . .'

'I didn't do anything to Claire. Really nothing. We were only talking.' I'm getting a little bit louder. It's not nice to be accused of things you haven't done.

'Talking about what?'

'Just things. I like talking to Claire and I think she likes talking to me.'

'Oh yes, she certainly likes you all right,' says Janet, and she sounds like she's only just holding herself back from screaming at me. 'Crazy about you. I just wonder what else was going on apart from talking.' I bet she did notice about the shirt buttons that time.

'He's said they were just talking,' says Mum.

'Are you accusing him of lying?'

'Well . . . you must admit it's a bit suspicious. I mean, no offence, but they are very different. Claire's so young for her age, very shy, very quiet. She's still a child. Joe's so streetwise, and he seems much older. What would they have in common?'

Streetwise is just one harmless word, but she rolls a lot more into it: dirty, violent, chav, liar, molester and ASBO, with just a touch of pram-face as well. I tense, waiting for my mum to explode.

'Maybe they were both a bit lonely and looking for a friend,' she says, and I could hug her.

'I didn't do anything bad to Claire,' I say. 'It's true. . . I totally respect her and I care about her and I think she's the nicest person I've ever met. To be honest, we did kiss twice, but nothing bad, really nothing . . . please ask her. Ask her if I did anything bad to her.' I'm almost crying by the time I get to the end of this speech, mainly from complete and utter embarrassment.

They're all looking a bit more sympathetic. This might be all right. But then I remember. I did do something bad to Claire. I did bully her. Here in this kitchen. Janet's watching me intently and she says, 'What's going on, Joe? Why do you suddenly look like that? Why are you chewing your lip?'

'I . . . just remembered something.'

They're all waiting. My mouth is completely dry.

'I . . . I was mean to Claire. Once. Here. But not in the way that Mr Naylor means.'

This means nothing to them as – thank God – they weren't there to hear what Mr Naylor had to say. But I've said enough anyway.

'What the hell did you do to our daughter?' shouts Gareth, and I think for a minute that he's going to punch me.

'I . . . I . . . she found out a secret and I just sort of scared her, sort of hurt her, just a little bit so she wouldn't tell. But I did apologise, I really did, and I think she understood.'

I catch a quick glimpse of Mum's face and have to look away. She's looking disgusted, frightened and sad all at once. Janet gets up. 'I think we've heard enough. I think you'd better leave now, Joe, and don't bother Claire again. And I'm going to tell Ellie to stop training with you as well.'

'But can't I just see Claire?' I ask hopelessly. 'Just to explain . . . to say goodbye?'

'I don't think that's a good idea, is it?' says Janet, and Mum says, 'Come on now, you've said enough.'

She gets up and turns to Claire's parents: 'I had no idea . . . no idea about any of this. He's never acted remotely like this in his life before. I can't apologise enough.'

We're walking towards the front door and I'm walking out of Claire's life forever and I don't know how I'm going to do it. And then I hear her voice.

'What's going on?'

I turn around. She's standing at the top of the stairs, wrapped up in a dressing gown, hood pulled up over her head. She looks pale and small and her hair is all over her face again. She could be about ten years old. I can't bear not to say goodbye. And I run up the stairs and pull her into my arms.

'You get down here at once,' yells Claire's dad, but I can't because Claire is clinging on to me. We must look like Little Red Riding Hood and the big bad wolf. I'm the wolf, obviously.

'Claire, I'm sorry, I told them about that time in the kitchen . . . and they're all furious with me, and they don't want us to see each other again . . . I'm sorry, it was my fault. . .'

Her face is buried in my shirt and all I can feel are her arms around me. Just for a moment I feel safe and loved. And then she takes my hand and sits down on the top stair, pulling me down next to her. She pushes her hair away from her face. 'We're going to talk about this,' she says. 'Joe's not going anywhere.'

It's quite funny really. They're all looking up at us cuddled together and no one's saying anything. Then her mum says, 'For heaven's sake, Claire, you ought to be in bed,' and Claire says, 'I'm not going back to bed unless Joe comes with me,' and she blushes bright red and I think I do too, because that wasn't the most helpful thing to say just now.

Mum says, 'Why don't we all go upstairs, then Claire can lie down and we can all talk a bit more?'

And everyone seems to agree that's a good idea, so we go into Janet and Gareth's bedroom and Claire gets into the big double bed and I sit down nervously by her side and the three parents stand over us.

Janet says, 'Claire, Joe's just admitted hurting you. We can't allow you to go on seeing him, love. You don't want friends like that.'

Claire looks tiny and pale and weak, but she's really determined.

'Mum, in case you hadn't noticed, I haven't got any other friends. Joe only hurt me for about twenty seconds, then he immediately started begging me to be his friend. He thought he was being all scary but I could tell he was just putting it on. He was scared, I could see. He apologised, and he explained and I understood why he did it. He would never do it again.'

I'm really hopeful after she says this, but then my

mum opens her big mouth.

'Claire,' she says, and she's not looking at me. 'Claire, it's never acceptable for a boy to hurt a girl. Never. Not even for twenty seconds.'

I can't believe she's doing this to me. I'm her son. Doesn't she care about me? How can she? Why?

And then she says, 'Believe me, I know what I'm talking about,' and I know. It's like I never knew and I always knew. I know why my dad disappeared out of our lives all those years ago. And I know what we're both scared of in me.

CHAPTER 27
When I Was Joe

Claire opens her mouth to argue, but Mum says, 'I'm going to take Joe home now, and we're going to have a talk, and I think you need to talk to your parents too. I'm sorry, but I think you'd better say goodbye for now.' She looks at Janet and Gareth. 'Maybe we could give them a few minutes?'

They go out on to the landing and we're left together. I put my head down on the pillow next to her. 'I'm so sorry,' I say, 'I've screwed everything up.'

And she says, 'You talk to her and explain and I'll talk to them. Don't give up. You're so important to me.'

'I don't know what's going to happen now. There's a load of stuff going on at school. Ashley. . .' But I can't even finish the sentence.

'It'll be all right,' she says. 'Don't give up.'

And we kiss, and it's the best feeling in the world to taste her sweet lips, and to stroke her soft hair.

But I have almost given up, and I think she realises.

Mum and I walk to the bus stop in silence, and we sit on the bus and get all the way home without saying a word. And all the time I'm getting more and more angry with her for interfering. And for all the things she hasn't told me. And for letting this happen. All of this. It's her fault. I think the anger is going to choke me.

I'm not talking to her about anything. I'm not talking to her ever again. I'm going to ask the police to provide a different appropriate adult. I throw myself down on the sofa and switch on the television. There's a new episode of *The Simpsons* and it's really funny. I concentrate hard on zoning everything else out of my head, and it works. I can do this. It's all about focus.

She gives me five minutes and then she marches in and switches it off. 'Hey! I was watching that.'

'For Christ's sake, Ty, don't you think it's more important to talk about what just happened?'

'No,' I say, and I switch it back on again.

'Ty, I want to know what's been going on. What did you do to Claire? Why?'

'Why didn't you find that out before you told her she shouldn't see me again? I'm not telling you anything.

I'm not even talking to you.'

I turn up the volume. She stands in front of the screen and puts her hand out for the remote.

'Give it to me.'

'No.'

'Give it to me.'

'Make me.'

She can't make me. I'm bigger and stronger than her. This thought freaks me out so much that after a minute's furious silence, I fling it on the floor by her feet.

'Leave me alone, you interfering bitch,' I say, but I mutter it in Turkish, so she ignores me.

'Right. Now. Tell me,' she orders.

'You know it. You know . . . I already told.'

'No, you didn't. You didn't tell us any details.'

'It was the day of the swimming pool thing. You were in the hospital with Gran. My contact lenses came out underwater and Claire saw that my eyes were green. So she asked and I had to . . . I tried to scare her . . . not to tell anyone.'

'What the hell did you do? Did you . . . you didn't hit her, did you?'

'No!'

'Thank Christ for that. So what did you do?'

'I took hold of her wrists . . . and kind of squeezed.'

'Oh. That wasn't a nice thing to do, Ty. A sweet little

girl like that. How could you?' She sits down in the armchair, which is better than having her stand over me. Her face looks all twisted and ill.

'I said I was sorry. And I explained . . . I explained why. . .'

I stop. Her eyes are wide and her mouth's dropped open.

'What do you mean, you explained?' she says slowly.

Oh, God.

'I just sort of explained . . . that it had to be secret. . .'

'What exactly did you just sort of explain?'

I'm not telling. I'm actually scared of her.

'Just that it had to be secret. . .'

'I don't believe you. Why did she say she understood?'

'She's very understanding.'

'Tell me exactly what you said. Or I will go back to their house and ask her, and I will embarrass you so much that when I've finished she will never want to speak to you again.'

I can't believe that my own mother is doing this. Gran would never ever treat me like this.

'I told her. I told her about witness protection and being Ty and Joe and everything. But she'll keep it secret. It's OK.'

'Ty! What were you thinking? You've put her in danger.'

'No . . . she won't ever tell anyone. Claire's sound, you can trust her. '

'You're not meant to tell anyone anything. How could you? She's in danger and you're in even more danger. What if she tells someone? What if someone gets their hands on her and does what they did to your gran? I'm going to have to ring Doug.'

'Please Nicki, please, *please*. . . I'm begging you, Nic, please don't tell Doug.'

'Jesus, Ty, what's happened to you? You used to be such a sensible boy, so gentle . . . so nice. . .'

'Shut up! I hate you!' My volume control has gone and this comes out as a shout.

'Don't talk to me like that,' she snarls. 'It's completely unacceptable for you to tell the truth to every girl you fancy. You were nearly shot, for God's sake. Think about Mr Patel's shop. Want that to happen to Claire? To Ellie? We can't mess around here.'

I go back to begging. 'Please, Nic, *please*. . .'

'Look, it's not so good for me either, right? I've just met a really nice bloke and it's all been screwed up. Story of my bloody life.'

She goes into the kitchen to phone Doug and I stamp upstairs and lie on my bed. I think about all the things I'm looking forward to as Joe. Running proper races over the summer. Joining the athletics squad. Maybe being in the football team one day. The end of term party – I'd been planning to give Claire a makeover and take her to the party and everyone would realise she was actually completely beautiful, and I'd be the one who had transformed her.

And talking to Claire, and going places with Claire, and kissing her again, and spending time generally with Claire.

None of these things are going to happen. I'm even feeling miserable about not being able to finish the lost property cupboard with Carl.

Mum comes upstairs and sits down on the bed next to me. 'What did he say?' I ask, and my voice comes out all shaky.

'He'll come as soon as possible with Maureen. They're going to talk about it with you and make a decision.' She puts her hand on my shoulder and I angrily shrug it off. 'But it doesn't sound good, I'm sorry.'

Doug and Maureen arrive about nine o'clock, just as I've decided they've had an accident on the motorway and we're never going to see them again. Mum talks to them first and then calls me to come down. I don't want to look them in the eye. It's Maureen who says, quite nicely, 'It's all gone a bit wrong, hasn't it, Ty? Doug had a call from your head teacher to say you were suspended again.'

They must have told Mum about it because she's looking even more devastated than before, and she stubs out her cigarette like she's trying to grind the entire ashtray into dust. 'How come you never told me?' she says. 'Bullying another girl? Suspended for the second time?'

'I never – she's just a liar. . .'

And then I remember Maureen and Doug heard me trying to get Ashley to come up to my bedroom and I shut up again. They won't believe me.

'It's no good, mate,' says Doug. 'It's a shame, but I think you're going to have to be moved on. Too much trouble here. You've become too visible. And we can't have you putting another family at risk.'

I don't say much. They're all sitting there looking at me and I know that somehow I've screwed everything up again. It seems such a big punishment for the one time I did something good. But maybe life works a bit like Tesco Clubcard points in reverse – you do your normal stuff and it all adds up without you thinking about it, and then suddenly you get a load of vouchers in the post. Or, in my case, you make lots of crap decisions and they all add up to your life falling apart altogether.

I pack my iPod, I pack my Man Utd scarf from Dad. I pack my photos and two lots of school books. I pack all Joe's cool new clothes, his running shoes, his contact lenses and his hair dye. I pack Claire's two scrumpled notes. I try very hard not to feel anything at all. And I lie down on my bed and remember the time when I was Joe.

When Mum's ready, they load the bags into the car. But I don't get up. I'm thinking crazy thoughts about running away. Going to live secretly in Claire's bedroom or her garden shed or something. Maureen comes and sits on the bed next to me. 'Time to go,' she says.

'I'm not going,' I say. 'It's not fair. I like it here. I need to be here.'

'You'll do all right somewhere else,' says Maureen. 'You can't hang on here and put yourself and other people in danger.'

'I don't care.'

'Think how your gran would feel if anything happened to you. She doesn't deserve to lose you. She's doing so well too, off to join your aunties any day. Think about how this Claire would feel if you were hurt because of her. Is she a bit special?'

And I can only nod and gulp, and Maureen gives me a hug and says, 'It'll work out.'

'Am I a bad person, Maureen?' I ask. It feels like

I've never known for sure.

She says, 'Seems to me you've always been a very good boy, very hard working, never in trouble. But a lot of difficult things have happened to you in the last few weeks and, just occasionally, you've not shown good judgement. Happens to everyone. Doesn't make you a bad person. I don't think you're a bully.'

It's reassuring, but she doesn't know the whole truth. And she's police, so I can't tell her.

CHAPTER 28
Mel and Jake

So now I have to get into the car and watch the street lights of this not-so-boring little town disappear into dark country roads. And then a motorway, lit up orange and eerie. And then we're checking into another hotel, another little room, where there's no room to unpack and nothing to do but watch a big screen TV.

It's different staying here though. The hotel is pretty similar, but we've changed. I go for a run every day, and there's a leisure centre where I swim and use the gym. Mum comes with me sometimes. And we talk a bit too, and I tell her a little about how awful St Saviour's was and how Arron and I weren't really friends any more. I don't tell her what the boys used to say about her. She doesn't need that. We avoid talking about

Claire, but I explain a bit about Ashley and she seems to understand.

One day I'm feeling brave and I say, 'What did you mean that day – you know – when you told Claire you knew what you were talking about?' And she replies, 'Oh, I heard so many terrible things working for a solicitor. I know how important it is for girls to realise that they mustn't take any kind of abuse.' I say, 'But it wasn't abuse,' and she shakes her head at me. And I know she's not telling the whole truth, and I think she knows that I know.

Maureen chops my hair a bit and dyes it a different colour, a kind of dark reddish brown, which doesn't look right to me. The eyebrows are still in place and she says I can go back to having green eyes, which I'm pleased about, but she wants me to wear glasses, which I'm not. I suspect she's designed my new look to make me as unattractive to girls as possible. She didn't try and change anything about my clothes though, so I still feel there's a basic Joe-ness about me. Joe with geeky specs and a bad haircut.

I try and find a computer to use, but there's no internet cafe and the only library I can find won't let you have a ticket unless you have a permanent address. So I can't even email Claire. And I don't know if I should anyway. I feel some scary emotion which is beyond sad whenever I think about her – you could call it despair, I suppose – so I'm working on blanking her out. It's like she's left an aching emptiness inside me.

Maureen comes to see us to talk about where we're going next. This time, she says, we can choose our own names. It's surprisingly difficult. I want a cool name, something like Spike. Mum is reading *Heat* magazine and suggesting stupid celebrity mother/son combos like Jordan and Junior, Gwen and Zuma, Angelina and Knox or Maddox or Pax. Pax isn't too bad, I suppose, but I think she's joking anyway. I counter with Marge and Bart but she's not having it.

Maureen says we're both daft and we have to be sensible. So we agree on Melanie and Jake. Mel and Jake Ferguson. I suggested the surname after Sir Alex. He's the manager of Man Utd and it'd be fantastic to be part of his family, except I think he'd shout at me a lot because that's what he's like.

And on a burning hot summer's day we leave the hotel and Doug takes us to another small town, a seaside town, with noisy seagulls circling overhead and a crumbling pier and a long grey beach.

This time we're in a flat and it's small, but it's bright and white and it smells of fresh paint and there's a stepladder which leads out on to a flat roof with a view of the sea. It's not bad. It feels a bit like being on holiday.

'Is this really a good idea?' says Mum. 'Don't these seaside places get a lot of visitors?'

'You're a long way from London,' says Doug. 'We think it'll be fine. This isn't a big place for day trippers. There's not much going on here.' Doug really knows how to sell a place.

We go and buy school uniform three days before the start of term. As I look at myself in the changing room mirror – dark green blazer, black trousers, grey jumper, white shirt, green tie, stupid red hair (I really don't like the hair) and steel-rimmed glasses – I'm trying to get an idea of what sort of a person Jake is going to be. He doesn't look as cool as Joe, that's for sure, but he's tougher than Ty ever was. He looks a bit miserable, to be honest, hiding behind his specs.

We get back to the flat and we're unpacking all the stuff, and Mum is talking about getting Maureen to call the Open University and see if her credits can be transferred to her new name so she can pick up her studies again. 'Only two more courses and I've got a law degree,' she says. And then we hear a knock at the door.

'Who on earth is that?' says Mum. 'Doug said he wouldn't be back until Tuesday to hear how your first day went.'

We both freeze, looking at each other nervously.

She says, 'You go out on to the roof and I'll see who it is.'

So I'm lying on the roof, watching the seagulls circling overhead and pretending they are vultures about to pick out my eyes, when DI Morris and DC Bettany step out to join me. 'Don't get up,' says DI Morris, and he sits down next to me. DC Bettany gets out his notebook. I'm beginning to hate that notebook.

So there's nowhere to run when DI Morris says, 'I've been talking to a friend of yours and I'd like to ask you some more questions.'

'Oh, yeah?' I say cautiously, watching three gulls fight viciously over a piece of fish. I'm wondering if he's been to see Claire, and hoping he doesn't mean Ashley.

'I want to ask a bit more about what happened before you got to the park,' he says.

And I know who he means. He doesn't mean Ashley. He doesn't mean Claire.

He's been talking to my friend Arron Mackenzie.

CHAPTER 29
Rio

Arron promised. He promised me. 'I'll never tell it was you,' he said. But of course six months in a youth offenders' institution can change anyone. I wouldn't blame him if he's told them what I did. But that doesn't mean I'm giving anything away right now.

I sit up. 'I thought you weren't meant to be talking to me without a lawyer here. Or my mum, anyway.'

DI Morris says, 'Here she comes.' And Mum's climbing out on to the roof as well. She sits down and says, 'Are you sure you don't want to come back downstairs? It's a bit more comfortable.'

'We shouldn't be too long,' says DI Morris.

Oh. That doesn't sound like. . . I'll just wait and see what he asks. No point rushing into anything.

He's asking about the paper round. About whether I ever saw anyone using the bags to transport anything other than newspapers and magazines. Whether any little packages were involved. And I say no, I was always the first one to get my bag and I had the longest round and they were all finished before me. It's true. I don't know if anything else I tell him will be.

Then he says, 'I want to ask you about a meeting that you and Arron had with the youths that you identified as being with Arron in the park. Julian White – known as Jukes – and Mikey Miller. Is that correct?'

'It wasn't a meeting like that. They were just there when we got off the tube on the way home from school. . . I thought maybe they'd been bowling. The bowling alley's just there by the tube station, you know. . .' Of course I realise now that Arron must have arranged it.

'I just knew them from boxing. Friends of Nathan, at least, I think so. . . '

They were scary, these guys. We met them by the bowling alley on the way home from school and walked with them down to the bus stop. We stopped outside one of those shops that sell knocked-off mobiles. 'What you want from us, boys?' asked one, and Arron said we needed protection. He'd been mugged the week before, threatened with a blade and robbed of his watch, and he was jumpy. That's when we both started carrying knives.

'You gotta earn dat protecshun,' said Mikey. He's one of those white guys who talk all the time in gangsta, have massive tattoos and go heavy on the bling. He had huge diamond studs in his ears and a gold tooth, and the sort of gold chains that you only wear in our area if you're tough enough to defend them. 'You gotta do some li'l jobs for us.'

I was too scared even to speak but Arron said, 'OK, man, no problem.' And they all laughed together.

'Wha' abou' 'im?' said Jukes, jerking his thumb at me. Jukes isn't one for the bling, and if you saw him in the street, the only thing that might make you look twice is the eagle tattooed on his arm. It's only because I've seen him fight at boxing club that I know how much power is packed into his stocky body. I shook my head and stared at the gum-splattered pavement, and the two of them laughed. And Arron joined in after a few minutes and said, 'He ain't got no bo'ul.'

'So you thought Arron was looking for protection from Jukes's gang,' says DC Bettany.

'No . . . yes . . . sort of. I didn't think they were a gang.'

'And you knew he was going to the park to do a job for them?'

'Umm . . . I didn't know exactly. He asked me to come along, and then he started talking about protection again, said I'd be a target for everyone unless I had it. But I said I wouldn't come. I didn't know what to do. I didn't want to get into trouble.'

I don't tell him that Arron wanted me to do the job for Jukes and Mikey. That he said, 'Prove yourself a man.' When I said no, he spat on the ground and said, 'You're letting me down, Ty. You're just a big girl.'

'You didn't want to get into trouble,' said DI Morris, and then, 'Well, you seem to have changed your tune recently. Suspended twice from school in as many weeks.'

'Sorry. It was an accident. I don't really know how it happened.'

'Don't let it happen again.'

'No,' I say, and think about what a completely boring person Jake Ferguson's going to have to be. He's going to have to make much better choices than Joe or Ty. I don't know if I'm up to it.

'So then you followed Arron?'

I've told them about this again and again. I'd followed him all the way to the lower entrance. It's only a small park. It stretches between two streets, up a hill, with a pond at the bottom and a children's playground at the top. Arron and I used to play a lot in that playground when we were younger. There's a wooden castle with walkways and a slide, and the usual swings and stuff.

We loved it there.

He'd gone in towards the pond and I ran around the perimeter fence, up the hill on the other side, and climbed over the fence at the top. No one was playing in the playground because it was getting dark and it was drizzling. I climbed into the castle, because from there you can see the whole path and everyone coming up the hill, but no one can see you.

'I followed him. Just in case he got hurt or anything. I didn't know what was going to happen. '

'Right. And when did Jukes and Mikey turn up?'

'They were walking up with Arron. They must have met him down by the pond. And then they all hid themselves and waited for someone to come along. But I've told you all this before. '

I'm thinking about that boy walking up the path towards them. I think about him a lot. He was singing along to his iPod. He was only the same age as me. He wore a hoodie and baggy trousers and he was eating chips and he looked just like all of us, except he was black and we were white. And I wanted to shout and warn him, but he wouldn't have heard because he was plugged into his music.

Arron leapt out at him. He had his knife out and he hit the boy's chips out of his hand. 'What've you got for me?' he said. You'd have thought the boy would have just given up right away, handed over the iPod and run away. That's what I would have done. But he didn't. He had his own knife. And he started waving it back at Arron.

If I'd done what Arron wanted and been the one mugging the boy, then I'd have dropped my knife and run away. And I can run so fast that there wouldn't have been a fight. But Arron didn't run. He was backing off, looking around, unsure what was going to happen next.

Jukes and Mikey jumped out and pushed him forward. 'Go on, man, don't let him disrespect you,' said Mikey. The knives waved in the air. I stayed frozen in the castle. What if I'd tried to help . . . shouted out . . . had some credit on my phone?

Then Jukes grabbed the boy's arm and twisted it. The knife in the boy's hand grazed Arron's ear, sending blood gushing over his shirt. And Jukes pushed the boy away, and he fell against Arron. And Arron's knife. And they splashed into the mud together and they were fighting, and all I could see was a tangle of bodies. And blood. And mud. And Jukes and Mikey running away.

And there's no point going through this with DI Morris because this was all in my original statement. They know this bit, every last detail.

338

'And how close did you get, before you called the ambulance?' asked DI Morris.

'Not close at all,' I said. I'd jumped down from the castle and run away. I could have just run and run and never come back, but I didn't. All the time in my head there were the two thoughts – first ambulance, then Arron. How to get an ambulance. How to help Arron. How to make certain he didn't take all the blame.

I got out on to the road and I saw the bus coming up the hill towards me. And I stuck my hand out to stop it. When the door opened I shouted, ' Ambulance . . . call an ambulance. In the park, by the playground . . . someone's really hurt.' And then I ran back.

'And then you helped Arron run away,' says DI Morris. 'Yes,' I say, and I wait. But he doesn't know. He doesn't know. Arron didn't tell him what really happened then.

'When did you realise he'd also been hurt?'

'When we were running. It all happened really quickly.'

'His idea to run, or yours?' he asks.

'Both,' I say firmly.

He's looking curiously at me, like he knows there's something wrong with my story. But he doesn't ask. He doesn't ask. So I don't have to lie.

He asks a few more questions, but nothing I can't

handle. And then he says, 'We're nearly there with the case that we're building but there may yet be some delays before it goes to court.'

'Oh, yeah?'

'Be patient. Keep your head down. We'll have a new statement which covers this meeting outside the bowling alley for you to sign in a week or so.'

'What about Arron? What's going to happen to him?'

He shakes his head. 'I can't tell you that,' he says.

I don't know a lot about courts and law but I'm hoping that, by telling DI Morris that Arron wasn't meaning to stab anyone, I can help him. Arron was injured as well. I'm sure he'll be able to argue self-defence. He's a lot younger than Jukes and Mikey. As long as the court believes me about what they did. I wonder what Arron's statement says.

'How come you never thought I was involved?' I ask. I want to make absolutely sure that I'm in the clear.

'Luckily for you, we found traces of your DNA on the castle, which backs your story, and the timing of you appearing on the bus route also seems to rule out much involvement. Anyone who'd been in that fight would be covered in blood and mud, and every passenger on that bus says you were spotless. It'd be hard to prove joint enterprise – that you were working with the others. Of course, you could have been acting as their look out, but we're not pursuing that line. We checked your computer as well and there's absolutely nothing on the hard drive to link you with any gang activity.'

I think about them checking my laptop, reading every message I've ever written, every word of the diary I kept for a bit – which was mostly about Maria at the tattoo parlour – and I feel a bit like someone's just gone through my underwear drawer or filmed me in bed at night. It's not good to be spied on. It makes you feel automatically ashamed.

'Can I talk to him, to Arron?'

'No, Ty, because you're a witness in the case against him.'

All these months I've been worrying that Arron and his family hate me for going to the police. All these months I've been confused about who's after me. But when I think clearly, I know who I have to worry about. I'm pointing the finger at the one who pushed the boy on to Arron's knife.

'OK,' I say, 'why can't you arrest Jukes's family? Because you know they were the ones that threw that bomb and beat up my gran, don't you? Why can't you lock them up?'

He sighs. 'It's a fair question,' he says. 'The problem

is proof. These are organised criminals. They're probably responsible for half of the drugs on the streets of North London. They control a large number of people and they have vast resources. Nothing that's happened to you will have been done directly by them. Getting people to testify against them is a problem, and getting hard proof that they are ultimately responsible for any one crime is extremely difficult.'

Fair enough, I suppose. It makes me feel a bit stupid, though, that I didn't realise what a risk I was taking when we went to the police in the first place. I wonder how they're keeping Arron safe in prison. Or did Arron even name Jukes and Mikey in his statement?

And then DI Morris says to me, 'OK son, behave yourself from now on,' and they leave me alone on the roof.

I lie on my back again and look up at the seagulls. And I'm back in far, faraway London, running back to Arron in the park.

I can see that the boy is dead. He couldn't look more dead. There is blood everywhere. But Arron is desperately shaking him and shouting at him, 'Wake up, man, help is coming, it's gonna be OK.'

'Come on Arron, leave him. You can't help him now.'

'Shut up, man,'

'Come on Arron, you can still escape.'

'Shut the fuck up.'

So I get out my knife. And I wave it in his face. And I say, 'You do as I tell you.'

'Make me, gay boy.'

I slash the knife at his arm. Harder than I meant to. And he's bleeding and gasping and looking at me like he never knew me.

The strange thing is that sometimes, when I remember it, my knife slices hard into his arm and blood spurts out in a fountain. And sometimes my knife just scratches his arm, leaving a straight red line which oozes little drops of blood. I have no idea which memory is right. I've been over it again and again in my head.

We run down the path, with the sound of sirens getting louder and louder. And we run through the trees and bushes to the bit of fence that backs straight on to his estate. Amazingly, no one sees us as we crash through the double doors leading to his block, and we call the lift.

Incredibly the lift arrives – it's usually broken – and we're all alone in the piss-stinking space. And it's there that Arron looks at me and says, 'I never thought you'd do that. Don't worry, I'll never tell.'

There's respect in his eyes for the first time for years – at last he sees I'm as good as him. He doesn't despise me any more. But then I wonder what sort of respect I've earned, and, ever since, that confusion has tangled my brain. Because I needed that respect, I was desperate for it.

Sometimes I dream of that moment and I'm high with relief – I'm not a pretty boy, I'm a real man – and then the joy drains away when I remember why he's looking like that, and I'm just a shapeless blob of nothing again. It's the worst dream because sometimes humiliation is worse than fear. And then I wake up and despise my selfishness because nothing that's happened to me means anything compared to what happened to the boy with the iPod.

By the time the lift stops, Arron's breathing is more of a gasp, and he's collapsing into my arms and we stagger along the last bit of walkway and fall against his front door. His mum hears the thud and comes to the door. And as we fall into the flat she sees the blood pouring down. And she's screaming and falling to her knees. 'He got stabbed,' I pant. 'You gotta do something.'

And luckily her nursing instinct takes over, and she makes a tourniquet and calls an ambulance.

After they've gone, I change into some of Arron's clothes. I put my bloody clothes into a Tesco bag and

I wipe the knife clean on them.

I go home and I boil up the kettle and pour steaming water over the knife, and then I put it back in the cutlery drawer. The Tesco bag goes under my bed and then I have a shower. I don't need to tell Nicki anything because she's down at the Duke of York for karaoke night.

I curl up on the sofa and all I can think about is blood and death and Arron and the boy. The way he was singing. The dead stare on his face. I'm shaking and crying a bit. But then I hear a knock at the door and I creep along and open it, and Nathan bursts into the room. He's sweating and shaking too, and he says, 'They've arrested him. The fu'in' hospital called de police to him. He's under arrest.'

And then he pushes his face next to mine and tells me to keep quiet. And I say, 'Yeah, yeah, I'm not saying anything.' All these months I thought he was threatening me. But now I wonder if he was trying to protect me, to keep me out of it. Nathan's scary, but he did always seem to like me. And maybe he knew what Jukes's family were capable of.

The next day I say I'm ill and I can't go to school, and Nicki calls Gran and asks her to come and be with me. And Gran makes me toast and tea and puts her hand on my forehead and says, 'Maybe you're running a temperature, my darling. Go back to sleep.'

But then she reads the paper and listens to the radio. She calls my mum and asks her to come home from the office. When she does, Gran sits both of us down in front of the lunchtime news and we watch a press conference. It's about a murder which may have racist motives. A press conference given by Mr and Mrs Williams, the grieving parents of Rio Williams, aged fourteen.

They're appealing for help, for anyone who was in the park that day to come forward. In particular for the boy who stopped the bus. There's a pretty clear description of me – green eyes, brown hair, grey hoodie – and Gran just looks at me. Then she says her bit about the precious child. This poor family's precious child. And then we go to the police.

The police take my statement, which names Jukes and Mikey and Arron, and then they take us to the canteen where I eat crisps and custard creams. Then they take us home and, well, you know what happens next.

CHAPTER 30
Fish and Chips

Another first day at another school. This time the school is stricter, more old-fashioned, more like St Saviour's in fact, minus religion but with the yes sir, no sir and the tons of homework. Mum will be over the moon.

It's only for boys. Doug and Maureen obviously decided that I need to be kept away from girls. I don't like it, it doesn't feel natural to me. You can't grow up among women and then easily flip over to everyone being male. Or I can't, anyway. I feel flat and gloomy. I'm worried it's going to be St Saviour's all over again.

They put a boy called Nigel in charge of showing me around and making sure I get to the right classroom at the right time, and he does it, but he's not really interested. At break he talks to his friends and I stand around until he's ready to take me to our History lesson. By lunchtime I'm so fed up that I tell him I'm OK by myself and just wander around a bit. I'm not hungry, just waiting for the day to end. And then I see the sign saying Library.

I push the door cautiously and see a room with hundreds of books. It's twice the size of the library at St Saviour's and I don't think there was one at Parkview – they had a learning resource centre instead. What's most interesting here are the computers.

'Hello,' says a woman who's got the most amazing ginger curls. 'We don't usually see many people in here on the first day of term.'

'Can I use the computers, please?' I ask. 'Is there internet?'

And she says yes, and I sit down and I log on to the email address that Claire set up for me.

There are twenty messages. Twenty. All from Claire. She's been writing and writing for weeks, even though I haven't replied. I can't believe it. I'm happy and sad and excited and terrified all at the same time.

The first messages are just short: *Call me, write to me, where are you? We need to talk, what's happened? Are you OK? I'm worried about you.* That kind of thing.

She wrote:

I found out what Ashley said about you and I told the head teacher that she'd been bullying me, and that you were only good and supportive to me. I know it's too late for you, but she's on full report now. I'm not going back until next term, and I think they'll move me to another class. I wish you were still here.

Then she wrote about a month ago:

At last I know what's happened to you. A nice lady called Maureen came to see me. Mum thought she was just a friend of your family, but she told me who she really was and how she knew you. She told me why you'd had to be moved away and that you were all right. I was getting really scared for you.

  I'm going to keep writing and maybe one day you will reply. Surprise me! You know I'm not angry with you. I wish other people hadn't interfered with us. I know they were just trying to be protective but I wish they'd have left us alone. I love you. Claire.

And then she writes message after message about her life, about how things have changed and how her mum's asking her all the time how she feels and is taking her shopping and stuff.

One message makes me stop and think for a bit.

I thought about what your Mum said about you hurting me and I want you to know that I didn't even mind at the time.

All the time I was thinking that you were actually touching me, someone like you had noticed me. Any pain came second to that. It's OK, you mustn't feel bad about it.

When I read this I *do* feel really bad, because I realise that Claire's quite screwed up about all sorts of things, and I see more what my mum was going on about. I wish Claire and I could have worked it out together though. She needs so much love and friendship and I have it here for her.

The last message was written yesterday when she went back to Parkview.

The first day is over and it wasn't as bad as I'd thought. Did you ever meet the school counsellor? They rushed me off to see her as soon as registration was over. She's a bit annoying to talk to – really nosy, assumed all sorts of things about you and me – but she had a good idea. She suggested that I pick about four girls in my new class, and then she got them to come to her room so I could talk to them about what had happened and they could sort of protect me in the classroom, tell other people to leave me alone, that kind of thing. I asked for Evie, Anna, Zoe and Jasmine from my PE group – did you ever meet them? They're OK, I think. They never teased me, just ignored me.

They were quite shy when they came in, and Miss Wilson

explained what she wanted them to do and I thought, this'll never work. But then she left us alone and I talked to them a bit about why I used to cut myself and how it felt and why it all went wrong and how I'm feeling now. I felt really sick and ashamed when I was talking, but they were all kind and nice and they said they were sorry they'd never talked to me and known what was going on. Zoe is a specially nice person and she asked me to go shopping with her at the weekend.

They all wanted to know about you. They wanted to know if you were cutting yourself too, and I said no, absolutely not, he was the one who saved my life and made me stop. And I have stopped, I really have. They wanted to know why you suddenly disappeared and I told them that your mum wanted to go back to London.

After that we went back into class, and at break and lunch I went round with them, and no one else has bothered me. Carl and Brian both asked about you and I told them I thought you were OK, and I told them the London story as well. Carl said in that case he forgave you for leaving him the rest of the lost property to sort out, which was nice of him.

Are you starting a new school too? Could you write and tell me about it? Are you OK? I love you so much, Claire x

I finish reading this and I hit reply and then I stare at the screen a bit and try and think about what to say. And I don't realise it but my eyes are a bit watery and the screen is blurry when I try and type. I've taken my stupid glasses off. They give me a headache.

'Are you OK?' asks the nice librarian lady. 'Because the bell for the end of lunch went ten minutes ago.'

I rub my eyes. 'Oh . . . I'm in trouble on my first day.'

'Never mind, they'll understand,' she says. 'Tell them you got lost. Where do you have to be?'

I pull out my new timetable. 'Maths. A7.'

'Shall I show you where that is?'

'Yes, please, but I really have to write something first.'

I think any other teacher would have told me off and pointed to the timetable, but she waits patiently while I write: *I finally found a computer I can use. I'll write properly soon. Missing you, love you too, Jx.*

'I'm done,' I say and get up to go and she says, 'Don't you need to put your glasses back on?' and looks at me as though she thinks I'm a bit strange.

She takes me along a corridor and points the way upstairs.

'Through the double doors, turn left, second door on your right,' she says. Then she adds, 'Welcome to Trenton Boys. I'm Miss Knight and you can always find me in the library.'

'I'm Jo— Jake,' I say, and she says, 'If you need any

help just come and ask.'

When I get home Doug's sitting at the table in our tiny living room and I don't mind him so much now, so I tell him and Mum all about how hard I'm going to have to work, and how I'll be doing Spanish which is obviously essential for a Premiership interpreter, and that someone mentioned that they might set up a Mandarin class after school. And I think there's an athletics club. So I can keep going with the running too.

Mum looks really pleased and says, 'I'll get you into university yet,' and Doug says, 'We looked for a school which would keep you busy. Your Mum thought this one would be good because they specialise in languages.' He looks really smug, but that's just the way his face works. I grin at Mum because I recognise this as a peace offering.

And then Doug says, 'I've got some news for you, young Ty,' and Mum looks a bit strange. Happy but also kind of stressed.

'What news?' I ask and Doug says, 'Your gran is coming back to England and so are your aunts. Your aunts are going to live in Manchester – we're getting them a flat there and you'll be able to visit because it's not so far away.'

'What about Gran?'

'Aha! She's going to come and live with you here.'

'Yay!' I'm so happy I whoop out loud and I see Mum wipe away a tear.

'But how can she live here? It's really small.'

'There's a studio flat downstairs which is empty. We thought she could have that. It's not what she's used to but she'll be very happy to be with you both.'

'You especially,' says Mum, and she goes off to make me a cup of tea.

Later, when Doug's gone and I've changed into jeans and a T-shirt, we decide to go and get fish and chips and eat them on the beach. It's a sunny evening and it's kind of relaxing to watch the waves crashing in. I've been wondering about trying surfing – I can see it's a big thing here and Mum says she thinks it's a great idea.

'Are you OK?' I ask her. 'Aren't you happy about Gran coming to live with us?'

'Oh. Well. Of course I am.'

'No you're not. Don't pretend with me.'

She sighs. 'It's just that she's never really approved of me, you know, Ty. I was never the good Catholic daughter she wanted.'

'Neither are the others,' I point out, but she says, 'Pregnant at 15? Beat that.'

She goes on, 'She adores you so much, and of course we lived with her on and off until you were five, and, even when we had our own place, you spent so much time there. After school every day, in the holidays; I sometimes used to feel I didn't get a look in with either of you. Like my mother had stolen my son and my son had stolen my mother.'

'Oh. I'm sorry. I never knew.' I feel guilty but cross as well, because I never asked her to hand me over to Gran. Stolen is a bit of a strong word. And then I ask, 'Why did we live with her on and off? I thought we just lived with her.'

'It's a long story,' she says. 'We had a go at living with your dad, just the three of us. It didn't really work. I'll tell you properly one day. Look, it wasn't your fault. I let her do all the mothering. Thought she was better at it than me, and I was probably right, eh?'

'You don't do so bad,' I say, reaching over and nicking a big handful of her chips.

'You liar!' she laughs, and a seagull nips in and pinches the end of her fish.

'I miss our flat in London,' I say. 'I really liked living there.' And she takes that as a compliment and says thanks.

'But it's OK here, isn't it?' she asks, and I don't know what to say because some things are good, like fish and chips on the beach, and doing Spanish is massive, but some things are rubbish, like not having any friends and missing Claire so much that it hurts and not doing training with Ellie any more.

And there's the constant nagging worry about our safety, and the exhausting job of remembering to lie all day every day about the most basic things. But I suppose that's going to be the case for a long time wherever we are.

'I suppose so,' I reply, and she says, 'Missing Claire?' and I nod, and she says, 'Well, it's much better not to get too serious at your age. At least you can concentrate on your homework,' which is just typical.

'You can't help what you feel,' I point out, and she says, 'I'm hardly one to preach, am I?' Then she sighs and says, 'I'm sorry everything's so difficult for you. What a useless parent I am.'

'You're about a million times better than my dad,' I say, and she says, 'You're underestimating,' and then we walk along the sea front and back to our new home.

CHAPTER 31
Confession

Jake's social life is crap. Watching *EastEnders* with Gran, that's about as good as it gets. He's a sad git, Jake. Good thing he's not really me. Funnily enough, when I was Ty, I was quite happy to spend an evening in front of the telly. But now I've been Joe, I expect more.

We're halfway through *EastEnders* when some guy starts beating up Ian, slapping him across the face and holding him by the throat. Nothing terrible. Normal stuff in Albert Square.

And then I look at my gran, and her eyes are full of tears and she's trembling and looking away from the television, so I quickly change channels. Gran will never talk about what happened to her and she gets upset if we ask, but she doesn't like loud noises, and she'll only open the door if I knock three times, and she asked Doug the other day if there was any chance we could move to a bigger flat which would have room for all of us because she's nervous on her own. Which isn't like my gran.

Anyway. On Channel 4 there's a programme about knife crime. About all the killings and stabbings. About the crisis among Britain's youth. About what the government plans to do about it.

I grab the remote to zap on to something like sport or *The Simpsons*, but Gran shakes her head and says, 'No, Ty darling, you need to watch this.'

So she goes to make tea and I watch. London, they say is the worst place for knives. In other British cities, things are more organised. Gangs have guns. In London, it's a free-for-all. We all have knives, gangs or no gangs.

The Mayor of London – the weirdo blond guy off the telly – goes on about kids not having enough to do . . . needing more facilities. Youth clubs. Boxing. Latin. *Latin?*

Some woman says that kids should be taken into hospitals to see stabbing injuries being treated. That's totally random – I mean, you'd have to wait around for ages before someone with the right sort of injuries came in. And you'd get in the way of the doctors and nurses. She's obviously not thought it through. Which is a bit worrying because apparently she's the Home Secretary.

A police guy says it'll take a generation to change

things, that they can solve murders really easily, but it's another story trying to prevent them.

And then they show a slide show of the victims, the teenagers stabbed to death in London this year so far. It's only September but the pictures seem to go on forever. Face after face of boys – almost all boys – black and white, big and small. One guy has a silly moustache and I cringe for him – imagine having your life end when you've just started experimenting with facial hair and you look like a complete dickhead. One boy looks a bit like Arron. Another looks more like me.

And then there's Rio, filling up the screen, Rio with his big brown eyes and his black hoodie and a smile that I never saw. I'm curled up on the sofa now, rocking slowly back and forward, a fist against my mouth.

Gran sits next to me and says softly, 'I know it's terrible, darling, but it's important to watch. This is why we're here. This is what we're fighting against.'

They're interviewing someone in a young offender institution now. A young guy, tall and dark, skin the colour of a frappuccino when you've stirred in the cream. For a moment I think it's Arron, but it can't be. He's not been to court yet. No one's found him guilty.

This guy is guilty. 'I carried a knife because my brother gave it me,' he says. 'He told me I needed protection.' I sneak a little look at my gran. She's shaking her head.

'The boy you stabbed – was he threatening you with a knife?' asks the interviewer. Slowly the prisoner shakes his head. 'I was drunk, innit?' he says. 'He disrespected me. I just shanked him.' He looks at his hand like he can't believe what it did.

He's serving four years for GBH. That could be me. That ought to be me. That might be me if the police ever find out the truth.

Here's another politician. A posh one. The one my mum likes – he talks a lot of sense, she says. You can tell from his smooth, certain face that he's had a pretty easy life. I bet he never worried about being attacked on his way home from school. He doesn't live in a world of fear.

He says that everyone who carries a knife should be locked up. I try to imagine how many prisons they'd need – hundreds and hundreds – and I laugh out loud. My gran gives me a look and I shut up.

The programme ends and she switches off the television. I hide my face in my cup of tea and she says, 'They should bring back National Service.'

'Why? Then you're just teaching people to fight.'

'Give these kids a bit of discipline,' she says. 'Give them a trade. Teach them some responsibility.'

She pats me on the shoulder. 'I'm so glad you're not like them, Ty darling.' I disappear into my mug again.

'Do you like it here, Gran?' I ask after a bit. I have to change the subject.

She shakes her head. 'I'm a Londoner, darling, I'll never adapt to living somewhere this quiet. Please God they'll find a way that we can go back home one day. This is fine for a holiday, but it's not real life.'

Then she smiles and says, 'But I popped into the church around the corner and introduced myself to the priest – very nice man, comes from Walthamstow, looks a bit like what's-his-name . . . George Clooney . . . and he says they've got a nice congregation on a Sunday. I don't suppose you'll come with me, will you? I do think it'd be good for you.'

'Umm . . . probably not. I've got a lot of homework,' I say. 'Actually, I'd better go and do some now.'

I go back upstairs to our empty flat – Mum's got a part-time job three evenings a week behind the bar at the local pub – and then I realise I actually have got quite a lot of homework, and some of it needs research, so I decide to go to the internet cafe. By thinking very hard about Jake's geography project I manage to shut out the thoughts of knives and prison and Rio and all those other faces – at least I shut them out of the front of my mind, but I know they're hiding in the back.

On the way I pass Gran's church and I wonder why you'd become a priest if you look like George Clooney. For one crazy minute I think about going inside and sitting in the confession box and telling the whole story to a dark iron grid. And finding out what Father Clooney would suggest for penance and contrition, and whether it's really true that priests keep the darkest of secrets.

But I'd be there for hours because it's so long since I last confessed. And I'd have to tell him all about Ashley and that. I think not. Just the idea makes me shiver and hurry on past the boxy grey building. Confession isn't meant for me. It's for people like my gran who only do good things.

But a memory is nagging me: assembly at St Saviour's and Father Murray telling us that confession was about the future as much as the past. 'It's Jesus's way of giving your soul an insurance policy,' he said, and everyone laughed because we imagined Jesus popping up on telly selling us a no-claims bonus.

Anyway, no one'd give my soul insurance now because I'm like a driver who's had too many accidents and I never really knew how to drive in the first place.

I go on into the cafe and get myself a Coke and log on. I spend fifteen minutes researching the Zuiderzee dam and printing out pages. And then I switch over to hotmail to see if Claire's sent me any messages. She has. Just a short one. Enough to take me through another few days.

Is it fair to lean on Claire when she doesn't know my whole story? Is it right? I'm already wondering if the Claire I'm relying on is real or a kind of made-up Claire that I've magicked up in my head. She's my best friend and I love her, but really I hardly know her. And she certainly doesn't know me.

And I know it's not fair to dump it all on Claire, but I have to tell someone and she's better than George Clooney hiding in a box or Jesus with his fully comp cover. She won't mess around with prayers. She'll either go to the police or she'll trust me. My fate is in her hands. It's a better place than anywhere else I can think of.

Hey Claire, my Claire.

I've been thinking a lot about why we got so close so quickly, and it's still a mystery. One minute I was being mean to you – and I am so sorry, you know, don't you – and we were fighting, and the next I just felt this incredible closeness and trust. I always will, even if you never want to speak to me again when I've told you this. I have to be honest with you. It's what we're about.

I'm a liar, Claire. I'm lying to the police and if I get into court as a witness I'm going to lie there too. I'm not just a liar, I'm someone who did something terrible. I hurt someone. I've never admitted it to anyone before.

It's up to you what you want to do. You could ask me lots of questions, and I will answer them all. I'll tell you anything. Maybe you will understand why I did it and forgive me.

You could never contact me again and I will understand. Or you could pretend you never got this email. It's your choice. Whatever you do, take care of yourself. I'm trusting in your strength. I love you. I always will. You are my best friend.

I know you think of me as Joe, but it was Tyler who did this and that's who I want you to love or hate or forget.

Ty x

The End

Read on for an exclusive preview of the
first chapter of the continuation of Ty's story in

ALMOST TRUE

CHAPTER 1
The end of Fake Jake

They come to kill me early in the morning. At 6 am when the sky is pink and misty grey, the seagulls are crying overhead and the beach is empty.

I'm not at home when they arrive. I'm the only person on the beach, loving my early morning run – the sound of the waves and the smell of seaweed. It all reminds me that my new name is Jake and Jake lives by the seaside.

Jake's normally a bit of a sad person – no friends, poor sod – but here right now, working on my speed and strength, I'm happy that wherever we are and whatever my name is, I can always run, my body is my own.

For a bit I even forget that I'm supposed to be Jake and I run myself back into my last identity, which was Joe, cool popular Joe. I miss Joe. It's good that I can be him when I run. I never want to be Ty again, my real name, the basic me, but I still dream of being Joe.

Joe never feels lonely, running on his own. It's Jake who's miserable at school, where no one talks to him.

Jake never thinks about Claire – *my* Claire, my lovely Claire – because just her name throws him into a dark pit of despair, but when I'm Joe I pretend I'm running to see her and I let myself feel just a little bit of joy . . . excitement . . . hope.

So it's a good morning, and even when I get near home and have to readjust to being Jake again, there's still a kind of afterglow that clings to me. A Joe glow for Jake the fake. I'm hot and sweaty and that's as good as Jake's life ever gets, but then, when I turn our corner, there are police cars everywhere and ambulances and a small crowd of staring people, and they're putting up tape to stop anyone getting through.

'Get back, get back,' a policeman is shouting, but I push on forward through the crowd to the edge of the tape.

And then I see it. A dark pool of blood at our front door. For a moment the world stops, and my heart isn't even beating. I'm swaying, and everything is going whiter and smaller and I'm like one of the seagulls flying overhead, looking down on the crowd and screaming to the sky.

I don't know what to do. I think about just running away, so I never need find out what happened. Then arms hug me tight and it's Gran, oh God, it's Gran, and she's pulling me over to a police car. My mum's hunched up in the back. She's making a weird noise – a kind of gasping, howling, hooting noise. It reminds me of when Jamie Robins had an asthma attack in year three – it was scary then and it's hideous now.

All her face is white, even her lips, and she's staring right through me – and then Gran slaps her face hard and Mum stops the terrible noise and falls into her arms. They're both still in their dressing gowns. There's blood on Gran's fluffy pink slippers.

Gran sits with her arms around my mum rocking her back and forth and saying, 'You'll be OK my darling, stay strong Nicki, you'll be OK.'

'What . . . who?' I ask, but I know. I'm already beginning to piece together what must have happened.

They must have rung our doorbell. Most days it would have been my mum stumbling down the stairs to the front door. If she had, then I think they would have grabbed her, dragged her upstairs and searched the place for me. When they found no one, what then? Kept her gagged and silent until I came back, then shot us both, I should think.

But Mum didn't open the door. She's sitting here in the car, retching and sobbing, doubled over like she's in pain. It must have been Alistair who went downstairs. Alistair, the guy she had just started seeing before we had to move here.

Alistair, who spent the night in her bed.

Alistair, who turned up last night, out of the blue.

No one bothered to tell me why or how.

Alistair, with his gelled hair and muscled arms. He looked like a prat from a boy band, but he was OK really. He was a good cook. My mum liked him a lot.

Alistair who worked in a gym and trained Ellie so well that she's going to the Paralympics next year. She was the first person to realise that I've got potential as a runner. Ellie's sister is Claire, my Claire. I'm probably never going to see either of them again.

Anyway. Alistair opens the door. He knew I was going out running and he probably thought I'd forgotten my key.

He's half asleep, hair all over the place. And they shout at him, 'Ty? Ty Lewis?' He stares, yawning and bewildered – he doesn't even know I have a real name, let alone what it is – and they must take that as a yes because then they shoot him. His hands are trying to keep his brains from spilling out. Then he drops to his knees on the doorstep and blood leaks from his broken body and he dies right there on the path. And they don't hang around because they think they've done their job. They've killed me.

This isn't the first time that someone's tried to silence me forever. It's just the first time that someone else has died instead.

My mum's woken up by the noise of the shots. She's standing at the top of the stairs, screaming and screaming, and then my gran, who's lived downstairs for the last few weeks, wakes up too. Gran spots Alistair's body – the blood. She screams and rushes to hug my mum. And then she calls the police.

Then the cars arrive, sirens shouting and the tape goes up and I get home from my run.

At the police station, they put us into a room on our own and say they'll send someone to take our statements. Gran pulls her mobile out of her pocket and starts ringing: first my aunties, then Doug, the policeman who's meant to be keeping us safe. Our witness protection officer. The man who's meant to keep us safe from the people who want to stop me testifying in court.

It seems like hours, but then they all start to arrive. Gran's trying to explain about witness protection to the local cops, and my Auntie Louise just says, 'Take us to whoever's in charge.'

Then Gran and Louise disappear into a room with the police guys and when Doug arrives he goes in there too. Doug looks incredibly rough. He doesn't even say hello to us. Mum and my Auntie Emma and I sit side by side in the corridor outside and I'm straining to hear what's going on. All I can hear is Lou's raised voice. She's good at shouting – she has to be, she's a teacher.

Mum is still shaking and crying and no one is doing anything to help her except Emma who's hugging her and saying, 'It'll be OK, it'll be OK,' in a really unconvinced voice. Deep, deep inside me there's a tiny muffled scream

– he's dead . . . he was shot . . . that should have been me – but shock has sucked all the feeling out of me and I'm getting that distant feeling again. It's like I've been laminated.

'I'm fed up with this,' I say. 'I'm going in there.'

Emma says, 'Ty, you can't just interrupt,' but I say, 'Watch me,' and I push the door open. They all go quiet as I barge into the room. It's almost funny to see Gran sitting there in her pink dressing gown in a room full of coppers.

'Look,' I say, 'we've been sitting here for hours. My mum's just seen her boyfriend shot. We all know they wanted to shoot me. What's going on?' I top it up with a lot of words that I don't usually say in front of my Gran.

Louise shakes her head and says, 'Just because there's been a murder is no reason for you to be foul-mouthed.'

'Oh for Christ's sake, Lou, you're not in the classroom now,' I say and I can see the police officers smiling. I sit down at the table with them. She frowns at me, but I'm going nowhere.

'Right,' she says, 'I think we've finished here anyway. Ty, you're coming with me. We've lost confidence in witness protection for you. We'll coordinate with the police when it's time for you to give evidence. But only if we're satisfied with their security arrangements.

'Your Gran's going to stay here with Nicki so they

can make their statements, and maybe someone'll be thoughtful enough to get them some clothes and then they'll have a discussion with Doug about where to go next.'

What does she mean? How is she going to look after me? What's going to happen to my mum? And Gran? Will the police even let me go?

Doug says, 'We'll give Ty 24-hour protection now this has happened. I don't think you should be too hasty.'

Louise is very near completely losing her temper. I can tell by the way the end of her nose has gone pink.

'As far as I can see, Ty is pretty safe right now. The bastards who are out to get him think they've succeeded. Until you release the victim's name that'll be the case. I'm assuming you won't do that right away. So I've got time to get Ty somewhere where no one will know where he is. And that includes the Metropolitan Police, and every other bloody police force in the country.'

'Are you suggesting *we* had something to do with this?' says Doug, who sounds pretty upset himself.

'I'm suggesting you launch an inquiry right away to find out how they got Nicki and Ty's address. I'll bet you'll find there was a leak somewhere close to home. And just in case you don't do that, I'm going to get on the phone to the Police Complaints Commission just as soon as I've sorted my nephew out.'

She's not finished with Doug. 'I want you to go to the flat and pack all of Ty's things, so I can leave here with him in half an hour. And then you can concentrate on making sure that Nicki and my mum and Emma – oh and me as well – have somewhere reasonably safe to go. You can keep your 24-hour protection for us.'

She leads Gran and me out of the room. Doug follows, and when he sees my mum he says, 'Nicki, I don't know what to say,'

Louise snaps, 'An apology would be nice, but that's not allowed, is it Doug? That would be admitting liability.'

Then she asks for some privacy to make phone calls and a policeman takes her away down the corridor.

Emma's rocking Mum back and forth, and Gran holds me tight.

'Ty, my love,' she says, 'this isn't going to be easy, but Louise knows what's she's about. She's rock solid that girl, always made the right choices, she'll know what's best for you.'

'I want to stay with you,' I say. 'I only just got you back.'

Gran's always been more like a mother to me than my own mum. I nearly fell apart without her these last few months. I can't believe I'm going to be taken away from her again. I cling on to her like I'm a baby monkey, not someone who's going to be fifteen in just over a month.

She kisses my forehead and says, 'I'm always with you darling, I always love you. But Nicki needs me more than you do right now.'

And that's it. Doug comes back with my bag, and puts it into Lou's car. I have a final hug with Gran and Emma. My mum is throwing up in the Ladies, so we wait for her, and I give her a hug too, even though she smells of vomit. She can't stop crying and I'm not even very sure that she understands that I might not see her for . . . for weeks? For months? Ever?

'Take care,' she says. 'Take care. Lou, take care of him.'

Louise says, 'Don't worry Nicki, I'll do what's best.'

My mum stops crying, mid-sob. She does an enormous sniff, which doesn't even begin to retrieve the snot on her face, looks Louise straight in the eye and says, 'He's *my* son, Louise, don't you forget that.'

And my auntie says, 'No one's ever in danger of forgetting that, Nicki. I'll be seeing you soon. Take care of yourselves.'

Then she puts her arm on my back and leads me away, underground where her car is waiting.

Acknowledgements

This book was conceived and mostly written at City University's Writing for Children evening classes. A big thank you to Anna Longman who suggested that I take the class and has made many excellent suggestions ever since. Amanda Swift was a great tutor – inspiring, encouraging, generous, insightful and always entertaining. And thanks to everyone on both courses for putting up with my copy flow.

I am completely indebted to Tony Metzer for his legal advice; likewise Jeremy Nathan on medical matters. Sue Demont introduced me to the concept of restorative justice in schools and Michelle Patoff checked all things Catholic.

Thanks to my agent Jenny Savill and her colleagues at the very cool multilingual Andrew Nurnberg Associates. And to everyone at Frances Lincoln Children's Books, especially Maurice Lyon.

Many thanks to Phoebe, my first reader, for many clever ideas, thanks also to Tom, Hannah and Avital and to Judah for fantastic proofreading. Deborah Nathan gave helpful tips on the ways of fourteen-year-old boys, and Alun David was a top-class critic. Thanks to Mum for her encouragement and Dad for lending his name. Thanks for reading and more, Valerie Kampmeier, Cindy Yianni, Katie Frankel, Emma Cravitz, Laura Blaskett, Ann Maher, Mandy Appleyard, Yvette Genn and Anne Webbe. And thanks to Nicky Goldman for some well-timed advice.

Last, but most, my thanks to Laurence for everything.